CW01636693

[illegible] WAY

An absolutely gripping British crime thriller full of twists

JUDITH CUTLER

Fran Harman Mysteries Book 3

Originally published as *Still Waters*

JOFFE BOOKS

Revised edition 2024
Joffe Books, London
www.joffebooks.com

First published as *Still Waters* by Allison & Busby Ltd
in Great Britain in 2008

This paperback edition was first published
in Great Britain in 2024

© Judith Cutler 2008, 2024

This book is a work of fiction. Names, characters, businesses, organizations, places and events are either the product of the author's imagination or are used fictitiously. Any resemblance to actual persons, living or dead, events or locales is entirely coincidental. The spelling used is British English except where fidelity to the author's rendering of accent or dialect supersedes this. The right of Judith Cutler to be identified as author of this work has been asserted in accordance with the Copyright, Designs and Patents Act 1988.

Cover art by Nebojša Zorić

ISBN: 978-1-83526-590-1

*With thanks to Leslie Norman for his generosity
to Oxfam & Jersey Hospice Care.*

CHAPTER ONE

The fifth-floor room was so neat it might never have been occupied. Only the hotel swipe card on the table and, parked unobtrusively beside the bed, the overnight case with a collapsible handle and little wheels showed that someone had entered. The kettle, however, was warm, and the cup and saucer missing from the hospitality tray; they were washed and draining in the otherwise immaculate bathroom. From the evidence in the bin, someone had drunk tea with no milk. The two biscuits, a chocolate digestive and a Genuine Scottish Shortbread, remained inside their wrappers.

The curtains were still pulled back in swags, though the nets heaved and billowed.

The glass door opening onto the balcony was ajar, despite the unseasonably cold wind and the torrential rain, which would soon soak into the carpet.

Blue flashing lights strobed over the street below. The slanting rain might have made them look more like lights on seaside rides. Instead, it rendered them even more cold and clinical.

The brightwear of the men and women scrabbling diligently in their intermittent illumination — someone had already sent for incident tape and floodlights — turned a harsh green. As for the blood from the shattered body they were attending, that too a far-from-natural colour, it was already trickling into the drains and sewers and would soon be borne, via the new and expensive sewage plant that Ofwat had forced upon Invitaqua, to the sea.

CHAPTER TWO

After thirty-five years in the police, Fran Harman knew all about fear. The dry mouth. The sweating hands. The racing heart. Even, on a couple of occasions, the failure of vital muscles. At least this Friday evening she hadn't got as far as that. But, much as she despised herself, the first three symptoms were very much in evidence.

'For God's sake, relax, Fran!' Mark told her, waving a full bottle and an empty glass enticingly under her nose.

'I told you, I'm not touching a drop until everyone's sitting down and eating. Maybe not even then. Hell, facing a killer with a gun's got nothing on this.' At least she was beginning to laugh at herself.

'I'm sure the new Deputy Chief Constable — please note all the capital letters! — would be delighted with the comparison,' he said dryly. 'Come on, it's not as if he's a stranger, even if he's not exactly a friend.'

'He could have changed a lot in — what? Twenty-five years? He was always . . . no, he never laughed at my jokes, never enjoyed the puns the others on my various teams — and I — made on my name. When I said we should be like doctors, taking the Hippocratic Oath: do no harm. Or when

I talked about us all having to put ourselves in harm's way, but not unless it was vital.'

'Not to mention your "apparently harmless" questions.' His eyes crinkled as she winced.

'Quite. Let's say he was always very self-contained. But on recent showing, he's as tight as an oyster, isn't he? Mind you, he'd need to be, to have run the Met's Rubber Heel Squad.' She sank down on a kitchen stool, pushing back her hair. It took her a moment to realise that the hand doing it was still in one end of an oven glove.

'Quite. But it's not a job I'd fancy, knowing every time you walked into the canteen people would stop talking because your job might mean you were fingering their mate's collar.' Mark brushed her hair back towards her face, inspecting his handiwork with a little smile as he tweaked it into shape.

'Or their own collar, of course. No, it takes a particular sort of person to get inured to that. Which is a good thing, isn't it? It's going to be hard for Simon, coming back to Kent as the chief's sidekick.'

He poured her a drink, which she took absentmindedly. 'Hard for you since you were his boss, once.'

She drank more deeply than she'd intended, and put down the glass with an accusing tap. 'Goodness, if I got resentful when all my protégés got promoted over my head . . .' It might be different for Mark, of course. The arrival of a deputy chief constable meant an effective demotion for him, at an age when other men might have been thinking about one last push for a top job. He had been phlegmatic about the new layer in the hierarchy coming in between him and the chief, but she knew better than to prod the bruise on his ego too often.

'Actually, you always seem pleased,' Mark observed. 'Proud, even. "This is the chief constable of X and I remember her when she laddered her tights on her first day and burst into tears."'

'Yes, I suppose I was some sort of promotional midwife.'

'You still are, aren't you? You're always pushing good officers onwards and upwards. Look at Jon Binns. Or young

Arkwright. It didn't take him long to get his sergeant's stripes, did it?'

She smiled fondly. 'Tom would have done that without my help.'

'You always say that.'

'And I usually mean it. But I certainly can't claim any responsibility for Simon Gates' meteoric rise. Apart from making him rewrite his evilly tortuous reports till they were in decent clear English, I suppose. They were models of their kind by the time I'd finished with him.'

'Which may explain why he's so keen on reports now. He'll be after you to go on some of his committees, you mark my words.'

'Let him try. God, do I smell burning?'

'No, you don't. Fran, I promise everything'll be fine. I know you'd be happier taking them out to a restaurant than cooking yourself. I know this is my kitchen and you'd rather be in your own. But truly, you're a great cook and there's something special about inviting people into your home, isn't there?'

She responded with a hug. For months Mark had hated their relationship being public knowledge, but something — perhaps their joint purchase of an eighteenth-century house called simply the Rectory — had flicked a switch, it seemed, and here he was preparing to host their third supper party in as many weeks.

They still occupied their two houses alternately, the Rectory being as yet uninhabitable. Fran's was a cottage in the rural village of Lenham; Mark's, in Loose, almost a suburb of Maidstone, was a house she still found forbidding, either because of the stern Edwardian aspect or because of its associations with his late wife. She felt it resented her presence almost as much as Mark's grown-up children did. In vain she told herself houses could not be inimical, or that Sammie and Dave were being illogical in their opposition to their widower father finding a new love. She still felt a chill about the place, and, as Mark had observed, always donned a bathrobe to flit about the house, while she was content to pad mother-naked around her own.

'Listen to that rain,' Mark said. 'It sounds more like October than April. Still, we do need it. And it makes drawn curtains and candles all the more appropriate.'

'Rather knocks out drinks on the terrace, though,' she grumbled, looking at her watch for the umpteenth time.

* * *

The first guests to arrive were an environmental health officer, Maeve Burton, and Bill, a man they'd never met whom Maeve had enthusiastically described over the phone as 'my new chap'. Maeve was a woman in her early forties, once the victim of a psychotic rapist. Fran had supported her from the moment the crime was reported, through the horrors of internal surgery to repair the damage done by the perpetrator's broken wine bottle and the vicious cross-questioning by defence counsel to the moment the judge sent her assailant down for life. The women had always liked and respected each other, but the friendship had not really developed until Maeve had crawled out of her depression and was functioning fully again. Bill, who was probably the same age as Maeve, was a vague and wispy man, and it was hard at first glance to detect what Maeve might see in him.

Next to arrive were a couple of academics whom Fran had met and liked during the course of one of her investigations, Hattie and Edward Wallace. Once lecturers at Manchester University, they immediately seized on Bill's bookishness and entered into a spirited conversation that allowed Fran time for a final, prayerful baste.

* * *

'A cop! Not me,' Simon Gates was saying firmly, sipping a spritzer. 'Not anymore. I used to be.' He stopped.

'You were certainly a cop when you worked with me,' Fran agreed, though she could of course have said, *worked for me*. How much longer would they want to dawdle over their drinks? How soon could she shoehorn them into the dining room so that the food wouldn't dry out? 'And a very good one.' She smiled, her glance including all their guests.

In his later forties, Simon Gates was still a bachelor, but the adjective *gay* — in either sense — did not seem to apply to him. Even in these days of smart casual and open-necked shirts for dinner parties, she guessed he had in his pocket an emergency tie he'd much rather have had knotted tightly round his neck. Everything about him spoke of discipline: brightly polished shoes, sternly groomed hair, even his eyes, the coldest grey she'd ever seen, now she came to think of it. The only time she'd ever known him less than confident was when she had asked him if he wished to bring a guest with him. For a few seconds only he had looked like a child offered a lolly. But then he had shaken his head sternly and said there was no one. She had filed the information away for future reference but made no comment. She and Mark had agonised about finding a *spare* woman, the ironic italics very definitely Fran's, for Simon to partner, but in the event had agreed that matchmaking wasn't part of their brief.

'How can a deputy chief constable not be a cop?' Hattie Wallace demanded.

'Just as all too easily an academic becomes an administrator and ceases to be a teacher or a researcher,' Simon responded, with a gallant bow. 'Far from chasing baddies with bags of swag, I'm responsible for—' he numbered his functions on the fingers of his left hand '—professional standards, corporate communications, and organisation and development. In the latter are included change management, strategic planning, delivering best value and service improvement, service inspection and performance analysis.' A charming smile suddenly lit his face, taking ten years off him and even half-warming his eyes. 'Now, does that sound like being a cop?'

It sounded to Fran perilously like a man who, if he were in the private sector, would make swingeing cuts in staff in the interests of efficiency and to hell with security of tenure.

'But you wear uniform?' Maeve pressed, her slightly widened eyes suggesting he would look very good in it.

'Of course.'

'I've never seen Fran in uniform,' Maeve added, with a swift smile at her hostess. 'You were in CID when I knew you. But you must have worn it.'

'Before and after your case. In fact, I was back in it until quite recently. Then I was seconded to CID for a particular investigation.' She smiled at the Wallaces, whom she had met while she was on that case. She would much rather have smiled at Mark, who had been responsible for her move. 'And I've been there, dressing as frivolously as I like, ever since,' she joked. Even in mufti, she dressed in dark, sober clothes as if she was about to appear in court. But out of the corner of her eye she could see that Gates' face had briefly hardened, as if he was making a mental note she suspected was quite at odds with the conviviality of the evening. 'Now, you must all be starving . . .'

* * *

Saturday promised to be a glorious day. The previous evening's torrential rain, which, as Mark had predicted, had somehow added to the intimacy of the supper party, had washed everything clean, leaving a dazzling spring morning.

Ignoring the chaos of the kitchen and grabbing her coffee, Fran stepped out onto the terrace, which further forays into domesticity had seen her decorate with a couple of hanging baskets and some promising tubs. Mark would be back with the Saturday papers any moment now, and then they could plan their day. Part of it must be spent at her cottage — they were determined to eradicate the brambles from the flowerbeds — and then the rest could be devoted to a further visit to the Rectory, just to reassure themselves it was still there and still as beautiful. Even to think of it, to think of other mornings when they could breakfast outside looking at their little estate, brought a smile of simple joy to her face.

Even the irritable ringing of the phone did not wipe it away. But the voice at the other end did its best.

'My father, please.' Sammie used the tone that Fran reserved for particularly delinquent constables failing to produce what they had promised.

Nonetheless, Fran kept the smile in her voice. 'He's out at the shop at the moment. But he won't be a tick. Can I—?' *Take a message? Ask him to ring you back?* She mouthed to the humming dial tone. She wrote and left on the front-door mat a careful note asking — possibly telling — Mark to phone Sammie immediately, and retired to the shower, lest she make the mistake of telling him exactly what she thought of his ewe lamb. Later, when he'd done his duty, she wouldn't even ask what Sammie wanted, though she would listen if Mark wanted to tell her. She herself rather thought that Tina, the young woman's late mother, would probably have recommended a good firm talking to. Tina had been a woman who never thought being a good mother meant indulging her children's bad manners.

* * *

At least she still could wash the plates that weren't dishwasher-proof, empty the dishwasher itself and then tidy the kitchen, and so be reassuringly noisy while Mark returned Sammie's call from the most distant phone extension, the one in his office. It hurt that he should make the call before even yelling to say that he was back, and before dropping the papers on the kitchen table for her. But that was how he always responded to Sammie: when she told him to jump, he simply asked how high.

Fortunately both of his children had been out of the country at the start of their relationship, otherwise it might never have blossomed as it had. Dave had returned briefly, established that his room remained unsullied despite her invasion of other areas, and left for the States again. But Sammie's husband Lloyd had now taken a job in Tunbridge

Wells, and it was reasonable for Mark to want to see more of Sammie and of the two new grandchildren he'd hardly met. Fran was prepared to adore them as grandchildren she would never have otherwise, and her credit card was willing to bend over backwards to indulge them. But so far it hadn't been called on to demonstrate its flexibility, Mark having been requested to meet the babies solo so that their infant sensibilities wouldn't be overwhelmed. How a man used to wielding authority could be so supine she could not comprehend.

God, had she chipped that? How stupid to let her anger get the better of a rather nice Royal Worcester plate — one of a set, Mark had let slip, that he and Tina had been given as a wedding present and was well on the way to becoming an heirloom. Never having been married herself, she could only guess at the significance of such inanimate objects. But injuring one in a temper tantrum worthy of her putative daughter-in-law was beneath her. She polished, checked, stacked and at last returned everything to the china pantry the house was spacious enough to boast.

Surely the phone call must be over by now?

At least she would go in search of the papers.

They were sitting on the hall table. She flicked through her favourite sections and then checked her watch. Surely Sammie had said enough for this time in the morning? With a grim smile Fran set the coffee machine going — Mark was almost Pavlovian in his response to the smell of fresh coffee.

And here he was. His glance took in the pristine kitchen and the breakfast things, but he did not appear to register anything as he sat down heavily enough to make the stool protest. In silence, she poured coffee; in silence, he drank it.

'Maybe,' he said at last, 'I didn't smack her often enough when she was a child. Or maybe I smacked her too often. I don't know. I'm sorry she was so rude to you.'

Despite herself she asked, 'How did you know?'

'Once upon a time I was a policeman,' he grinned, reaching for the apricot jam, 'and I learnt to make deductions from evidence. Today I had a succinct note and a daughter fuming because I hadn't been at the end of the phone the second she wanted me. So I gather she didn't make polite conversation with you.'

As supine as he, she temporised. 'She sounded quite stressed.'

'She might well. Lloyd's thrown her out, she says.'

'He *what*? The bastard!' She pushed away from the table. In such a crisis, especially one with children involved, she could forget past irritations.

'What are you doing?'

'Going to clean her room, of course. And the spare one. And we'd better go and buy some bunks for the spare room, or whatever babies sleep in.'

'Not until we've had breakfast, anyway.' He spread and munched and dabbed up crumbs assiduously. And irritatingly.

So there was plenty of time for Fran to work out what was wrong. He hadn't denied that Sammie would be staying here, had he? And naturally with the children. Had Sammie refused to accept the offer of a safe haven until its pollutant had been removed? Was she demanding that Fran be excluded from what was fast becoming her home too? On past performance, Fran wouldn't put it past her. At the very least Fran had a feeling that Mark would no longer be assuming she would stay over every night they weren't sleeping in Lenham. That he would ask her, with great embarrassment, to understand.

So what line should she herself take? Righteous anger? Or acquiescence, on the grounds that a father owed his flesh and blood more than he owed his lover?

At last, Mark quite visibly gathered his courage.

'Fran, I've got the biggest favour to ask.'

She took a deep breath and gave what she hoped was an encouraging smile. And was glad she had when he spread his hands helplessly.

'I'm torn down the middle, Fran. I want to be with you. I've made that clear to Sammie. But she claims Lloyd hit her, and in front of the kids. Now, you and I both know what women's refuges are like.'

'You couldn't have your grandchildren going to one of those,' she agreed, glad she could see eye to eye with him about that at least. 'But she could surely exclude Lloyd from the marital home. If he has hit her, he can be done for assault, and a spell for him in the cells would enable her to make all the proper legal moves.'

For a moment he looked almost shifty. Then he said, 'I don't actually believe he has struck her. Certainly, when I pressed for details she became evasive, really evasive. I think they've just had a tiff and she wants out to give things time to cool down. OK, a big tiff—'

'So if we — if *you* — offer her refuge here, we're colluding with her.'

'Or offering a breathing space for them to kiss and make up. I don't know. You don't suddenly get a dose of wisdom when you become a parent, you know.'

She was hardly in a position to argue. Instead, she asked, 'So what's the favour?' Some of her former resentment seeped into her voice.

He looked up, startled. 'Didn't I say? I wondered if, just until they're back together, of course—'

'Assuming they get back together,' she interrupted sourly, and wished she hadn't, because his voice took on an acidic note.

'—that as *you* suggested, they stay here. Sammie and the babies, I mean.' Before she could say anything, he rushed on, 'She'll pay a nominal rent, of course, and I shall get a solicitor to draw up a tenancy agreement. I can't have Dave thinking she's going to walk off with the whole lot while he gets nothing. I've always tried to treat the kids fairly, if not equally.'

Fran had managed not to say anything, but she sensed that it was her very silence that made him say, 'And they'll both have to wait until after we're both dead, Fran, to get their claws on anything. Both of us,' he added firmly.

'Some people think it's better to give their kids stuff when they need it,' Fran countered, sensing a huge rainbow casting the previous clouds into perspective.

'That's what I'm doing. Giving her shelter when she needs it. But this house is going to pay for my care in my old age, Fran. I've learnt my lesson from your parents. When I'm senile, I don't intend to batten on my nearest and dearest — and that includes you. A luxury padded cell for me!'

'And she's happy with that?'

'I know you think I'm a pushover. I probably am. It was Tina who did all the disciplinary stuff, and then I thought indulging them would temper the pain of losing her. But on this I did make myself clear. I also said that I expected her to treat you as part of the family from now on, and if she wanted to see me, she saw you.'

Now that was a treat in store for them all.

'But what's the favour? I'm not arguing with anything here.'

'You might. I'm tempted to tell her that you're part of the deal. Perhaps I ought to insist. In other words, that you treat this place as your home, and that's going to continue.'

She nodded slowly, trying to reserve judgement while she waited for the rest of the deal.

'Do you see that working? We come in at seven or eight at night, expecting a bit of peace and quiet—'

'Or something altogether less restrained,' she said.

'And falling over the toys she never gets round to putting away; finding nappies blocking the loo; getting woken up by yelling kids; finding her in the bathroom first thing when we've got nine o'clock meetings . . . It wouldn't work for me. If it did for you, you'd be a saint. So the favour is this. Can I move into your cottage full time?'

It took a moment for this to sink in. Then she beamed.

'What are we waiting for?' she asked. 'Start packing now!'

CHAPTER THREE

That evening saw Fran dressed up again, though Mark, watching from the bed as she preened herself, was still in jeans and a filthy sweater.

'Are you sure this is a good idea? I really don't want to poop Jim's party,' she said as she fastened her earrings.

'Are you sure you can use the verb like that? Yes, you look perfect: smart but, with luck, not too smart. Sweetheart, of course you must go, even if it's just for a few minutes. A man only retires once. How long did you say you've known Jim?' He got up to fasten the pendant he'd given her the previous week.

'Thanks. Since I was twenty-two — and kindly have the decency to do your maths in your head.'

He made a great show of counting on his fingers.

She grabbed them. 'Jim was my very first CID sergeant. He terrified the socks off me. But he scared all the lads too. I think he protected me, without them — or me! — realising it. And he stayed a sergeant for years and years, while I kept on getting promoted. A lot of men would have been bitter, but not Jim. He was always the first to congratulate me. A really magnanimous man.'

Mark laughed, but said nothing.

'And a great trainer, too. I know Maureen wanted him to retire properly at fifty-five and toddle off to the Costa Geriatrica, but I'm glad he didn't. Think of all the young officers who've been through his hands in the last ten years. He's really made a difference, Mark.' She applied one last dab of make-up. 'Are you sure you won't come too?'

'I shall pop my nose in when I drop you off, and stand a round for everyone, but no more. Come on, Fran, someone my rank hanging round? You can get away with it, since you worked with him, but I'd really put the kibosh on things, wouldn't I?'

She didn't argue. 'OK. We'd best push off then, if you really don't mind giving me a lift. But I insist on getting a taxi back.'

'Of course I shall take you there. Actually, it's just an excuse to grab another load of my things from Loose.'

'And to see your grandchildren in the bath. Give them a hug from their absentee quasi-granny. You could even point out to Sammie that if we got to know them a bit we might be able to babysit for her.'

'The last refuge of the desperate grandparent! I shall say that and a good deal more, I can tell you.' He looked around, rolling his eyes at the heap of well-filled bin-liners in the corner. 'You don't think it's too late to make another deposit in a clothes bank, do you?'

'I think we've pretty well filled Sainsbury's Oxfam skip. What about moving across to a Sally Army one on another supermarket site somewhere? Funny,' she added, fishing a blouse out from the nearest bin-liner for one last look, 'I used to think I was the bee's knees in this. Now I all I can think of is how closely I must have resembled Mrs Thatcher.' She shoved it back in and tied the bag's ears firmly. 'Who, as I recall, was Jim's heroine.'

'Well, none of us is perfect,' he said crisply, hefting the sack and a couple of others. 'Come on, party time!'

* * *

Jim's face had lit up as she and Mark entered the heaving pub. Mark bought drinks all round, clapped Jim on the shoulder and made a discreet exit. As soon as he could, Jim shepherded her into a quiet corner, and sat cupping a hand round what he insisted was his better ear.

'I hate this sort of thing,' he confided. 'I'm all for a bit of a lark, but all this drinking and folk yelling at the tops of their voices . . . And that bloody loud music! How old do they think I am? Thirteen?'

Sympathising more than she cared to admit, Fran peered round for a face she recognised. A few quick words and the musical part of Jim's problems was cured.

'I did think I'd have liked a proper sit-down meal, but then I wouldn't have been able to talk to everyone, would I?' he continued wistfully.

She was painfully aware that he had begun to age. His waist had thickened to the point where he supported it with his belt, and brown spots speckled his hands and forehead. The startlingly handsome young man — she might have had a crush on him for a while — was now in senior citizen territory.

Fran happened to know that there'd be a couple of minibuses arriving any moment to take Jim and twenty of his closest mates to just the sort of bash he wanted, where his wife, who'd been told to make a great show of telling him to go and have a night with the boys, would be waiting, plus the said boys' wives. In fact, Fran had organised everything, from the restaurant to a last-minute visiting hairdresser to titivate Maureen.

'I just wanted to tell you how much I appreciated all you'd done for me,' she said, squeezing his hand. 'You were more than my sarge, Jim. You were my mentor.'

'You've not done badly. Mind you,' he added with a sad shake of his head, 'I did have you down for a chief constable. In fact, I had a tenner on your being the first woman chief in the country.'

'I'm sorry I lost you your bet. But my not being desperate for a really big promotion was partly your fault, Jim.' Not to mention her long-distance care for her parents, which had made doing even her existing job as a chief superintendent well-nigh untenable for some time. 'It was you who taught me to get interested in the people behind a case, not just the crime statistics,' she explained with a smile. 'And though I've crunched a few numbers in my time, thanks to you I'm never happier than when I'm getting my hands dirty with a spot of detection. Anyway, it's too late now. I shall be retiring myself any day now.'

He looked at her quizzically. 'They do say you've shredded at least two letters of resignation, maybe three.'

'You've done your share of that,' she countered.

'I get fond of them, that's the trouble,' he said. 'The ones I teach, I mean. Taught! They kept me young.'

She knew the cue. 'You certainly don't look sixty.'

'And you know full well I'm sixty-five, so cut the cackle. When I had to leave CID, though, young Fran, I really missed the buzz. I always wanted to know the whys and wherefores, as well as the hows and whos and whens. Take this suicide business down in Hythe — at the Mondiale, that new hotel on the front.'

She was hooked at once. 'What's that?'

'I wouldn't know anything about it, and I don't officially, mind.' He touched the side of his nose, just as she'd known he would.

'But . . . ?' she prompted.

'Seems this man — he'd be about my age, Fran — he lived down there, in one of those nice flats overlooking the sea, with a balcony for a few pots and a couple of deckchairs . . . Seems he took himself off to the new posh place, the Mondiale, you know, the one that looks as if it's just dropped in from outer space. I don't know what the planners were thinking of, do you? And he puts his little overnight case beside the bed, makes himself a cuppa, uses the loo, and then hops off the hotel balcony. Just like that. I heard it from young Pete Webb, over there. So what I want to know is, why should anyone do that, eh? Why go to the Mondiale when he'd got a perfectly good place to jump from at home?'

'You're right. There's something that doesn't add up there.'

'Tell you what, I've asked Pete to let me know what they find . . . But you can see what he's got his mind on.'

Fran looked at one of her CID officers and a young woman whose bodies were apparently glued together. 'Not so much his mind as his hands, I'd say! So who is she?'

Once she'd have been able to get away with a dress like that. So why had she never risked its equivalent in her youth? Because her mother would have thought the colour common — she thought it a most stunning cerise — and there was no disputing it showed rather more than it concealed. Vulgar, Ma would have called it. And somewhere along the line Fran had omitted vulgarity from her life.

'Jail bait,' Jim declared. 'You wouldn't think to look at her that she's one of the best forensic accountants in the force, would you?'

'I wouldn't have associated her with that sort of figure, I will admit.' A couple of old-timers limped their way across to Jim's table. She grinned. 'It's time for Trev and Denis to have their turn with the party boy, is it, guys?' She got to her feet and bent to kiss him. 'Tell you what, Jim, why don't I keep an eye on this Hythe case and let you know what they find? Then I'll drop in on you and Maureen from time to time and tell you all about it over a cup of tea.'

His face lit up. 'Would you, sweetheart? Whoops, I'm not supposed to call you that, am I?'

'I don't think Mark'd mind.'

'It's not Lover Boy that worries me, it's the Thought Police! All this political correctness, Fran! It's driving me to drink! Hey up, now what's going on?'

The minibuses for the inner circle were at the door.

As she waved them all goodbye, Fran had a pang of regret. Should she have gone with the gang? No, she'd had her five minutes with Jim, and would keep him abreast of the Hythe suicide. Presumably there was no doubt it was suicide?

Not a cleverly staged murder? Despite herself, she, like her old mate, was intrigued.

* * *

The house was horribly quiet when she let herself in, and for a moment, as she leant against the front door, she could have been quite dismal. She'd certainly have liked Mark to be there to welcome her back.

At least her — *their* — bedroom was tidy. She stripped off her glad rags and was running a well-deserved bath when the Hythe suicide came back to her mind. She could understand killing oneself. God knew she'd come close to it when Ian had died. And she could understand wanting to make a good job of it — imagine taking tablets and waking up a few days later with an irrevocably damaged liver and wishing you could change your mind. So the lemming-jumps at Beachy Head or the Forth Bridge made obscure sense and at least would be dramatic. You could leap off yelling 'Geronimo' or whatever. But going to a hotel and leaping off its balcony, not your own — that was weird. She turned off the taps and reached for the phone. And then she put it down again. The suicide wouldn't be going anywhere, as police parlance had it, in a hurry. It'd be much better to leave her questions till Monday.

When she picked up the phone the second time it was to phone Mark. She thought they deserved a takeaway after their day's efforts and he could choose an Indian or Chinese, depending on how little either took him out of his way on the way back. Correction, his way *home*.

CHAPTER FOUR

Mark nibbled a fraying cuticle. How could you tell the woman who's just got rid of half her clothes to make room for yours, who'd ditched cherished CDs and a whole bookshelf of paperbacks, that you didn't after all want to live in her house because the water tasted strange?

Answer: you thought your way round it. A poke round in the loft might reveal a drowned bird in the water tank, not at all a rare occurrence, and you'd deal with it as if — surprise, surprise! — you'd just happened to check and there it lay, waiting to be found.

Next he must work out how to open the hatch to the loft, ostensibly to stow his cases out of the way, though they could equally well have lain under the bed in one of the spare rooms.

Fran was currently cooking his breakfast. Very occasionally they would allow themselves a sinful fry-up, though it was always cooked under the grill and the wicked eggs poached, never offered sunny-side up. The smell rose enticingly up the stairwell, and would permeate the loft too, once he'd managed to open the bloody hatch.

At last, furious with himself, he had to trundle downstairs and humbly beg her assistance.

'After breakfast?' she asked. Surely this tough woman, who could change government policy with a glare at a civil servant, wouldn't ruin breakfast just to indulge his whim!

She was filling the kettle. No, he couldn't face tea. Coffee would disguise the taste better.

'Why do you want to get into the loft, anyway?' she asked, tipping, to his amazement, a fluffy pile of scrambled eggs onto his plate.

'To get rid of some of my rubbish,' he said.

'Can't you take some of it back to Loose? There's plenty of room there, surely, if Sammie has her old room and the babies the spare room. By the time they're big enough to want their own rooms, either we shall be in the Rectory or Sammie and Lloyd will have been reconciled — or both, with luck.'

'Don't tempt Providence. To be honest, I don't want to go back for a couple of days,' he said, surprising himself with the confession. Why was it easier to talk about a row terminating in your daughter's hysterics than about your lover's tainted water?

'It must be hard,' she began, obviously feeling around the subject with some delicacy, 'to go back into a situation so similar but so very different from the one you were used to. To have Sammie there again—'

But no Tina, and Sammie quite a different girl from the one he had created in his memory. He wouldn't mention Tina, but said, attacking the bacon, 'I shall always love Sammie — she's flesh and blood, after all — but just at the moment, between ourselves, I don't like her very much. As for the kids — well, Benny's only a baby, and I've only seen him asleep or screaming, and Ella must be embarking on the Terrible Two's somewhat prematurely. I'm afraid,' he summed up, 'we said things that both of us are probably regretting. No, actually I should have said them before when they might have done her some good. Ten years ago. Maybe fifteen. Anyway, I think I'd rather let the dust settle for a bit.'

Fran nodded without commenting. He had an idea she wanted to say something but wasn't sure how to broach it.

But, surprisingly, she said, 'You know, this ought to be a special weekend, oughtn't it?'

What was he missing? He made a swift dive for safety. 'Every weekend with you is special.'

She gave a mocking bow.

She'd said 'weekend', not 'day', so presumably it wasn't her birthday. He flannelled again. 'So how would you like to celebrate?'

'How about a picnic out at the Rectory? I picked up some finger food yesterday at Sainsbury's. I thought if it rained I could shove everything in the freezer for another day, but the weather forecast's good.' She sounded almost apologetic, asking for such an innocent treat.

'Or we could try that pub at the end of Rectory Lane.'

She was definitely shamefaced. 'We can't. It's booked solid, as I discovered yesterday. I phoned, you see . . . I thought with all our removals we might not want to cook.'

'It's very hard,' he declared, his voice as plaintive as he could make it, 'to kiss a woman shovelling egg into her mouth.'

* * *

'No, try again,' Fran urged. 'I'm teaching you to fish, Mark, not giving you just one meal.'

He poked again at an invisible point on the trapdoor. At last it opened, the flap falling floorwards to reveal an aluminium ladder. One yank, and up he could go. The hatch was so small — how had she managed with it so long? — that he would have to get up inside while she stood below and passed him the cases. Not a lot of time for a quick inspection of the water system, then.

'It's a good job you had a floor put in,' he called down. 'Is there anything you want me to reach while I'm up here?'

'I'll come up and have a look. It's ages since I had a poke round. I bet there's at least another carload of stuff for Oxfam.' Her head appeared through the hatch. 'No, it's not too bad, is it? I had a purge once when I . . . It was the thought of being like Ma and Pa, who never threw anything away . . .'

What had she meant to say?

As for the tank, he'd brazen it out. He peered into it, sniffing. In the general mustiness of an old roof space it was hard to be sure, but he could swear it did smell.

'A galvanised tank!' he said. 'I thought they went out with the Ark.'

'If this one ever springs a leak and has to be replaced, we'll have to cut a hole in the landing ceiling or have it cut to bits. I've measured and it wouldn't go through the hatch,' she said, joining him. 'You know, I really ought to have had all these lead pipes ripped out and replaced, oughtn't I? And a plastic tank. What are you looking at? Or rather, for?'

Now she had asked, he could tell her. But it would come more as an observation than as an accusation. 'Sniff.'

'Sniff the water?' She looked at him quizzically. 'Water isn't supposed to smell, is it?'

'All the same . . .'

She sniffed, but shook her head. 'Ian's sister's always telling me to take zinc or something to improve my sense of smell. That's why I don't wear much perfume — I can't smell if it suits me or not.'

'I shall buy you some today that suits you,' he declared, suddenly realising why she had declared the weekend important. It was their first officially under just one roof. 'After all, it's our special weekend, isn't it? I know Boots isn't very romantic — hell, let's go to France! Come on! We can pick up a ferry!'

'Of course we can. But first tell me what you can smell. You've got me worried.'

'Have you got a torch so we can have a look? It may be a bird's found its way through a crack in the roof and committed suicide. I had a squirrel do it once.'

But the water was clear.

* * *

Their day in France had ended so late that for the first time in their joint lives they had overslept. But even the fact that Fran had to dash off to the village to buy milk didn't stop breakfast being an amazingly good-humoured and leisurely affair, considering that they both had meetings in their diaries. In fact, it wasn't until she was parking the car at police HQ in Maidstone that Fran said, 'You know you thought the water in my tank smelt funny? Well, Mr Patel — you know, the lovely old guy at the corner shop — was saying a number of his customers were saying the same. I wonder what's up?'

He hauled himself out and said, 'Whatever it is, it'll have to wait. I've got one of Simon Gates' financial policy meetings in ten minutes, and I've an idea he's a long meetings man.' Long meetings? Long knives too, and most of them in expensive senior officers' backs, he suspected, though he wouldn't burden Fran with his fears yet.

His reward was a sunny smile. 'Don't you believe it. I taught him, remember. It'll all be done and dusted in an hour.'

* * *

What was all this smelly water business? In the ladies' loo along the corridor from her office, Fran filled a hand bowl and bent down to sniff. No. Nothing. Maybe the tiniest hint of chlorine? She gathered some in her hands and sniffed again. Chlorine and the faintest hint of that exceedingly expensive perfume Mark had bought for her the previous day. What a wild pair they might end up in their old age, if they started acting on impulse. She had a feeling that she and Mark had always responded — as he had done on Saturday — to the demands of others, not themselves.

She had a meeting of her own to go to, this one about devolved budgets. Then this afternoon, after lunch with Mark, she'd talk to Pete Webb about the Mondiale suicide. The only thing she had to do was find an excuse to bomb down to Divisional Headquarters in Folkestone to talk to him. Since Hythe only boasted a police office working fewer than shop hours, any serious crime was dealt with by Folkestone CID.

As detective chief superintendent, she was entitled to visit and talk to any CID unit in the county to appraise its current performance. Some visits were formal, involving chewing off the ears of recalcitrant officers. Others resulted in her carrying desperate appeals for extra funding, equipment or personnel back to HQ. But she'd like this to be altogether lower key, though she didn't know Pete Webb well enough to admit that she was simply being nosy on Jim's behalf. Perhaps Mark would have an idea. Or maybe she'd think of something during the dratted meeting she was about to be late for.

* * *

'You could say you're in the area — unspecified reasons — and just thought you'd pop in to congratulate them all on the success of Jim's leaving do,' Mark suggested, trimming fat off the ham with his salad.

She did likewise. At their age flirting with cholesterol didn't seem an option. 'Pete only went to the first half.'

'You were in the area and just thought you'd drop in? Come on, Fran, with your seniority and reputation you can do pretty well what you want.'

'I don't want to acquire a reputation for eccentricity — at least, not yet.' She felt her chin go up in something like defiance.

'Why not?'

'I don't want them to think I'm gaga,' she admitted, chin going down again. 'Every time I lose my specs, Mark, I think of my parents. And no, I won't buy one of those cord things to hang them round my neck. It'd be support tights next!'

'So you tell him that you were in the area buying a Zimmer frame and thought . . .' He broke off to respond to his beeper. 'The chief. I'd better be on my way.'

CHAPTER FIVE

It would have been nice simply to drop into a CID office and see what was really going on. However, that was no longer possible. Obviously, these days unauthorised people off the street must not stroll beyond police station front desks. Moreover, Fran's rank made her recognisable to most CID officers and a lot of reception staff too. So the element of surprise was lost, and before she was within yards of it a whole CID room could be transformed from a bantering gang of rowdy teenagers to a particularly docile and industrious group of professionals.

As she popped her head into the office of Folkestone CID, she gave DI Pete Webb the benefit of the doubt. His desk looked as if its owner had been toiling since dawn on a variety of projects, most of them no doubt unrelated and many incompatible.

Webb struggled to his feet, making a feverish attempt to adjust a non-existent tie. 'Ma'am.' He looked older by daylight than in the pub, perhaps forty-five, and decidedly less lecherous.

'Hi, Pete. How's things?' She patted the paperwork. 'There are obviously plenty of them.' When he didn't reply, she continued, 'The new DCC's making everyone dance, is he?'

He managed a grin. 'And Mr Gates has got a very complicated tune, ma'am.'

'Guv. Or, since I'm here not on official business but because of something Jim Champion said, Fran will do. Good party, wasn't it?'

He flushed to his ears.

Dimly Fran remembered a Mrs Webb, who had been big with twins last time they'd met. And Pete was already playing away from home, was he? Fran would have to make sure he was too exhausted at the end of his working day to do anything other than sink into his wife's arms. Not that it was any of her business, of course, she told herself, moving a pile of files from the visitor's chair and sitting down.

Trying to sound casual, he said, 'Decent bloke, Jim. One of the old school.'

Whatever that meant. It probably included her, come to think of it.

'I just hope he lives to enjoy his retirement,' Pete was saying.

'Is there any reason he shouldn't?' she demanded, anxious.

'Only the statistics,' he said. 'Longer you work, sooner you die.'

'Well, there's an encouraging fact,' she said. 'Actually, Jim was talking about someone else's death. Possibly a suicide. But maybe not.'

He stared, clearly not placing the case immediately. Then light dawned. 'Ah! Alec Minton. The old guy who topped himself in Hythe. Ten days back.'

'Definitely topped himself?'

'No evidence so far to the contrary at least.'

She nodded. 'Any idea why? It was his choice of venue that intrigued Jim — and now, of course, me. It's infectious, isn't it?'

Pete looked as if curiosity was a bug he didn't have time to catch.

'I suppose the hotel room is no longer preserved as a scene of crime?' she prompted.

He shook his head. 'The SOCO team gave it the spring-clean of its life. Considering the hotel's only been open a year, there was a remarkable amount of grime. Makes you think, doesn't it? Anyway, there was no evidence at all of any foul play, so it's back in use, I should imagine.'

'But not popular with the punters, unless they happen to have a dust allergy!'

'His flat is still as he left it, though. No relatives that we can trace.'

'Any chance of a conducted tour? OK, an unconducted one, since you're clearly going under.'

He shook his head and reached for his jacket. 'Maybe a breath of sea air would clear my head — and I mean literal sea air. The place is right on the front at Hythe, one of those modern blocks you pass if you walk eastward along the promenade. And maybe seeing the place with a fresh pair of eyes would cast some light.'

'Great. Meanwhile, can you get someone to photocopy the file on him? Just the main pages, at this stage. I can pick them up when we get back.'

* * *

Fran had always liked Hythe, a small town that still managed to clutch some vestiges of individuality about it, though every time she walked down the pedestrianised High Street a familiar shop seemed to have gone belly up to be replaced by another charity outlet. Some obliging author had included the place in a book of crap towns, presumably because it didn't have much appeal for *youf*. Fran, however, whose career had taken her to many towns she thought far more deserving of inclusion, thought it had a great deal to offer the retired, with all the shops — including a couple of supermarkets — being within walking distance and more or less on the flat, too. The town was bisected by the Royal Military Canal, a relic of the Napoleonic war, with broad paths either side to tempt cyclists and joggers, or even wheelchair users. The seafront, on which the supposed suicide victim had lived, looked out to Dungeness to the west, Folkestone to the east, and, on a clear day, to France. It was always windy, and thus bracing. What must put families off was the fact that the beaches were steep and shingly, though there was always an angler or two with huge lines on stands, the owners as often as not huddling in mini-tents. They certainly needed shelter today.

Pete held the communal door open for her and headed purposefully up the stairs. At least he didn't consider her decrepit enough to need a lift.

* * *

Fran's mother had always augmented the last-minute packing and milk-cancelling preparations for their annual jaunt to Burnham on Sea with a rigorous house-clean. Her rationale, if such it was, was that if a rail crash, or, later on, when a Ford Anglia became their proudest possession, a car accident should wipe out the entire family, at least the place would be decent for those left. Who those might be, Fran had never known.

It seemed as if the late Alec Minton had followed the same philosophy, even to a couple of air-fresheners, so powerful that even Fran could register them, to stop the place smelling musty.

'Unusual, those, aren't they?' Fran said quietly. Even after all these years, it always seemed natural to speak in lowered tones in the house of the dead. Reverence was hard, however, if you were padding round in protective gear, to avoid contaminating the scene.

Pete didn't share her sensibility. 'Smells like a polecat's boudoir, doesn't it?'

'As if — and I'm only thinking out loud here, Pete — he might have expected his body to be found here, and wanted to overcome the smells of mortality? Though the fresheners would have to be pretty pungent to do that for long.'

'And he'd have needed automatic fly-sprays too. Unless he meant to pack his own cadaver with ice.'

She laughed as she had to at the gallows humour. 'No sign of a bath full of ice cubes? You'd need industrial quantities.'

'More than for your average party, all right.' He stopped short. 'Guv — er, Fran — what you saw on Saturday, it wasn't like it seemed.'

She gave a snort of dry laughter. 'It's no business of mine who you shag, so long as it's not in police time.'

'But I'm not shagging her, Fran. Not with Elaine and the twins at home. Honestly. We're friends, that's all,' he pleaded.

Since he'd raised the topic, she'd let him have it. 'If you ask me, friendship that *close*', she leant on the word, 'can be just as hurtful as a full-blown affair if you're a woman at home whose life is dominated by two kids. How old? Four? Three! God, nervous breakdown time! But as I said, it's none of my business. And Alec's kitchen is. Shall we have a look?'

It had the same unused look as her own before Mark came on the scene. But the cupboards were stocked with china and glass and there was a set of good saucepans. But when it came to food, the cupboard — together with the fridge-freezer — was bare. The pedal bin had been emptied.

Back to the living room. It was dominated by a state-of-the-art TV and hi-fi system, with very few books. A stack of DVDs suggested, at a quick glance, a fairly conventional taste in both music and film.

'Those newspapers — how do they correlate with the date of his death?'

He peered with the air of a man who ought to be wearing glasses. 'The *Telegraph* for the day before. The local rag — the previous weekend. *Radio Times* . . .' He flipped it down.

'Can I look? Is he the sort of man to mark the programmes he means to see?'

'So we'd know if he meant to go on living beyond the day he seems to have topped himself?'

'Exactly. And here we are. He dies on a Tuesday and he wanted to watch *The Bill* on Wednesday and Thursday. What's that?' She picked up an A5 magazine. It looked strangely familiar.

'A freebie from another part of the county, up your way. *Lenham Focus*. God knows how he got hold of that. And why.'

'Have you got a really junior kid you could put on to finding out? Just out of interest.' She gave it a quick glance. She never got round to reading it at home, always consigning it to the paper collection in her scullery and wishing she could intercept the person delivering it to tell him or her to omit her cottage from their round. She bagged it for him, watching him jot down the details. Come to think of it, she might have a copy for a more recent week still in the recycling sack at home.

'The bedroom next?'

'There are two. This one seems to be the spare — overlooking the road, no balcony, rather small.'

'And as tidy as if he never used it.'

'He did, as a matter of fact. He used it as his office. That cupboard opens to reveal a desk.' He pointed but didn't open the door.

'How clever. And you've checked his computer?'

'Not yet. I'll get one of the lads on to it.' He made a note, then realised her eyebrow was raised. 'Or one of the g — *women*.'

She nodded. Everything seemed to be pointing to a suicide, except for that business with the newspapers, which slightly puzzled her. 'And the master bedroom?'

'Here. He'd stripped the bed and left it as you can see.'

The duvet was neatly folded and topped with two pillows.

'So what has he done with the bed linen?'

He shrugged.

'You could get someone on to that, too. What a lovely room.' She wondered over to the window, a huge affair with double doors leading onto the balcony. Green shoots were already poking out from the pots he'd planted. Only one of the chairs was left without a green waterproof cover, the one he regularly used, no doubt, as he sat and scanned the sea and watched passers-by strolling along the broad promenade. 'Bathroom?'

He led the way. Once again, it was immaculate, giving nothing away. She was glad when he said, 'I wonder where his dirty towels are? Same place as the sheets, no doubt.'

'Which sounds like a launderette. Possibly one with service. All this fossicking around! Why didn't the wretched man have the grace to leave a suicide note? Sorry!' He stepped to one side to take a phone call. 'Sorry, Fran. There's an urgent problem back in Folkestone . . .'

* * *

'So they've turned the job down? After stringing us along all these weeks? The buggers!' Fran could have wept all over her salmon.

Mark's hand hesitated over, then settled on hers. 'They said the Rectory was just too big a job for a firm their size. They'd need access to specialist restorers, people conversant with paints from the period, interior designers . . . You name it, they didn't seem to have it. I'm sorry.'

He sounded as disappointed as she felt. She turned her hand to clasp his, as much to comfort herself as to console him. 'It's not your fault. After all, it is a huge task, if we're going to get it right. Presumably if we'd found the restorer, et cetera, et cetera, they could have done the manual work. Or are the ceilings too high, the wood too much in need of repair . . . ?'

'The thing is, to pull all that together, you really need a clerk of works on site all the time, coordinating deliveries and everything.'

'Is it the sort of job I could do if I retired?' she asked, not knowing whether to sound hopeful or doomed.

'You could organise anyone and anything, Fran, but you need contacts and expertise, I suspect, so you don't get great skeins of wool pulled over your eyes. I don't think you'd enjoy it. I'm damned sure I wouldn't.'

She nodded glumly. 'I suppose we could just get it done piecemeal — at the risk of having to re-do some things if we got them out of order.'

'Let's give it another week, and we'll do just that. And pray this dry spell lasts — with the state of the roof another downpour might be fatal.

'Meanwhile we've got each other and everything's fine.'

Except, she added under her breath, for the smelly water.

'In the meantime — and I know I'm breaking our no shop-talk pact! — I wonder if you'd do me a favour? I need a senior CID officer to review a case, and till Henson's back to full fitness I don't want to put any extra pressure on him.'

'No problem. He's a chauvinistic louse, but I wouldn't wish another heart attack on him. Especially if it got you in hot water for failing in your duty of care.'

They shared a rueful grin.

'Quite. Now, there's a man doing life whose case is coming up for appeal any moment now.'

'One of mine?'

'No — it was two or three years back, when you were in one of your uniform phases.'

She grimaced. 'Ah, when I was working on all that community policing stuff that gave the Home Secretary the chance to do our job on the cheap, bugger him.'

'Exactly. So the case was in old QED Moreton's hands.'

They pulled identical faces. Detective Superintendent Sid Moreton was a cop, he liked to declare, of the old school, the one Jim Champion was supposed to be in. In other words, Moreton was not a man prey to doubt, or even the nuances of equivocation. Whenever he summed up evidence in a case, he invariably added QED — *quod erat demonstrandum* — as if what he had offered was as definitive as that in a geometrical proof. He was liked by his older colleagues, feared and resented by his younger ones, though his ability to bully the CPS into accepting slightly tenuous cases had its good side.

Mark continued, 'So would you mind reading through his files and seeing that we've got all our i's dotted and t's crossed? And liaise with the CPS? You know that these days the CIO can be investigated, even tried, for perverting the course of justice if he's made a hash of things, and I'd hate to see any of our CID ending up in the same nick.'

'So would I. Lead me to it.' They exchanged a smile at first comradely and then far from it. 'But not till tomorrow morning, perhaps.'

CHAPTER SIX

Despite Fran's example during his youth, Simon Gates let his meeting meander on interminably. Fran had to sit on her hands to stop herself doodling like a bored student. At long last, it dwindled to a close, reaching a few vapid conclusions, to be fed, no doubt, to the ever-open maw of the Home Office.

Their duty done, the officers were mostly too well disciplined to dash out of the seminar room like kids released into the playground after a very late break bell. Little groups coalesced and spread apart. Embarrassed that her boredom — that everyone's boredom — must have been patently obvious to him, Fran found herself in conversation with Simon himself.

'So once we went through hoops; now we're to go over them, or under them, or any damned way except through them,' he said, as if by way of an excuse.

'It goes with the territory,' she said, non-committal but disappointed in him.

He set them in motion, gesturing her through the door before him. 'How's your new territory going? The Rectory?'

'Don't ask! As we said on Friday, we wanted one firm to undertake everything if possible, so that they could adopt what I suppose you might call a holistic approach. Two — now three — have chuntered about how much they want the work; how much they need the work. And then they decide there's too much work. We need a miracle.'

To her amazement, Gates flushed. What on earth had she said? He asked with a diffidence she did not associate with him, 'How would you feel — I know this is a long shot, and they may not want such a big project either — how would you feel about a team of women doing it?'

'All women? For all I care, they could be a chained work-party of life prisoners from the Deep South of America so long as they did the work. Maybe without the manacles and the uniforms.'

He didn't laugh. 'They try to be all female. But if necessary they do deign to take on the odd man. They're very unusual, very much an acquired taste.' In a rush, he added, 'I could ask the boss to contact you if you like. They've done some really big projects. I'm sure she'd show you photographs and even give references.'

Why didn't he simply give her the firm's name? But never one to look a possible gift horse in the mouth, Fran nodded. 'I'd be very grateful. Thanks.'

'It's I who should be grateful. It was a very pleasant evening last Friday. Thank you very much.' And he scuttled off like a child given a fiver to spend in a sweet shop.

So all she had to do now was await a possible phone call from an anonymous woman who might or might not want to rescue the Rectory.

Meanwhile, however, there was work to be done on the appeal case coming up, even if she could only scratch the surface before meeting Mark for lunch. She retired to her office and started reading the good old-fashioned paper file, ready to make notes as she went. Before she could do more than pick up her pencil, however, the phone rang.

She pounced, first ring.

'Heavens, you're keen, guv! Pete Webb here.'

'You've got some news for me!'

'But it's not good news, I'm afraid, and it's nothing to do with the Alec Minton case. It's poor old Jim Champion . . . It seems he dislocated his knee over the weekend.'

'Heavens! It must have been a wilder party than we could have guessed at!'

'No. Some cricket match the following day. Anyway, he's on crutches. According to one of his mates, who was having a snifter with my guv'nor, he's feeling very sorry for himself.'

Thank God for old boy networks. 'I'm not surprised.' She scribbled a note to herself to send a card. 'Any news on the Minton front?'

'Nothing worth a phone call, if it hadn't been for the news about Jim. We've found the service launderette that did his sheets and towels. They've got half a dozen shirts, too. They're back in his flat now — there wouldn't be any evidence for the lab boys after what they've been through.'

'Did the launderette staff say anything about his demeanour?'

'Hang on.' She could hear him leafing through paper. 'They said he was always polite. Even when he dropped the last lot of stuff in.'

'Is that all?' She thought she might have got rather more out of them. 'Did he say when he wanted the laundry back?'

'The manageress said she just assumed he wanted his usual deal, a twenty-four-hour service. He didn't say anything different.'

'Well,' she observed, resorting to the black humour he had used in the flat, 'he might have said, "Don't hurry with these. I'm going to top myself; I shan't be needing them again."'

'It would have made our job easier,' he agreed.

'Indeed. Now, Pete, you were going to ask someone to photocopy the salient paperwork in the case, and I forgot to collect it.' It was hardly surprising. He'd more or less tipped her out of his car at Folkestone nick and hurtled off with a burn of rubber into some more exciting situation. 'You couldn't fax it over, could you?'

She could hear his sigh. 'Tell me, guv, why is Top Brass taking such an interest in this? I meant to ask yesterday, but you were so obviously caught up in the thrill of the chase I didn't want to interrupt you.'

'Because of Jim Champion,' she said simply. 'If an old-timer like him smells a rat, believe me, a rat there will be!'

'It still looks like suicide to me,' Webb said, his voice sounding little-boy stubborn.

'Oh, I'm certain it is. But why, that's the question, why? And why in that hotel, not his flat?'

* * *

'Because he didn't want to be traced back to his flat, of course,' Jim Champion said a couple of hours later, easing back into the sort of squashy, all-enveloping chair it would be hard to get out of with both legs operative, let alone only one.

If she had been asked to justify taking half the afternoon off to talk to an old-stager, Fran would have said he was germane to an inquiry. However, all she'd had to do was tell an interested Mark where she was heading, with a note to her secretary not to expect her till the following morning.

'I never told you,' Jim was saying, 'but apparently he gave a false address when he signed into the hotel. He paid cash upfront, including a breakfast. He said he'd lost his credit card or some such. He gave a false name, nothing like Alec Minton, and an address in Surrey, which convinced them — wouldn't have taken me in for a second, though. It was only because one of the paramedics recognised him from the shop where he used to buy his papers that they got a proper ID.'

'I'm slipping, Jim,' she said, sipping Maureen's over-strong builder's tea, the sort she'd loved until Mark had got her palate hooked on the weak green variety. Maureen had swiftly identified the visit as an opportunity for talking shop and had made herself scarce. 'I should have asked Pete Webb all this.' She didn't mention the still missing paperwork.

'And he's slipping, or he'd have told you.'

'He's got other things on his mind far more urgent than indulging my whims.'

'Other things including young whatshername, the one with—' He gestured large breasts. 'And I'll bet he's told you it's all above board, too, eh? The young. Think they've invented everything, don't they?'

The young. As if they were a different race. She'd never heard him speak like that before. Had it taken less than a week's retirement to change his perspective so profoundly?

'They certainly didn't invent sports injuries. Pete says you were playing cricket.' She just stopped herself adding, *at your age*. 'How did you hurt yourself so badly? And how long will you be on crutches?'

'It was at this church match . . .' He embarked on an explanation that she, as a non-cricketer, would have been happy to skip. And the answer to the second question involved equal quantities of medical jargon. But it seemed to equal a piece of string. It all depended on how fast he healed, if at all, but there might or might not be surgery, which might or might not be keyhole. It might have been one of Simon Gates' meetings. The gist was that he would be immobile for some time, and as he wasn't an officer who'd always craved time to work on a sedentary project he was not a happy man.

In the end Fran was grateful for the ring of her mobile. Excusing herself, and promising a return visit soon, she let herself out and took the call.

'Is that Detective Chief Superintendent Fran Harman? Paula Farmer here,' came a resonant voice, the sort that could be heard from one end of a football pitch to another.

'I'm sorry?' Fran prompted.

'Simon Gates asked me to contact you,' she added encouragingly. 'Didn't he tell you? Typical!'

Fran wasn't quite sure whether such inefficiency was typical of men in general or Simon in particular.

'You're from the restoration people? How wonderful of you to call me! Thank you so much.'

Her gushing deserved Paula's dry response. 'I'd save your thanks until we've seen the job and priced it up — and decided if we can take it.'

'At least you called me back, Ms Farmer. A lot of firms don't bother.'

'Oh, that's because they're afraid of the work and it's not macho to say so. Or some price the job so high you can't afford them. We don't work like that.'

Fran didn't think they would, somehow. 'And "we" are?'

'We started off as Paula's Pots, a small co-operative. That's what some of our clients still call us. Pact Restorers we are now. So where's the property and when can we do an internal inspection? This afternoon?'

Fran surprised herself by being taken aback. 'You don't hang about.'

'Gates says it's urgent. I should warn you, however, Detective Chief Superintendent, that good restoration work is neither speedy nor cheap.'

'It's urgent because I don't know how much longer the roof will survive. The other firms promised to protect the whole lot with scaffolding and sheeting, but they never showed up to do it.'

There was a pause. 'You love the place already, don't you? Where is it? OS map coordinates would be useful if it's remote.'

Fran gaped. 'There's an OS map in my car. Bear with me a minute . . . I can be there in forty-five minutes,' she added as Farmer read the coordinates back.

'Excellent. So can I.'

* * *

'Pact Restorers?' Mark echoed when she called him with the news. 'It sounds as if they ought to be operating under the United Nations mandate to police international ceasefires.'

'Paula Farmer certainly sounded at least as authoritative as any General Secretary, and more likely to smack recalcitrant leaders into order. She certainly doesn't rate our shiny new DCC over much.'

'Did you say Paula Farmer? The name sounds vaguely familiar . . .'

'Be that as it may, I'm meeting her at the Rectory in forty-five minutes. I must go. I daren't be late!'

Late she was, however, or Paula Farmer was early. Fran suspected the latter. In fact, she suspected that Farmer would deliberately arrive anywhere early simply to discompose the person meeting her.

At five-foot ten herself, Fran didn't meet many women of her own height, but Paula Farmer must have been at least that. At forty-ish, she carried more weight than Fran, but Fran suspected it was pure muscle under a suit as well cut as her own.

'It's a beautiful building. You were right to worry about the roof, though. Is there much damp damage inside? Last Friday's rain wouldn't have done it any good.' Clearly she had no time to bother with formalities. A Dictaphone clipped to her lapel, she carried both a powerful torch and a digital camera; she produced hard hats for both herself and Fran.

Fran stared. 'Are these necessary? Mark and I have been in quite often and—'

'It's a building site the moment I agree to take on the job. Hard hats, protective boots, high-visibility vests, Detect—'

'Fran, please.'

The other woman approved, nodding and rewarding her with a smile that lit up the whole of her otherwise inscrutable face. Fran thought vaguely of Dutch Interiors, as if the Girl with the Pearl Earring had filled out with age.

And she was on the move already.

Fran donned her hat and scuttled after her.

* * *

'I just want to hug the place and make it better,' Fran admitted, almost apologetically, as they looked out of an attic window at the surrounding countryside. 'I've never felt like this about a simple building before.'

'In that case it's the place you've got to live.' Paula spoke flatly, but with a tinge of the mystic, acknowledging a destiny not worth arguing with. She pointed at a van. 'Ah, I see Caffy's here. Caffy Tyler. She's responsible for the interior work. Don't expect magnolia gloss from her, by the way. She'll use appropriate materials — the sort English Heritage and the National Trust use. Probably the only places she'll encourage you to update are the bathroom and the kitchen.'

'We shall need more than one bathroom,' Fran objected. 'Some en suite.'

'She'll know what you can and can't do. Chapter and verse. Trust her, she's the most highly qualified of all of us — done a list of courses as long as your arm. Drat, who's that arriving now?'

Fran smiled. 'That'll be Mark. He loves the place as much as I do.'

'Mr Harman?'

'Assistant Chief Constable Mark Turner. Call him Mark.'

'Police titles are such mouthfuls,' Paula said, as if she had wide experience of them and condemned the lot.

They watched while a small woman passed Mark his headgear, and two yellow discs marched forward together.

* * *

'Hello. I'm Caffy Tyler — Caffy with two f's, not Cathy,' a gamine young woman just getting out of the predictable white van introduced herself to Mark as he got out of his car.

'Mark Turner.' Her name sounded familiar too, but her face certainly wasn't.

They shook hands, not so much an introduction, he suspected, but more as if they were sealing an unspoken bargain.

'What a place!' she said, beaming.

'We just want to make a start,' he said. He caught a pleading note in his voice and carried on, 'We thought we could do something ourselves in the garden.'

Caffy wrinkled her nose. 'You could make a start cutting back those hedges, I suppose, though the trees would need trained surgeons.'

He had his usual vision of people in masks and green gowns.

'And under all those weeds you might even have a proper Victorian garden with parterres and paths — you'd need an expert to tell. Wouldn't it be fun to restore that too!'

'We don't want to live in a museum. It's not as if it's National Trust or anything like that,' he objected.

'You wouldn't put furry dice and Darren and Sharon labels in that elegant car of yours, would you?' she asked scathingly.

Before he could concede that he would put nothing in his car that would distract the driver or limit visibility, the other woman was upon him too. And that was how it felt, as if he was about to be overwhelmed by the sheer force of their personalities. He and Fran both — he'd rarely seen her looking so punch-drunk. She threw him an ironic smile.

As for Caffy, she wandered off on her own, soon to be followed by the woman Fran had introduced simply as Paula, as if she were a long-lost cousin. He'd certainly been Mark immediately, though that was possibly Fran's doing.

Occasionally they could hear the women exclaiming over something, for good or for bad.

He gathered Fran to him for a kiss and a hug, the sort he and Tina had once shared when they'd entrusted a sick Sammie to the care of a hospital consultant. 'It'll be all right now it's in their hands,' he said.

CHAPTER SEVEN

'If there's really something wrong with the mains supply, I want to know what Invitaqua are doing about it,' Fran declared, unloading litre upon litre of bottled Malvern water from the car. Half of her couldn't understand why a pair of old toughies like them had become so obsessed with the issue of pure water; half of her, having seen so many deaths as a result of neglecting elementary precautions such as wearing seat belts, knew all too well.

'You're quite right,' Mark agreed, hefting the shrink-wrapped batches into Fran's utility room. 'Cost apart, this isn't at all environmentally friendly, is it? All this plastic, when you should be able to turn on a tap?'

'Not as bad as buying Fiji water — think of all the food miles that involves. All the same, I want proper home-grown Kentish stuff,' she declared, little-girl stubborn, stamping her foot.

'For the time being, you can have it, and you're welcome to it. You can have my share too,' he said, stowing the last load. 'At least we can shower at work . . . Nice cup of tea?'

'I think we've earned a beer,' she said.

He couldn't argue. On the way home from the Rectory, they'd called in at his house in Loose to collect the post

— he'd only just got round to having Royal Mail redirect it — and encountered, after the calm firmness of the two Pact women, the quasi-hysteria of Sammie, rendered helpless by her credit-card bill. Had it been her financial profligacy that had caused such a rift in her marriage? Neither he nor Fran now bought the theory that Lloyd had thrown her out: little things she let slip suggested that she had left in a major tantrum and now secretly wished she hadn't.

Mark had insisted that Fran went to the house with him, though she had offered to stay in the car.

'You've rights too,' he'd said, 'one of which is to be treated courteously. And I'd like you to meet my grandchildren.'

'I'm not very good with babies,' she said cautiously.

'Who is, without practice?'

In the event, she'd had to learn very quickly, Sammie leaving her in charge of them while she dragged her father off to see the bill, which for some reason couldn't travel to the living room. The gist of what she was saying was that she couldn't pay even the nominal rent he'd asked for; the subtext, he was sure, was that he should offer to settle her debts. Nearly four thousand pounds on one card alone, none of it, as far as he could see, on anything except clothes and shoes, apart from a manicurist and hairdresser. He was quite sure that Fran had at least half that on hers some months, as he did, since they both used plastic like cash, but they both, he knew, always paid off the complete balance. Fran's excuse was that the National Trust benefited from card use, while his chosen charity was Oxfam. The only people gaining from Sammie's recklessness were the bank's fat cats.

'Cheers,' Fran said, passing him a bottle, which he clinked against hers. She wasn't usually a beer-from-the-bottle woman, despite her usual air of mucking in with whatever the boys were doing. But, since it didn't need washing up — presumably glass recycling did all that was necessary to get rid of any bacteria — a bottle was definitely the drinking vessel of choice this evening.

'Cheers. I'm sorry to land you in all this.'

She slipped an arm round his waist. 'All what? We're together and at last the Rectory is in good hands. I liked the way Paula had organised the scaffolding people before we even left the place. They make a good team, don't they? Paula's organisational skills and Caffy's obvious idealism?'

'Do you think they're an item?'

'I hadn't thought about it. Does it matter? Let them have their private life — or lives. I'm sure they deserve them.'

He nodded. 'I just wish I could place them — I know those names from somewhere, but certainly I've never met them before.'

'Is that what's the matter?'

'Matter?'

'Something's been troubling you ever since we left Loose.'

'Ah. Well . . . I suppose Sammie's the matter.' It came out with a rush. He gave an edited version, just as he was sure her account of childminding had been somewhat censored.

'At *what* interest rate?' she demanded as he finished. 'Hell's bells! So what are we going to do about it?'

'You're not going to do anything. She's my problem.'

'She's actually Lloyd's problem, or more properly her own. All the same, what are we going to do?'

'I've told her to phone the company and explain. And to see a solicitor.'

'If she's declared bankrupt it's going to cause all sorts of problems down the line. Maybe for Lloyd too.'

'And me, of course, if she uses my address.'

'Bloody hell, yes. So what are we going to do?'

He could feel the anger that ought to have been directed against Sammie rising against Fran. 'I've told you, she's my problem, not yours.' Seeing her stiffen, he took a deep breath. 'Look, if she'd ever spoken a civil word to you, let alone a friendly, welcoming one, damn me if I wouldn't have there-there'd her and paid every last one of her bills. And if we hadn't had the Rectory to pour money into, of course.'

She didn't argue, but her face closed against him, as it always did when she was troubled — no, when he had troubled her. And now she was getting the dinner, in a sort of pained silence. They'd laughed over buying pre-washed microwavable vegetables, plastic glasses and paper plates, but that was before their visit to Loose. And why, while he laid the table, did she break off to do some jotting with which she clearly had difficulties?

She turned to him with a face lit as if by a minor triumph. 'Do you know how much interest she has to pay overall if she only pays off the bare minimum each month?'

'She's talking about changing her card, to one that charges no interest on your existing balance.' At least they were talking again.

'That's fine and dandy so long as she doesn't put any more on it. Or on any others. I take it you've established how many she has? Mark, you haven't, have you? Go on, phone her now and find out. Every last penny she owes. You don't have to tell me, but she needs to be honest with you so she can be honest with herself. And you might talk to her about Lloyd, too.'

* * *

While he did as he was told, Fran disappeared to the scullery, sifting through the sack of paper scheduled for recycling.

'I'd have thought you'd have had enough of rubbish after this weekend,' Mark observed, making her jump.

'I just have this niggle,' Fran said, still burrowing. 'Ah!' Triumphantly she flourished an orange-jacketed *Focus*. Presumably each issue was colour-coded — the one in Minton's flat had been green. Sitting on her haunches, she thumbed through. 'I ought to make a point of reading this, you know. Look, it's got details of everything that's going on: Borough Council Corner; Parish Affairs; Our Man in Westminster; Lenham Community Matters; Clubs, Groups, Societies, Organisations and Gatherings; Focus on Youth; Our Rural Environment; History of Lenham; Thoughts and Reports from St Mary's. And lots of local ads.'

'So it will be invaluable now you actually live in the village full time. It really is a very pretty little place, isn't it? Fran?'

She struggled to her feet. 'Drat. To think a couple of years ago I could go from squat to stand with no effort at all. More important, it's got a bit about our water in it. Here — continued reports of a strange smell . . . complaints to Invitaqua . . . Mr Patel was right, wasn't he? I wonder what the latest is. Come on, let's go for a walk,' she wheedled. 'Just as far as the corner shop.'

'Why there?' The chair in Fran's living room that had become his was exceptionally comfortable.

'Because Mr Patel will know the latest about the water — who's phoned, who's written, who's whatever.'

'OK, you've talked me into it. So long as we can stop off at the Dog and Bear afterwards for a glass of proper beer.'

She beamed. 'And whoever's behind the bar there will have the latest news too.'

* * *

Fran hooked her arm matily into Mark's as they strolled home. Funny, she remembered her parents doing that — never holding hands, as she and Mark often did. And she recalled heroes in classic A-level novels offering arms to young women, even without a romantic attachment. Why had it gone out of fashion?

'So at least twenty people have complained to Invitaqua about this taste — and one woman claims she found a greeny-blue thread in her hand bowl. And Mrs Green, whoever she may be, says she's found a blonde hair in her sink, as does Mrs Carter, but we can't trust her because everyone knows what a copycat she is! Is there anyone in the village the Patels don't have an angle on?' he demanded with a laugh. 'But so far nothing appears to have been done,' he summed up more soberly. 'Why not?'

She laughed. 'I can feel your spine straightening and see your chin taking on its official jut! I should imagine it's because no one's got through to the right person. You know how these enterprises work, all pre-recorded messages and press this and then press that. Everything's designed to make people give up.'

'You wouldn't give up.'

'I wouldn't try the conventional way in the first place. And since a good half-dozen have tried writing and had zero response, I shan't be doing that either.'

He laughed. 'So what will you be doing?'

'One of two things — maybe both. The obvious people to contact are Ofwat, since they're in charge of all the water companies. But I suspect they'll tell me to go through all sorts of official complaints channels, forgive the pun, and you know how I'd love doing that.'

'The other, then?'

'Pull in a favour.'

He drew her to a halt. 'Is this legit?'

'Would I ever bend a single rule? Little me? Well, I should think it's legit, but Maeve Burton will soon tell us if it isn't.'

'Maeve as in wispy little Bill?'

Fran suppressed an inapposite joke. 'Maeve's pretty senior in Environmental Health, remember. She's always telling us to call on her if we need something doing.'

'People often say they owe you a favour without meaning it,' he warned. Fran always took them at their word.

'Perhaps it isn't a favour — just one organisation helping another organisation. It's got to be a criminal offence, selling dodgy water, and the police and Environmental Health would naturally work in tandem.'

It was easier to agree. 'Your phone call or mine?'

'Mine. Tomorrow morning. When we did Shakespeare for A level there was something about beer provoking the desire.'

'And the rest of the line says it takes away the performance!'

'I'm quite sure it doesn't . . .'

* * *

‘What I was thinking,’ she began the following morning as she drove them into work, ‘about Sammie, is this. So long as she cut up her cards in front of you, we could pay off all her debts — and she could pay us back, interest free.’

‘For “we” read “I”,’ he countered, wondering how long she’d been hatching the idea. ‘But it’s a good idea. If we can afford it. We predicated buying and restoring the Rectory on income from letting one of our houses and selling the other. With Sammie *in situ* we shan’t be able to let my place and — according to Paula — there’s no chance of moving into the Rectory for several months, so we can’t sell yours. And Pact are not going to come cheap, are they?’

‘Paula assured me that they operate on very tight margins.’

‘She’s not about to admit to being a multimillionaire, is she? And we know the materials won’t be your bog-standard Homebase stuff — they’ll come dear as well. Which is why we’ve agreed to pay their bills as they crop up. No, hear me out. I shan’t begrudge a single penny, believe me. It just means we shan’t have as much money to throw around as I’d like. And that includes on Sammie.’

‘I could retire and cash in my lump sum,’ she said in a thin voice.

He patted the hand on the gear-lever. ‘Just at the moment your monthly salary cheque’s probably more useful.’

‘If I got another job, we’d have the lump sum and a monthly cheque.’

‘If I got another job, we would, too.’

She almost stalled. ‘You what?’

‘You’re not the only one who can retire, you know. I’ve an idea life’s not going to be much fun under your thin-lipped protégé. I must be able to pull in some sort of job even at my age. There must be firms who actively recruit the more mature.’

‘Homebase does, I believe. Or is it B&Q? Now there’s an idea. You could stack the shelves there and get us staff discount on our gutters.’

* * *

Maeve Burton answered first ring.

'Fran! And I've got the thank you card for the dinner party stamped and ready here on my desk.' Knowing Maeve she probably meant it. 'How's the romance? I saw you were wearing an engagement ring.'

It suited police ideas of respectability, but there was, of course, the problem of what it actually meant. 'It's got to the shared mortgage stage,' Fran said, without further explanation. Given Maeve's history, she still tried to exercise tact when it came to talking to her about her personal life.

'No wedding bells yet?'

'At our age?' she asked derisively. But it hurt — like a tooth with over-hot tea — that Mark never mentioned marriage, and was consistently evasive if she mentioned it, which, to be fair, she did about once a month. Perhaps that constituted nagging and was counterproductive. 'How are you and Bill? He seems very nice.'

'He is. Don't let that mild exterior put you off. He's wonderful when it comes to unsafe buildings. Now, I've just sorted out some mammoth cockroaches in the kitchen of an extremely posh hotel — when you do get hitched, you will remember to consult me about the venue for your reception, won't you?' Maeve deafened Fran with a whoop of laughter.

At one point Fran had thought Maeve would never laugh again. But it seemed she was indomitable.

'Of course I will. And invite you — if you'd care to come.' Not every woman who had been raped so viciously that she could never have children and whose fiancé had consequently jilted her would enjoy seeing other people celebrate their unions.

'So long as I can bring Bill,' Maeve declared.

'That goes without saying.'

'The wonderful thing is, he's not bothered about children.' It might have sounded like girlie gossip, but to Fran — and presumably Maeve — it was far more than that. 'And to prove it he'd actually had the snip before he met me. Well, three kids already, all grown up. So no worries on that front.'

Not unless the children were like Mark's. Fran, however, said all that was proper and encouraging. And meant it. But how on earth could she turn from gossip to what she wanted?

Why not be as direct as she usually was? 'Actually, Maeve, wedding reception venues apart, I was wondering if you could do me a favour.'

'Ask away. I can always say no.' Her voice suddenly lost its buoyancy.

Was she having a flashback? At one point she confessed to finding it hard to use the simple negative without recalling the event when she used it in vain. Fran held her breath.

'But I'm sure you wouldn't have asked if it weren't important, so fire away,' Maeve continued in her normal voice.

'I don't know if you've heard about our village water supply? There's a funny smell — and taste — to it—'

'As if there's a dead dog in an aquifer or something?'

'I hadn't thought of that precisely,' she said.

'But it would certainly explain the milk in the coconut. I suppose it does come from an aquifer? Or a reservoir?'

'I've no idea. Just out of a tap.'

She was rewarded by a cackle of derisive laughter.

'Anyway, a number of villagers have already tried complaining to Invitaqua direct. Some have phoned, others have written. But no one has had a response.'

'Anyone can get water tested, Fran. Is that what you're asking me to organise?'

'Could you? Unofficially at this stage.'

'No problem. OK, I'll send someone round to collect a sample or two from your very own tap. No, tell you what, we'll have a meal — our shout — and come back and I'll take the sample myself. Actually, perhaps we'd better eat somewhere a good distance from Lenham . . .'

* * *

Fran's encounters with colleagues in the canteen or elsewhere might have looked casual but rarely were. Today when she saw DI Jon Binns lurking by the water cooler, she found that she too was thirsty, although she'd just downed a mug of tea.

Jon Binns had moved from forensic accountancy into the more general area of CID, where he had attracted Fran's attention for his loyalty, occasionally misplaced, and his acumen. He also seemed to like her as much as she liked him, and even if passing the time of day with him didn't elicit the information she needed she wouldn't consider it time wasted.

Pleasantries exchanged and over, she said bluntly, 'Jon, I need to pick your brains. You've got a business degree, haven't you?'

'Fancy your remembering that!'

Fran usually did recall things she might find useful one day, but she grinned noncommittally, implying, she hoped, that she always took an interest in promising young officers' backgrounds.

'Tell me, why should a firm risk failing to respond to customers' letters and calls?'

'They probably don't think it's a risk at all. People aren't persistent.'

'People like me are persistent. People like me smell rats if Customer Relations never phone them back.'

'You needn't always. It can simply mean that the firm doesn't employ enough poor drones to respond to all their complaints.'

'Not that it doesn't care?'

'It's all to do with balancing variables, guv. And very few customers are going to make a fuss if no one rings back.'

'OK, so you give up phoning and write. And still nothing happens. What then?'

'Someone makes a stink. Goes to the media. And then things start to happen.' He narrowed his eyes. 'Are you thinking of a specific organisation here? Because I'd have thought a call from someone like you, speaking with the authority of your rank, would work wonders.'

He was good, this lad. *The authority of your rank!* What he meant, of course, was that Fran could bully her way through most situations. She smiled silkily. 'So you think I should give Invitaqua one of my grade-one bollockings?'

'Invitaqua? Aren't they in the process of being sold?'

She rounded her eyes encouragingly.

'They've not been a UK company since privatisation, I know that, and I've an idea they're owned by some German-based multinational, which is now selling it off to some off-shore holding company. Venture capital . . . Do you want all the details? The story was in the *FT* the other day — I can look it up if you want.'

'I'm not sure that's necessary, thanks, Jon. But the gist of what you're saying is that they're currently in a sort of financial limbo—'

'That's right. It's no one's baby at the moment, and all people are interested in is the price of shares. But that shouldn't affect the day-to-day running of the company.'

'I should hope not — it'd be bad if they turned the taps off until they'd completed their negotiations.'

'What were you going to complain about, guv?'

'The village water supply tastes odd and smells a bit, some people claim. Would it reduce the share price if there was a water-quality scandal?'

'Only if it was big enough.'

'So they might be covering something up until the deal goes through?'

He looked her straight in the eye. 'I don't see them covering you up, guv.'

'Like a noisy budgie in a cage? I should like to see them try!'

CHAPTER EIGHT

Reaching at long last for the file that Mark had asked her to read, and this time getting to the stage where she even checked her pencil was sharp, Fran was again interrupted by the phone. It was Simon Gates' secretary, inviting her to yet another meeting.

'This afternoon? Sorry, I can't possibly. Would you send Mr Gates my apologies and tell him I'm tied up with a job for Mr Turner?'

Two minutes later the phone rang again. It was Gates himself.

'I wouldn't have requested your presence if it hadn't been essential,' he said without preamble.

An essential meeting with no prior preparation? Surely not. All the same, she temporised. 'We've got a case coming up for appeal shortly. Mark wants me to check the validity of our case before the CPS start picking holes in it.'

'Such reviews are Henson's responsibility.'

Surely he knew about Henson's heart problem? Lest he hadn't, she spelt it out. 'Detective Chief Superintendent Henson was off sick for some months after major heart surgery. OK, he's back now, but he's still very much on light duties, and he's only on seventy-five per cent of his hours.'

With the connivance of both the chief and Cosmo Dix, head of Human Resources, Fran, who'd had to take over a case or two from him, had continued to stand by to pick up odd bits and pieces so that Henson wouldn't be under too much pressure. 'So I support him whenever—'

'I'll expect you at three, DCS Harman.' He cut the call.

The bastard. Double bastard for betraying her belief in him.

Even she had to respond to direct orders, so, with great reluctance leaving the file behind, she took herself off to the meeting. Predictably it overran lamentably and predictably made not a jot of difference to the sum total of things. She'd have done more for the world by touting a collection box outside Sainsbury's for the Police Benevolent Fund.

Two hours later, then, gasping for a cup of tea, on her return to her office, she was greeted by an A4 internal post envelope. Forget the tea! A quick look inside told her it was what she'd been awaiting for some time, the background information on the Alec Minton suicide. She knew local CIDs were overburdened not just with cases but with the concomitant paperwork; all the same, Pete Webb had been decidedly dilatory. She glanced at her watch — it was now nearer seven than six. Mark would be waiting for her. Hell's bells, they were supposed to be meeting Maeve and little Bill at eight. All the same—

'No you don't,' Mark announced, popping his head round the door just as she lifted the flap.

She dropped the envelope guiltily on the desk.

'If you open it now, Fran, you'll still be here at midnight, scribbling here, jotting there.'

'And of course, I'm not supposed to be looking at cases — I'm Meetings Woman now.' She explained, watching Mark's face tighten with anger at having his own request countermanded. 'I can't even wipe my damned nose without having to minute it or write a paper about it. And I thought Simon was good!'

'He was at the rank he was on when you met him. He's just like practically everyone else at his level — promoted just beyond his capacity. And he knows it and makes up for it by making everyone else work three times as hard as they ought simply to cover his back.'

'You never do. And you're also answerable to the chief direct.'

'I have a wonderful team, and a guv'nor who insisted that dealing with a spot of real crime from time to time was good for one's brain and kept one in touch with the workers.'

She shook her head. 'That cock won't fight. He's got the same guv'nor and pretty well the same team, plus you as support.'

'Or me looking over his shoulder, as he may see it.'

She would rather blame herself than Mark. 'Perhaps I overestimated his abilities.'

'If you did, everyone else on his career path has too. We shall see. Meanwhile, why don't you have a word with the chief, Fran, and get him officially to support your position as Henson's backstop — yes, in writing for preference — before Gates gets you back into uniform.'

'What did you say?' she gasped, not knowing whether to be furious or afraid.

'No, don't panic — it's only a feeling. I suspect Gates doesn't like anomalies of any sort,' Mark explained, 'and your position isn't exactly regular.' They exchanged a smile — it was he who had suggested it, after all, at which point their relationship had burgeoned. 'Now, hadn't you better nip off and change? We don't want to be too late.'

All the same, when she returned, no longer severe in a trouser suit but almost flirty and feminine in a calf-length skirt, he had fished out the photocopies and spread them on her desk.

'Mine! Mine! Gimme!'

He held a fistful behind his back. 'You'll have to pay with a kiss first . . .'

* * *

'I'm getting too old to eat so late,' Mark admitted, reaching across the dressing table for the Rennies.

Fran begged one too. 'I forgot when I agreed eight that Maeve has never arrived early in her life, and that she likes a good chinwag before she so much as opens the menu. And the service was slow, you must admit that.'

'Slow! Like tortoises on bromide. And all of us coming back here to fill those special sterile bottles of hers with water whilst under the influence of whisky didn't help.'

'And neither did Bill wanting an attic-to-cellar guided tour as if he was on a National Trust outing. Or casing the joint.'

'But Maeve did say she'd get someone to run preliminary tests at the reservoir tomorrow if our water showed the merest hint of anything dodgy. So the evening was mostly a success.'

'Not for my tum.'

'Nor mine. No dessert next time, anyway.'

'No dessert ever, ever again . . .'

* * *

Considering how long it had taken Pete Webb to get the material on the Alec Minton case, there wasn't much of it for Fran to look at when she arrived at her desk on Wednesday morning. Half of Fran wanted to shake his officers for such perfunctory reports. The other half agreed with what she was sure had been the tacit, possibly even the open, decision of the investigating team: it had been a suicide and the sooner they could report their findings to the coroner the sooner they could get on with investigating some real crime.

The information they'd gathered gave a bald outline of his life. Alec Minton had been born sixty-three years ago in Leicester. After secondary school he'd been employed as a clerk first by Leicester City Council, where on day-release he'd studied and obtained appropriate qualifications. After ten years or so he'd moved to Birmingham City Council, and thence to South Staffordshire Water, where he'd steadily progressed up the promotion ladder. He seemed to have taken no further courses or exams. He'd not married and sold his parents' house on their death to buy his own in Erdington, a suburb of Birmingham. When the Thatcher government had forced privatisation on the utilities, he'd finally left the Midlands and headed to Manchester City Council. In nothing like a top post, he'd retired at the age of sixty, settling, as many other people his age did, in Hythe, where he'd joined the library and the bowls club.

Why had he bothered killing himself? In his place Fran would have simply died of boredom.

And why had he gone to a hotel to do it?

His bowls club colleagues reported him as having a very equable temperament, surrendering to neither of the impostors, triumph and despair. Only once had they ever seen him lose his temper, but it was agreed it was fully justified. He'd apologised to the committee. His neighbours said he was the ideal man to have living above or below, he was so quiet. His car service log was up to date.

'Alec, Alec. What secret propelled you to your grave?'

'Talking to yourself, Fran? Not a good sign.'

The chief! Fran was on her feet in a second.

'For goodness' sake,' he said, waving her down again. 'On second thoughts, you wouldn't have a cup of tea on offer, would you?'

'Tea or coffee,' she said. 'And some home-made biscuits.'

He settled himself with the air of one who intended to stay for some time. Bother him. The rest of Alec Minton's file apart, she only had half an hour before the next bloody Gates meeting and had meant to prepare for it properly, in the hope that the benefit she got from it might be proportional to the effort she put in.

'You weren't on the interview panel for the DCC post, were you, Fran? Coffee, please. No, some of your nice soothing green tea.'

'No, of course I wasn't! I've sat on more appointment panels than I can shake a stick at but never for posts above me!'

'Ah,' he said gloomily, staring at the straw-coloured liquid in the mug she set before him. Perhaps it had been his choice that made him so downbeat.

Sighing, she sat and waited. To prompt him she fished out the tin of biscuits. 'Don't for one moment think I made these!'

He smiled. 'Young Tom Arkwright's auntie?'

It was his memory for details like that that earned him not just the respect but affection of his officers. Less liked was his habit of quoting Shakespeare at apposite moments.

'Tom still thinks he needs to look after me, sir. He drops by for a natter when he gets his weekly consignment.'

'You enjoyed working with him, didn't you?' He smiled.

'Very much. He's a nice kid — should go far. In fact, he's about to take up his first posting as sergeant down in Ashford.' Where was this going?

'You'll miss the biscuits then.'

'I shall have to make an effort to bake my own.' And why not, now she was back in her own kitchen at weekends instead of being overawed by Tina's?

He chewed appreciatively and sipped with less enthusiasm at his tea. 'Gates is running a pretty tight ship, eh, Fran?'

'Wall-to-wall policy meetings, sir. Just what the Home Secretary ordered. And just as Gates has nailed one document, the Home Office changes its mind and we're supposed to be focusing on something else — business as usual, in other words.'

She was rewarded by a guffaw of dry laughter.

'But he's doing all right?'

She made a tiny rocking motion with her hand. 'Maybe sweeping a tad too clean, sir. If only he could time-constrain agenda items. You know my feeling about meetings anyway,' she added, as if to temper the criticism. 'Especially when I've got other things on my plate I consider should take priority.'

His laugh was ironic. 'I do indeed. But this is a general feeling?'

'I only ever speak for myself, sir.'

'Not for Mark? He isn't feeling his nose has been pushed out, is he, Fran? I wouldn't want that.'

'Would you expect him to tell you how I feel, sir? Well, then, how can I possibly answer that?' she asked with a conclusive grin, which, to his credit, the chief returned.

'Nice to see Henson back in harness,' he said unexpectedly.

Mark's warning about Gates' intentions ringing in her ears, Fran smiled. She hoped he would not realise her duplicity. 'Until he's able to work a full week, you can rely on my continuing to help him out in whatever way I can. In fact, sir, I'd really like my position to be confirmed, just for the record.'

'You don't think you'd be more use giving Gates a hand? Mentoring him a bit?'

'Dogsbodying for him you mean?'

She had gone too far. The chief got to his feet. 'I'm sure you'll always fulfil whatever role you're called upon to take. And no skiving off meetings, Fran — not without a very good reason.'

'Sir,' she said, also on her feet. But she spoke to an empty room. So she stuck her tongue out at the closed door. Now what? Should she see the chief again and push her point, or memo him formally? Neither was a good move, and might well be counterproductive. He was a man who always liked to think he'd had ideas first.

* * *

Halfway through the afternoon's meeting, even more tedious because she'd not had time to prepare at all, let alone adequately, she scribbled a note to herself. 'Why was Alec Minton reading the *Lenham Focus*? Which edition was it?' As an afterthought she added, 'What did he look like?' That seemed about the most productive moment of the whole afternoon. Especially when Gates, mistaking her enthusiastic jotting as a sign that at least someone was involved in the proceedings, bounced her into leading a sub-committee dealing with the needs of divisional CIDs. It wasn't an unreasonable move. After all, she had been compiling the information on her own initiative. But she had an idea that he was staking a claim on her, and, given the chief's closing words, he would win. And she would become no more than his minion, no longer — in her eyes at least — a free agent.

At last, feeling as if she bore on her shoulders the whole weight of future policing in the South East, she trailed past her secretary's office on her way back to her own. She gave no more than a languid flap of the hand, but Pat waved vigorously and pointed at the phone. Fran responded by breaking into something more energetic than a depressed saunter, and, in the safety of her sanctum, picked up the handset.

'Maeve! Already!'

'Bill insisted he could smell something funny too. He's got a wonderful nose, Fran — always chooses my perfume for me. He saves me from making the most expensive mistakes.'

Fran made little winding gestures. One's own middle-aged infatuation was one thing, someone else's another, even if it was Maeve's.

'Anyway, Bill thought there was something fishy — or more probably animal! — in the supply. So I didn't bother testing your tap water but went straight for the reservoir check — you know, with that clever portable machine I was telling you about.'

'And did it—?'

'I told you that they can test for conductivity, pH, dissolved oxygen and temperature? Well, there was sufficient evidence to go for the full investigation.'

'Excellent news! Or is it?'

'It's not very good at all, from your point of view — because it does suggest that there is some sort of pollutant. And the other bad news is that it'll take a whole week to get the results.'

'A week!'

'That's how long science takes, Fran. But—'

'There's a but?'

'This is a good but. Invitaqua are required by law to take regular samples. So I can demand to see their results. And if they've found impurities and have done nothing to investigate the situation, we can have them on toast.'

'Boiled alive in their own dodgy water would be more appropriate. Maeve, I'm so grateful.'

'It's my job, Fran. In any case, I always like returning a favour.'

Fran overrode the thanks. 'So what do I have to do next?'

'Absolutely nothing. Which will be a change for you, won't it?'

It would indeed, and a nice one considering there was still the urgent matter of the appeal case file to go through. Was she getting slower or the days shorter?

'We'll work in tandem with the Environment Agency,' Maeve continued. 'We serve an order and they do the enforcing.'

'And then?'

'They'll flush out the pipes and you're back with nice pure H2O.'

'You are my heroine — and Bill my hero,' she added as a tacit apology for ever doubting Bill's perfections.

CHAPTER NINE

Fran was so determined to get stuck into the case Mark wanted her to study that, having dropped him at the station to catch an early train for a Home Office meeting, she slipped into work almost secretly, with a banana and an apple for breakfast at her desk. Any chance phone calls would be diverted to her secretary, the caller being disappointed since Pat Harper, the saint officially on the payroll as her secretary, didn't officially come in till eight-thirty. Pat was usually in long before this, but used the time to catch up on other work uninterrupted.

Fran rolled up her sleeves, literally and metaphorically, and opened the file.

Three photos, all passport size, stared up at her. The first was of Janine Roper, a woman in her thirties. The unsmiling, face-forward pose did her no favours, but it was clear that she had good features and well-cut hair.

Janine Roper had been eight years younger than her husband Ken, a local government officer. His photo showed an anxious-looking man in his early forties, hair already thinning. He'd been wearing either spectacles or sunglasses before he was snapped — two marks showed on the bridge of his nose. Janine had lived with him in a semi-detached estate house in Ashford. Neighbours said they were an ideal couple, never arguing and having mercifully quiet hobbies. The only minor bone of contention was Ken's dinghy, which he kept on his drive, with the result that he was in the habit of parking on the road in what others regarded as their spots. Ken was a keen amateur sailor, his friend Maurice Barnes crewing. Someone said Janine, a classroom assistant, was given to extensive reading; at least she was always talking about visits to the public library. Colleagues at school reported that she often seemed tired and listless, but she'd mentioned nothing apart from insomnia. In confirmation, packets of herbal and homeopathic sleeping pills had been found beside her bed.

If she and Ken were a model couple, everyone reported how affectionate Janine was towards Maurice, the other man in the case. Maurice was a big but gentle-looking man about Ken's age, who'd permitted himself a winsome turn of the mouth that had somehow escaped the notice of the smile-resistant Passport Office. Apparently Janine was given to hugging him and linking arms with him when they went about as a threesome. Yes, the press had gone for a three-in-a-bed angle, but swiftly dropped it, preferring the jugular of a suddenly jealous husband who had killed his wife and blackmailed his friend into helping. And Maurice might have been susceptible to blackmail. A biochemist working at a perfume factory near Ashford, he was a local councillor hoping to be adopted as a Lib Dem parliamentary candidate, so the less scandal in his life the better — at least until after he was elected.

The police thesis was that Ken had killed Janine in their home just before or during the spring bank holiday weekend — they'd found spots of blood in the bathroom that Ken insisted must have been caused by one of her frequent nosebleeds, though there was no medical confirmation than she had a nasal problem. Then, the allegation went, the two men had bundled her body under the tarpaulin that always covered Roper's dinghy when it was on the drive, and then, hitching the dinghy to the Ropers' Fiesta, set off to the sea. Neighbours had seen them waving her goodbye; the police believed that the men had waved to an empty house. There was CCTV footage of them arriving at Whitstable, the dinghy still covered in its tarpaulin. But the cameras hadn't actually picked them up as they set sail, so there was no saying whether the vessel was lower in the water than it should have been with only two aboard or indeed if there was something still mysteriously swathed in tarpaulin by their feet. An obvious flaw in the police case was that, even allowing for the waywardness of tides and currents, no body remotely matching Janine's had ever been washed up where they would have expected it. Neither had one appeared further afield.

Both men had vociferously protested their innocence. Neither had a record of violence, sexual or otherwise.

Meanwhile, Barnes agreed that Janine had been in his bed. His claim was that she had had a sick headache when she was round at his house with her husband, but that was considered a likely tale, though at least there was medical corroboration that she suffered from severe migraines.

So the DPP had been convinced, the jury had been convinced and the men were now doing time.

Fran leant back and rubbed her neck. Her colleagues seemed to have done a business-like job in unearthing and presenting adequate evidence, even if almost all of it was circumstantial. As for the SIO's notebooks, she had a nasty feeling — an instinct, nothing she would have mentioned to anyone but Mark — that old QED Moreton had put in just enough to satisfy the regulations, and that there was as much omitted as admitted. What about other suspects? He had made very little effort to trawl through other people who might have wanted Janine dead, colleagues or even sex offenders. She made a note — in her reckoning, this was a real weakness.

Another note — this one to Pat Harper — to contact the Home Office to arrange permission to visit Roper and Barnes as soon as possible. Whom should she take with her? Tom would be ideal, but it would be wrong to distract him from his new promotion. DI Jon Binns? This legwork might be a bit lowly for him. But Tom's new girlfriend, Sue Hall — she might do. A quick phone call reached her.

'Me? Really? Oh, ma'am — guv! — that'd be terrific.'

Was it pure or applied delight? Fran's protégés — or protégées — tended to swarm briskly up the promotion ladder. But since Sue was seeing Tom, the most naive of men, Fran gave her the benefit of the doubt.

'We'll need to look at the evidence, of course. Two pairs of eyes are better than one. Are you tied up with anything really urgent this week?'

'Nothing I can't fix. Oh, guv, wait till I tell Tom.'

'I'll give you a call the moment I can clear my diary. Love to Tom.'

Tempted though she was to drop everything and go down to the evidence store immediately, Fran thought she would preface the visit with what she always caustically dismissed as playing politics. Mark, however, more worldly wise than she, had thought it a good idea for her to attempt another pre-emptive strike against any plans Simon might have in mind for her, so that was what she must do.

Having achieved nothing with the chief, it was fortunate she got on very well with Cosmo Dix, head of Human Resources. She phoned to invite herself down to share his first — always excellent, she'd heard — coffee of the day. He served China tea in thin china cups, complete with saucers; she'd be interested to see how he took his shots of caffeine.

In white, almost translucent, Rosenthal espresso cups, that was how.

'The trouble is,' Cosmo agreed, passing a plate of expensive-looking chocolate biscuits Fran reluctantly declined on her scales' behalf, 'that the chief will get ideas into his head that are so hard to shift. One needs to replace them gently, discreetly. A bit of circumnavigation is called for, Fran, dear. Or do I mean circumlocution? Circumspection?'

Fran shook her head. 'Are you sure there is an appropriate word?'

'Who cares? What I have to do is foresee a series of events that positively require him to keep you in CID, just as long as you want to stay, of course. I think it might be something to do with DCS Henson's health, don't you? We wouldn't want to put any pressure on it, would we? Or do I mean him?'

'I've already tried that tack with him, and with Gates, who wasn't at all sympathetic.'

Sighing, Cosmo took what in anyone else would have been a swig from his cup. 'Much better to leave it with me, Fran — and for God's sake, don't get in any fights. Everything by the book. Softly, softly.' He touched the side of his nose.

She finished her coffee, refusing a second cup on the grounds that she needed to sleep sometime before the week was up. 'So I'd better go and start the homework he's set me. A report on the needs of divisional CIDs.'

He smiled. 'With you writing it, who knows, they may even get what they want.'

* * *

Fran went so far as to open both a computer document and a paper file. Simon had implied she should draw on her own recent experience of divisional CIDs, but — though she would never have admitted it publicly — she had been at HQ in Maidstone for so long that she felt that any recollections she had would be unreliable. So she would sally forth to talk to a few CID officers, in particular one Pete Webb.

Why not? It was a nice day, and if Folkestone was hardly the most inspiring of towns, it had sufficient sea breezes to blow away any tangling mental cobwebs.

And she wanted to nag Webb some more over the Minton case.

In fact, the ostensible reasons, as she freely admitted to Pat, when she popped into her office to say she was leaving the building, were the supplementary ones.

'Take your bucket and spade and make a day of it,' Pat suggested.

Fran and Pat had worked together only a few months, but they liked and approved of each other. The fact that they used the same HRT and were anxiously eyeing the prospect of elasticated waists was now less important than a sense that they were allies.

'Go on, Fran. You know I'll be in touch if you're needed here — before anyone notices you're missing. If you took an unmarked vehicle from the pound, they'd see yours in the car park and assume you were in some meeting somewhere.' Pat smiled with a wholly feigned innocence.

Fran grinned her thanks, too grateful to pose the question that immediately sprang to mind — where on that shingly stretch of coast would you find a grain of sand?

* * *

'Will this committee actually deliver what we want down in the divisions?' Webb asked suspiciously.

'How long have you been an officer, Pete? Well, then, you know the answer as well as I do. But at least if you ask for the sun, the moon and the stars you may get a few new light bulbs. And when you've given me your wish list — and please be as imaginative as you like — you can have a treat.'

He groaned. 'I know your treats. You want another look at the Minton case, don't you?'

'You know what, I wouldn't mind a look at Minton himself.'

'You're joking. Hell's bells, Fran, is there anywhere in this new wish list policy of yours that allows you to tell a detective chief superintendent she's off her head?'

She regarded him coldly for a second. All these days of hierarchical meetings had made her first impulse to bawl him out. So her rueful grin was directed both at him and at herself. 'It depends whether she was announced by her title or by her name, I should imagine.'

'In that case maybe we should compromise on "guv",' he replied.

'So I'm only slightly off my head?'

'Must be all those meetings,' he said. 'Do you fancy a cuppa before we start on this 'ere list?'

'Not half.'

* * *

At last, over a matey canteen lunch after all their efforts, she asked, 'Now, Pete, why should Alec Minton have a copy of a Lenham freebie paper and why should he have kept it? And — most important of all — did it have any connection with his death? You haven't a spare minion you could ask to check, have you?'

He spread his hands in clear disbelief. 'Christ, guv, haven't we just spent the past hour saying spare minions are a thing of the past? Not that you've ever let us use the word, anyway. All *junior officers* are too busy getting buried under paperwork.'

'I know, I know. I'd do it myself but—'

Her phone rang.

It was Pat, who dropped her voice conspiratorially. 'Fran? DCS Henson's secretary's just phoned me. He's not well — just a bad cold, I think — and he's gone home. And guess what—'

'He wants me to go to one of Gates' meetings for him. Oh, Pat, and I haven't done more than have a quick paddle.'

* * *

There was no doubt that Gates registered her late arrival, so she stayed behind, schoolgirl-like, to apologise.

'I wouldn't have thought it necessary to conduct all your interviews face to face,' he said, not unreasonably. 'Have you never heard of email or the phone?'

'Sir.' There was no point in trying to explain the impossibility of getting hard-working men and women to respond to a cold email they believed would have no tangible results when twenty other things cluttering their desks screamed for their attention. 'And I have to tell you, sir, I shan't be available tomorrow.' His eyebrows shot up even as she drew breath to explain. 'I shall be in court. All day, I expect.'

And even he couldn't argue with that. Could he?

He said coldly, as if he'd like to clap her into detention, 'Surely they'll recess for the weekend at lunchtime.'

'And if they do, sir, rest assured I shall be back at my desk.'

* * *

As she returned from court — it looked very much as if the case was going their way — the sun came out, turning the trudge from the car park into a stroll on a spring day. Accordingly, she took the long way round, a route which took her past the knot of miscreants in smokers' alley. The — largely male — conclaves had always worried her, as inevitably the nicotine-stained bonding created an out-group of those who never touched cigarettes. For years the implication had been that if you were a real man, or aspired to be one, whichever gender you were, you were out there puffing in all weathers, and by way of recompense acquiring inside information. Now that official policy actively discouraged smoking anywhere in the environs of HQ, only the hardiest gaspers still congregated, and normally, hoping to escape detection, in twos or threes at most. Today there must have been nine — no, ten.

About to give them a few choice words, Fran stopped herself short. These weren't rookies idling the afternoon away, but men — and a few women — of a similar rank to hers. She smelt not cigarette smoke but the sharp odour of conspiracy.

The huddle broke up, absorbed her, and re-amalgamated. She didn't expect them to come straight to the point, nor did they, but it didn't take long for her to realise which way the conversation was drifting. Once she'd seen a ballet — what the hell was it called? Drat these senior moments! — in which primitive people had circled round a maiden, persuading her that she had been chosen to represent their needs to the gods. So far so good. But it seemed that the maiden had to dance herself to death to put their point across. Fran had a distinct feeling that she was the one round whom the elders were gathering, and though dancing was not on the menu, some sort of intercession most definitely was.

'Organise a petition about Gates? You've got to be out of your collective minds!' Fran said, once she'd got the drift. 'This is the police, for God's sake. It's not some golf club committee worried that some new member wears the wrong socks.'

'But we all agree on the problems. So what about a round robin to the chief—?'

'Are you *serious*? You can't go over Gates' head!'

'But—'

'If you have a problem, you should have the guts to tell him. To his face.'

A couple of heads nodded, as if that was what they had been urging all along.

George Marshall, a uniform chief super the same age as herself, said, 'Of course, you've known him ever since he was a constable, haven't you?'

'I have indeed. Though I could never have known he'd turn out this way,' she said.

'So you — having been his mentor, as you might say, Fran — would be well placed to have a word in his ear.'

'On the contrary, anything I said could be construed as sour grapes. If anyone is going to say anything to Gates — and what, for goodness' sake, can anyone say? — it's got to be someone with no axe to grind. Obviously those of you still expecting promotions here or elsewhere can't be involved. But I can see a couple of faces as old as mine. Come on, George, you could manage a fatherly word. Or you, Terry. Or even both of you, over a quiet beer.'

'I bet he only drinks Chardonnay.'

'Even if he's straight TT, which he isn't, you should still make a nice informal approach. Hell's bells, we're not some kids snitching on a mate.' Suddenly she recalled the name of the ballet. *The Rite of Spring*. She'd known the music for ages, of course, but had found the stage version, with its costumes and movement, strangely disappointing. It was best watched with her eyes closed, as it were. The rest of the conversation was accompanied by irritating snippets of Stravinsky in her head. *Thump*-thump thump thump. *Thump*-thump thump thump.

'Will you back us, anyway?' *Thump*-thump thump thump.

'Only if you do it properly, with no messing around with petitions and round robins. But for once in my life, I'm not going to lead from the front. Sorry.'

Thump-thump thump thump. 'Of course, being with the ACC means you don't exactly have a free hand.'

'My hands are as free as the next person's, but it's still no.'

'I suppose you couldn't get the ACC to—'

'Absolutely not! Him tell his immediate boss he couldn't run a piss up in a brewery? I think not! I tell you, it's got to be done properly or not at all.'

There was a murmur from her colleagues, a couple grudgingly acknowledging she might have a point.

'So George and Terry, you think?'

'It's what *George and Terry* think,' she countered. 'Or any of you who feel strongly enough — and brave enough,' she added under her breath.

Turning away, she found herself falling into step with a snuffle-nosed and coughing DCS Henson, a man with whom she had shared a mutual loathing ever since his first day with the Kent Constabulary. Presumably he still thought her a superannuated old whore, but today he flickered a faint smile in her direction. Hers to him mirrored her concern; if anyone looked as though he ought to be tucked up in bed with a couple of aspirins it was Henson.

'I never got round to thanking you for helping out so much when I was in hospital,' he said, startling her. 'And since.' Perhaps during his near-death experience he'd seen a vision warning him to change the error of his ways. He must have shed three stone at least; sloughing off the fat had left his newly pale skin curiously loose, and his once brisk pace was now an amble. It came as no surprise that he was still unable to work full hours — there was a frailty about him she associated shockingly with her late father.

In an effort not to give way to a sudden pang of emotion, she said curtly, 'No problem.' That was too brusque, so she added more conciliatingly, with a hint of a grin, 'We're both old pros, aren't we, Dave — we get on and do the job.'

His cough sounded painful. 'Instead of calling meetings and—'

'I'm no fan of Gates, but that's what he's paid to do, call meetings — not as many as he calls, I grant you, and not such bloody long ones.' Again she softened. 'How on earth do you manage to fit them all in with your workload on your reduced hours?'

'More delegation than I like. Thing is, these drugs I'm on sap your energy.' He certainly sounded weary. 'And you do your bit, I suppose.' Gee, thanks. 'In fact, if it was up to me, I'd put you on extra cases and have you go to less meetings.'

She was so flabbergasted that she forgot to be enraged by his use of less, not fewer. 'I'm glad to hear that.' For a moment she nearly told him what she feared Gates had had in mind for her, but thought better of it. She and Henson might be speaking, but that didn't mean anything more than an armed truce. She certainly wouldn't trust him not to rat behind her back. She changed the subject. 'Actually, I've got quite involved reviewing a murder case that's coming up to appeal. One of old QED Moreton's — I think he was before your time.'

'But he was legendary for taking short cuts — even I've heard that.'

'There's no clear evidence of that so far. But I want to have a look at all the case material myself. Wouldn't you?'

'I bloody would. And I'd rather do it than go to another of his lordship's fucking meetings. Didn't you know? There's one at four o'clock — three line whip.'

* * *

'And exactly what were you discussing at that mothers' meeting of yours?' Gates demanded.

True to her promise to herself, Fran had been a model committee woman, alert and indulging in not a single doodle. She'd not put forward any new ideas, but since the topic wasn't one of which she'd had any particular experience that was excusable. She had however supported some colleagues if their ideas seemed good and had pointed out flaws in others' arguments. It had been practically gold star material. So Gates' question, shot at her as she left the room with the others, had come as a shock.

'I beg your pardon?'

'I asked what you were talking about with that smokers' group. Not that you smoke, as I recall.'

Smoke? She positively flamed with anger, especially as out of the corner of her eye she could see those she suspected of having been ring-leaders scuttling away to the safety of their offices. 'Do you want me to talk to you here or in private?'

'I want you to tell me in the presence of the chief. Now. This instant. I won't have you plot behind my back, you old bitch.'

'Sorry, sir,' she said with feigned cheeriness, refusing to wince at the venom in his voice, 'you can't use "old" as a term of abuse. Not even to me. Oh, for God's sake, Simon, take a look at yourself. We've hardly had Henson back five minutes after his heart attack and now you're planning one for yourself. Get a grip.'

He pointed. His arm was quivering with fury. 'In the chief's office! Now!'

Stopping legs apart, arms akimbo, Fran shook her head. 'No way. Stop making a fool of yourself, Simon, lad. Your office or mine, if you insist, but never wash dirty linen in front of the chief and put him on the spot.' She turned on her heel and led the way back to his office, less subject to underlings' scrutiny than her own. She was acutely aware of all the ears listening intently to their progress.

Without being asked, she sat down. He might take the opportunity to tower over her and bully her, or he might react by sensibly sitting himself.

He chose to tower. She folded her arms across her chest but realised how combative she must look so released them to clasp her hands meekly on her lap.

'You were asking me about the gathering outside,' she prompted.

'Well? What were you up to?'

'As it happens I was urging caution to a lot of hotheads. But since it wasn't my meeting I can't tell you how it started or, indeed, who convened it. Nor would I if I knew,' she added under her breath. 'Look, Simon—'

'I believe you're supposed to address a senior officer as "sir". And I don't believe I gave you permission to sit.'

'So you didn't. Do you mind if I do, sir? It's easier to have a pleasant conversation sitting down.' She could feel things slipping beyond her grip. She didn't mean to wind him up, but knew she was perilously close to doing so anyway.

As for him, he was getting angrier by the moment, and had she not trusted all his years of police training, she would have been afraid that he would strike her.

'Simon. Sir. This is getting out of hand. You saw me in conversation with a load of other old lags like me and now you think I'm organising — what?'

'That's what I want to know. Now. What?'

'I'm organising nothing. Full stop. As for our colleagues, I simply can't tell you. I came in at the tail end of a private conversation. Then I walked away with DCS Henson asking him how he felt and how he was coping with his return to work.'

'Everyone knows you hate each other's guts.'

Now who had told him that? 'You can't run into a colleague who's had an illness as serious as that and not ask about his health,' she said reasonably.

'Very plausible.'

'And very true. He's still far from well, as it happens. I admit that a year ago I'd have wished all his toenails to grow in, but now the poor bugger's a shell of what he was.'

'I'm not interested in Henson's health.'

'But you should be.' How much easier it was when she was sure of her ground. 'In human terms, we don't want him to have another — possibly fatal — heart attack. In corporate terms,' those words should appeal to him, 'it would be a disaster if we forgot our duty of care and drove him to an early grave.'

'Your meaning?'

Did he really need anyone to spell that out? 'I shouldn't think it's really your bag, more Cosmo Dix's, but I'd have thought the occupational health people should be reviewing his workload.'

'You're very good at sticking your nose into things that aren't your brief, aren't you? So it comes as a constant source of amazement to me that you won't do those things that you ought to do.'

For a moment she was back on her knees at confirmation class. Shutting the door on the memory she said, 'Henson's far too macho to volunteer, without being prompted, the information that he's struggling. All I'm doing is watching out for the colleague whose role I took over when he was ill, on the grounds I'd done it for years enough in the past.'

'Things have changed, Harman.'

She shook her head. 'Officially my job description hasn't been changed yet. At my level, any radical alterations have to be agreed with all parties. All. Changing my role either overtly or by stealth is not in your gift, Simon.'

'I think you'll find it is.' He tapped a file on his desk. '*My* job description, if you want to read it.'

'Let's get Cosmo to talk to the Superintendents' Association rep, shall we? I didn't want to make trouble—'

'Bloody hell, that's rich coming from you! Trouble's always been your middle name! We used to call you the Mouth. Speak first, engage brain second.'

What had turned him from a model trainee to an embittered boss? As for the accusations, they hurt, no doubt about that. She'd always seen herself as assertive, standing up for the underdog. He was casting her as an abrasive menace.

'Simon,' she said, getting to her feet, 'this is clearly getting neither of us anywhere. I don't need to listen to things that on reflection you might have preferred not to say. So I suggest we both do what we're paid to do — a spot of police work. Good afternoon.'

And with what she hoped was dignity, she walked out of the room.

And what next, eh? Should she stomp off to Cosmo, to query whether her job description could be changed at Simon's whim? That would mean a third party knew that she and Simon were now actually at war. Or wait for Mark's return, when he would lovingly coax her out of her fury? That could compromise him, something she'd tried to avoid the moment they'd become an item.

She sat at her desk, head in her hands.

She'd no idea how long she'd been like that when Mark phoned, apparently breathless.

'I've managed to get hold of tickets for *The Producers*,' he announced. 'And you have to catch the next London train.'

CHAPTER TEN

Monday morning saw Fran return to court, to be recalled to the witness box by a stupid and bumptious defence counsel, whose fatuous questions she was able to parry with what the judge described as wit and grace. She hung about for a while, just to be sure in her own mind that she and her team had done everything possible to make a watertight case, before returning to Maidstone too late to lunch with Mark.

She checked her desk, post and emails to ensure that no gremlins had conjured yet another meeting from thin air. No, not one! But before she could celebrate Pat Harper came in bearing a pile of paperwork requiring her instant attention and the news that Henson was off sick.

'He looked pretty bad on Friday,' Fran said, non-committally. 'Has any arrangement been made to allocate his workload?'

'Come on, you know they'll land you with anything they can't manage. Now, could I have this lot checked and signed by four . . . ?'

* * *

Halfway through the afternoon, she'd cleared all the paperwork Pat had inflicted on her. What next? Gates' report? Not likely. She picked up the case file Mark had asked her to look at. Should anyone query her activities, she minuted that it was a matter of priorities. She did think of suggesting that every extra day innocent men spent behind bars was sinful; instead, she referred to recent judicial criticism of the police and CPS for deferring appeal cases *ad nauseam*.

In response to Fran's phone call, Sue Hall met her at the evidence store. Fran recalled her as having a hairstyle so disciplined she might almost have been in denial about its auburn beauty. Today it was slightly looser — Tom's influence, perhaps? — but her suit was as severe as Fran's own, her only ornament a small gold crucifix on a fine chain. It was clear she was apprehensive. She'd never worked solo with Fran before, but surely that couldn't be worrying her? Surely she was made of sterner stuff? All the same, Fran resolved not to bark or snarl — certainly not at her and possibly not about other people. The obvious way to make her relax was to talk about Tom, but Fran wanted her to feel valued for her own sake.

So she plunged straight into the case; as she spoke, she found her vague fears solidifying into doubts. 'But don't get me wrong. I'm sure everyone did his or her best. But we've taken some criticism in the media recently and I'd rather find any holes in the case and plug them before anyone else spots them.'

Almost visibly brave, Sue said, 'There's a distinct lack of other suspects, isn't there, guv?'

'Exactly. Just as having no body is a real problem. Now, I don't want to waste your time, but if later on you could check every database you can for other possible perpetrators it would be enormously helpful. Just so we can eliminate them. Right, let's see what the dead woman's clothes tell us about her.'

The answer was: not a lot.

'Is this all they have of hers?' Sue demanded, tossing the few sealed bags on top of each other as if rooting through a sales bin.

''Fraid so. What would your next move be?' she asked with what she hoped was an encouraging smile.

'To gain access to their house and check her wardrobes and so on. Find out if she used make-up. What her hobbies were. Do we have time?'

'Technically, yes. But another question looms.'

'"Does the budget run to it?"' Sue asked in a pseudo-official voice.

'Got it in one. There's a fine line between checking that all that's necessary has been done and starting an inquiry from scratch.'

'But you're starting from the premise that all has not been done, aren't you, ma'am? Guv?'

Fran nodded, a rueful grin matching her protégée's. 'And that's going to come expensive.'

Sue's face fell. 'Does that mean you just rubber-stamp everything and give up?'

'I shall have to take it back to the ACC. But I shall tell him we both feel there are areas that may warrant — less complacency, shall we say? Trouble is, Sue, just because Mark and I are together, that doesn't mean I can influence him when his head and his budgets say no.'

'But surely his budget would stretch to talking to Barnes and Roper again.'

'It better had. Or he'll be cooking the supper for a week.'

They turned together and signed out.

Fran pointed to Sue's gold cross. 'Do you believe in all that?'

'I got talked to by a vicar, guv, during an Alpha Course. A nice woman.'

'Not Janie Falkirk, by any chance? The priest in charge of St Jude's, that run-down church in Canterbury?' And instrumental in solving the tricky case she and Sue had worked on. Or perhaps it had been the doing of St Jude himself, the patron saint of lost causes. 'Don't look so embarrassed, Sue. She's a good woman. But if you did happen to believe in saints and things, it wouldn't hurt to have a word with St Anthony, would it?'

'Janie's a bit low-church for saints. Why St Anthony, anyway?'

'I've an idea he's the guy you pray to when you want to find something. In this case, poor Janine Roper's body.'

* * *

'You know I trust your instincts absolutely, Fran. If you think there's something dodgy, there is. But in the current climate we need something pretty concrete to justify reopening a case for which, after all, we got a conviction.' Mark looked across his desk. It was a matter of principle with them both that any discussion of this sort should be as official as possible, with discussions and, more important, decisions, properly recorded.

'I realise that. But I do feel that, at the very least, we should reinterview Roper and Barnes. Roper is here in Maidstone nick for goodness' sake — it wouldn't take much longer than popping to the dentist.' She spoke so innocently there had to be a catch.

'And Barnes? Don't tell me — Dartmoor or somewhere equally inaccessible. Oh, Fran—'

'It's not my fault they move the prison population round like so many pawns on a chessboard, with far less reason and rationale. Durham,' she confessed at last.

'Jesus Christ! How do his family manage to visit him?' He slammed his hands on his desk in exasperation. 'Rehabilitation, returning to the community? All we do is lock the buggers up and shuffle them round and then we're surprised prison doesn't work. Go to Durham if you must, Fran. But why not try Maidstone first?'

'I intended to — he's the husband, after all.'

He expected her to end the official conversation with a quick private one. But she didn't say anything, didn't move.

And her face was so blank that he knew she was up to something. Worse, that she wanted him to do something. From the quality of her silence he knew exactly what she wanted. She wanted him to get on to his friend in the Prison Service and whisper that Barnes should be moved again — yet again? — and this time somewhere nearer home. Still neither spoke. At last he simply flapped his hands, and she left without so much as a wink.

He'd better get on the phone, hadn't he, and have a conversation he must absolutely never have had.

* * *

Fran was just shrugging on her jacket when someone knocked on her door. But it wasn't Mark she beamed at. It was DCI Joanne Pearce, a woman Fran always felt she could do business with, though she always wanted to tell her to dress less for a night clubbing and more for a serious job, especially when the clinging and revealing clothes she favoured clung too tight and revealed rather too much forty-year-old flesh.

'It's just courtesy, really, ma'am,' the younger woman said. 'But with DCS Henson off sick and likely to be for some time, we thought you ought to know what we're up to.'

Fran nodded her thanks. 'Which is?'

'We've picked up a guy with a long history of domestic violence. And other things.'

There was clearly a story here. 'Sit down and tell me all about it. Coffee?'

'No thanks. Not a lot to tell, guv. We've had our eye on him for some time in connection with the death of a prostitute in Ashford. We knew we'd get him eventually. There was some CCTV footage of a hooded man and plenty of DNA at the scene.'

'But it's one thing to have DNA, another to find out who it belongs to,' Fran nodded.

'Quite. Anyway, uniform got called to a domestic — quite a serious one, in fact — and as a result of the gob-swab they did on him then, we've got him for the murder of the tom.'

Fran tried not to wince at the term she loathed. 'How serious was the domestic?'

'She died. We think it was accidental — I mean, if you really enjoy knocking a woman about, why spoil your hobby by killing the punch ball?'

Fran wasn't entirely happy with Pearce's cynical tone but said nothing. Everyone dealt with their anger in their own way, and if that was Pearce's so be it. So she asked, 'Do we have any other unsolved murders on our books? Going back however long your man — did you tell me his name, by the way? — has been in the district?'

'Dale Drury. Aged thirty-seven. Lives in Stanhope.'

'Part of Ashford.'

'Right. And not the loveliest. It'll be better without him, anyway. He's been this close to an ASBO a couple of times, and he's only been there four years.'

'Lovely man. OK. Do all that's needful, Joanne, and call on me if there are problems. And do talk to him about any other crimes he might want to come clean about, won't you?'

'Any in particular, guv?'

However decent Pearce might be, Fran drew the line at confessing an illogical desire to find Drury had killed Janine Roper. 'Any unsolved murders, crimes of violence, whatever. Our clear-up rates could do with a bit of a boost. Or even any another force might still have on their books. Let's be Good Samaritans, shall we?'

* * *

Her jacket now on, and her bag in her hand, the last thing Fran wanted was another call. She had half a mind to pretend the office was empty, and let it ring on, but knew she would have to meet Pat's eye if she did. So with strong reluctance she did her duty, bracing herself for a last-minute summons from Gates.

'Harman,' she declared, in her flattest, do-not-interrupt-my-thought-processes voice.

'Fran?' It was a woman's voice at the other end.

'Paula?' Fran sat down, hard. Pact were going to give up on the Rectory, weren't they?

'Yes. Paula Farmer. We've got a tiny problem, Fran. No, nothing to panic about. It's just that we — look, this may be fanciful, but we've an idea someone's watching the house.'

'Watching the Rectory? But it's miles from anywhere! Why on earth?'

'Oh, lots of good reasons. Stealing to order for one. You've still got wonderful original fireplaces and other features *in situ*. And our equipment's worth a bit too. Would you mind if we took a few security precautions?'

'Do whatever it takes, Paula.'

'It'll cost a bit to do it properly. We have our contacts, of course. But if you've people in mind you'd rather call on . . .'

'How soon could you mobilise your people?'

'As soon as we end this call.'

'Please — just get on to it.' Before she'd reached the end of the sentence the phone was dead.

* * *

'It simply could have been Paula being ultra-efficient, of course,' Mark said, five minutes later. 'And no cause to panic at all.'

'All the same,' Fran said stubbornly.

'All the same, to please you — all right, to please me too — we'll drive past, just to make sure. Though of what, I don't know.'

'Nor me. But it'd be nice to see the place again, wouldn't it?'

The last of the rush hour traffic having had time to clear, they had an easy journey, following minor rather than major roads. As they approached, the lowering clouds thinned, and there was a suspicion of spring sunshine. Mark kept up a flow of low-grade gossip, and she responded in turn.

He slowed as he always did at the top of the lane so they could look down on it. Except they couldn't see the roof for scaffolding and huge polythene sheets.

'It looks more like some work of art by that pair who wrap buildings, doesn't it?' he asked, taking her hand and squeezing it. 'I wonder how many square metres of sheeting are up there.'

'Intensive care for buildings! It ought to be wired up to a giant heart monitor to let us know how it's progressing.'

'I wouldn't mind betting that Paula and her mates have got the buildings equivalent somewhere. You know, monitoring damp and movement and stuff.'

'You sound really professional. Shall we go and see? You know, I never expected them to move this quickly.'

'It's double-overtime for weekend work, that's the trouble,' he grumbled.

She shot a glance at him. Was there something else about Sammie and her debts he hadn't told her? 'Look, they're still there! No, we've just missed them.' A car pulled away from the entrance, heading briskly down the lane away from them. 'Brownie points for them working so late, anyway.'

'If it was them. I wouldn't have thought a BMW would be their preferred mode of transport. I only got half of the registration,' he said, jotting it down nonetheless. 'Well,' he added defensively, 'if they're worried enough to fix extra security, I'm worried enough to do my bit.'

'Let's hope it was someone just coveting our house. Anyway, they'd have to deal with that padlock. It'd keep Fort Knox safe, that.'

'Unless an intruder did this.' He scaled the five-barred gate with ease.

She did the same. With less ease. The house looked impregnable enough, with steel plates protecting lower-level windows and doors. Round the doors that were obviously in use, mesh barricades were padlocked together. Paula was certainly doing her best. But was it good enough? On impulse, as they turned to leave, she blew their new home a kiss.

CHAPTER ELEVEN

Tuesday saw Fran trying to enter a house as strongly fortified as the Rectory, but much less beautiful. This was the semi in Ashford previously occupied by the Ropers, and now secured until Ken had completed his sentence — or, of course, until his appeal was successful. It was in Singleton, once a fairly self-contained Nineties development, now a giant suburb of the sprawling town of Ashford.

'I'd no idea you could cram so many properties onto one hillside,' Fran said sadly, putting down her torch to fiddle the key into the lock.

'Without adequate infrastructure, too,' Sue Hall agreed with what sounded like genuine bitterness. 'I hope John Prescott's pleased with himself, that's all I can say. Concreting and bricking over everywhere down here. Have you seen that new development on the floodplain by the superstores? How long before the buyers get their breakfasts wearing welly boots, eh?'

Fran gave one final twist to the key and at last the front door opened. 'If only we could open a window or two!'

'The whole lot for preference. Doesn't it smell horrible?'

Stale and airless, yes, but not as bad as if a body had rotted in it — but perhaps Sue had been spared that experience so far.

Sue flicked a light switch in vain.

'They've turned off all the utilities, I'm afraid.' Fran switched on the torch. 'Where shall we start?'

There was very little to suggest any passions, least of all those leading to death, in the living room. The furnishing and decor were bland, with no pictures or trinkets about the place. Had some sympathetic officer or friend packed everything away, just in case vandals got in? She hoped so. The kitchen was so small it seemed as if it had been designed simply to heat TV dinners, not cook meals from scratch, but there were some good saucepans and utensils. Mercifully someone had cleared out the fridge and food cupboards.

Upstairs the beds were stripped in the two main bedrooms; the box room was too tiny for so much as a folding bed and was almost fully occupied by an exercise bike. Fran homed in on the larger bedroom, which had obviously had a make-over, if not an expensive one, with fitted furniture. Roper's side of the wardrobe contained mostly casual clothes, Janine's the sensible outfits you'd somehow expect of a classroom assistant. The dressing table and chest of drawers showed both wore standard Marks and Spencer undies.

'Do you suppose they ever went out at weekends and enjoyed themselves?' Sue asked sadly.

'The funny thing is that they did,' Fran replied. 'The case notes say that she read huge numbers of books, and he enjoyed sea-sailing. Not a lot of evidence of either, is there?'

'Well, maybe he kept his sailing gear at a yacht club or something.'

'He's supposed to have sailed from Whitstable, so you could check up there. But where are her books? You don't just borrow books from libraries: you buy them too, surely. You don't have to have shelves full of hardbacks, I admit, but you'd pick up the odd paperback with the week's shopping, that sort of thing. Tell you what, Sue, could you have another trawl through the file, to see if there's any mention of things being stored elsewhere? Or maybe I've remembered something that wasn't there . . . Look, we must lock up now — I've got a meeting to go to.'

* * *

Somehow the air in the meeting room seemed just as stale as that in the Ropers' house, perhaps because the main thrust of the agenda was penny-pinching, thinly disguised as restructuring. Gates carefully dodged the eyes of the older and most senior officers present as one would avoid watching turkeys discussing Christmas dinner. Cosmo Dix was sitting in, casting an occasional quizzical glance at the chairman but remaining remarkably silent. Dale Drury and Ken Roper were the official business in the forefront of Fran's mind, but occasionally she would have a niggle of anxiety about the Minton case. She was sure the Folkestone team just wanted the poor man buried and his case closed, and she was equally determined that the secret he intended to take to his grave should be revealed. But she must concentrate on the matter in hand. She had a nasty suspicion that Gates was about to streamline her and her colleagues — and possibly Mark and the other ACCs — out of existence.

* * *

Head down, she was walking back to her office after a very late lunch with Mark when Gates broke into her reverie.

'A moment of your time, please, Chief Superintendent,' Gates said, his voice as cold as his eyes. He ushered her into his office, retreating to the far side of his executive desk. 'And perhaps you would be so kind as to close the door.'

Fran found herself standing in silence before him. This time she waited for an invitation to sit but suspected it would not come. From the way he tipped back in his chair clutching a pen between both sets of manicured fingertips, he looked as if he was prepared to bollock someone and since she could see no one else in the room she presumed it must be her.

It would be a new experience. Oh, she'd had many rebukes from her superiors — what officer with her length of service hadn't? — but never from one who had once been very much her junior. How should she react? As if it had been any other person in the role of deputy chief constable administering it? The more she thought about it, it seemed that was the only professional way to behave.

What puzzled her was what she might have done wrong. She'd missed no meetings, had recently contributed at least three good suggestions to each one, and had got herself involved with at least one sub-committee. She'd criticised Gates to no one except Mark, who would have died rather than grass her up. Perhaps she had been a tad absent-minded at this morning's gathering, but then she had a lot to think about.

But he was speaking, with a shallow smile. 'I understand that several times in the recent past you've offered to resign but that for some reason the chief — or the ACC — has persuaded you to stay. May I ask why?'

What the hell? 'Why I've offered to retire? Or why the chief — Mark's never been involved — tore up my letter of resignation?' She smiled as duplicitously as he. 'You'd have to ask the chief that. But he's away at that anti-terrorist conference in Portugal, I understand. I'm surprised you're not there too, actually. Your experience of active policing is much more recent than his, after all.'

'I thought I could do more good here,' he said, clearly wrong-footed.

'The ACCs have always held the fort before,' she said. 'Heavens, Simon, you played a major part in sorting out that awful business in London. And you liaised with the Malaysian anti-terrorist branch at one time, didn't you? Your input would have been invaluable.'

'Well, I—'

'And such a conference would have held you in good stead, too — all those contacts, for goodness' sake! You've done well to become a DCC in this force, but surely your sights are set higher than that. Head of the Anti-Terrorist Branch, I'd have thought.' It was as if she was sergeant to his rookie again, her enthusiasm for his career driving her headlong.

For a moment his face lit up in response, but it soon closed again. 'It was more about *your* career I wanted to talk.'

'Mine's pretty well over, Simon,' she said frankly. 'OK, I do some special one-off jobs for the chief, and even without those I'm certainly not underemployed at the moment.' It wouldn't hurt to tell him about her current caseload. 'You know Henson's off sick at the moment with bronchitis so I've picked up—'

'It's a very expensive way of filling gaps. And surely the Superintendents' Association would have something to say about the practice. After all, you're blocking temporary promotions that would look good on someone's CV.'

So that was what drove him. His CV. Why hadn't she realised before? She would bet that Mark had.

'Nope.' She shook her head firmly. 'If you check the personnel files — sorry, Human Resources files — you'll find I've always recorded the need for precisely that sort of upgrading when it was clear that an absence was going to be protracted. I've always made sure someone else got the experience — and the salary! — they needed. Sometimes, though, an inexperienced super who's been moved up finds it useful to have an old-stager like me to turn to.' Let him chew on that. And let him invite the old-stager to sit down.

'And are you doing any special little jobs for the chief at the moment?'

If only he'd get that edge of sarcasm out of his voice. She said sweetly, 'You know I'm working on the Roper and Barnes case. Unless you want to overload Henson I'd like to continue with it, even when he returns. It seems to me we handled it very badly at the time, and if we're not bloody careful we could open ourselves to charges of conspiracy to pervert the course of justice.'

'Surely there are junior officers who—'

'Exactly. Junior officers. Inexperienced officers. They're not all as talented as you were, Simon. They need guidance.' She hoped he remembered all the hours she'd spent helping him write cogent reports. 'And as it happens I like helping to catch criminals and solve crimes.'

'Not sitting on committees and sharing your wisdom and experience that way.'

She didn't like the way his tongue had curled on the two nouns. He might well have been quoting the chief, come to think of it.

'I'd rather pass on anything I've learnt one to one, I must say,' she said with a smile. It wasn't meant as a confession but he leaped on it as if it were.

'So you don't think committees are productive.'

She raised her hands in exasperation. 'Committees are committees, Simon, and no organisation the size of ours, answering to both the public and politicians, can survive without them.'

'They'd survive without you on them.' His tone was just short of offensive.

Actually, it wasn't. It was bloody offensive. But she had a feeling it was better not to respond. So she shook her head in a puzzlement that was only partly feigned. 'Meaning?'

'Frankly, you're a waste of space. You come in at the last minute, dash off first like a school kid hearing the bell. You barely say anything and you sit and doodle as if you're bored out of your skull. I think it's time you resigned again. While the chief isn't here to change your mind.'

She hoped she wasn't blushing as the truth of his criticisms hit home. There had been times when she had behaved like a resentful schoolgirl, which was both disloyal and stupid. But she wasn't prepared to go at his behest. Not by a long chalk. 'It'd certainly save the force some money,' she said, folding her arms and rocking back on one hip, as if actively considering his point.

'Indeed it would.'

'And delivering best value is one of your remits, isn't it?'

Her affability clearly startled him.

'Yes.' He produced something suspiciously like a smirk.

'So you want to do — in the chief's absence — what the chief wouldn't do.' She felt better on the offensive.

His eyes narrowed. 'I've told you what I'd like you to do. Falling on your sword would be better than being forcibly retired.'

And, despite what he'd said about his job description, where on earth would he get the mandate to sack her? Despite the fizzing anger, she smiled gently. 'Simon, I couldn't possibly do anything like that behind his back. And he'd know, all right. Cosmo Dix would be on the phone to him before you could say pension.'

'He's another of your mates, is he? How convenient to have the head of Human Resources in your pocket. I bet he advises you on your suits, too.'

She blazed. 'If that's what I suspect it is, a homophobic remark, I suggest you withdraw it now, Simon. And take care never to utter another one in my hearing. Over the hill I may be, but I helped draw up the present UK guidelines and I will not tolerate their violation, from a DCC or anyone else.'

'How dare you!' He was white to the lips with anger, breathing unevenly through flared nostrils.

She dared say no more.

Suddenly, disconcertingly, his rage subsided. He even laughed, if grimly. 'If only you were like that in the committee.'

'I was — believe me, I was. When we were drafting the guidelines. And drawing up other vital policies. I suppose I find it easier to care about protecting people than saving money,' she said seriously, shifting her weight to the other hip. 'And spending weeks drafting documents that the Home Office will tell us are redundant the day we submit them.'

A glimmer of the old Simon showed. 'Is that why you never went for ACC or DCC yourself?' He sounded genuinely interested, with an underlying disbelief that someone he'd once possibly liked and respected didn't share what seemed to him an obvious ambition. What would he make of officers who were still constables when they retired, simply because they preferred their regular contact with the public and thought they could make a difference?

She responded with honesty. 'Partly. There were other factors.' But she wouldn't tell him the whole story — that she also had very sick parents who depended on her to commute down to Devon every weekend to care for them — lest he see it as yet another sign of culpable weakness. Neither did she add that only Mark's sympathetic and imaginative intervention had saved her from the sack, or at least a disciplinary hearing. She was sure of that, though Mark had never admitted it.

His phone rang. He answered it as curtly as if he were chair of some huge corporation whose every second cost money. 'Of course. Right away.'

'I'm sorry,' he said, in the manner of one with no regrets about anything. 'I've got a visitor.' He stood to indicate the interview was over.

'So you won't argue if I continue with the Roper inquiry?'

'I know that you've had one or two notable successes,' he conceded.

Patronising bastard.

'But my view is that you should return as soon as possible to Uniform where you are at least administratively useful. You've seen the latest statistics, Harman. They're not good.'

At least? She was getting angry. 'Would taking one of your most experienced active crime fighters off a murder case and telling her to minute meetings help our figures?'

'I told you, I have a visitor. I'll think it over and come back to you later in the week.'

'And with whom lies the final decision? You or the chief?' she asked.

But he was holding the door open for her, and she was damned if she would have a row with him before the interested gaze of his secretary and a Japanese officer with extraordinarily long hair.

'I'll take that as the chief, then,' she murmured. But he was already greeting his guest and it was quite possible he didn't hear.

* * *

She never knew why being angry about one thing should make another idea pop up of its own volition. Of course! Given the current climate of blame, she doubted if any of QED Moreton's original investigation team would give her the low-down on the case. But if anyone would know someone prepared to speak off the record, it would be Jim Champion. And it was about time she did her duty and took him a bunch of grapes. It was just a matter of finding the time.

At last she could shake the dust off her feet and head for home. 'I'm in a bit of a mood,' she told Mark. 'In a sulk, even. Maybe you'd better drive . . .'

* * *

Mark wished he could ask her point-blank what had upset her. He didn't think anyone else would realise there was anything wrong. After all, she'd grinned broadly as he regaled her with a spot of gossip about an ACC from another force he'd been meeting, and she responded with all the appropriate prompts. But there was a slight glitter about her eyes, a tension about her shoulders that made him think for a moment she might be feverish. He'd seen her popping into Gates' office, but she'd not yet chatted, as she usually did, about whatever had been said. Had she discovered just what a hard-nosed mean-minded little bastard he was? She'd be as upset finding that a protégé of hers had feet of clay as he had been discovering that his daughter was a heartless spendthrift.

He ought to talk through with Fran all his doings with Sammie — the girl had even tried to wheedle him into leaving Fran on her own and spending Sunday with her — but he was ashamed both of his anger and of his helplessness. He was Sammie's father, for God's sake. He had brought her up better than this. He had cherished her, as she should be cherishing her own children in turn — but was signally failing to. He had taken her to open her first bank account, explained about overdrafts, counselled against credit cards unless you could be sure of paying off the balance.

As for love, surely Sammie had had a living example in his marriage to Tina. Whatever the situation, and towards the end of Tina's life there had been many crises, Tina and he had always dealt honourably and honestly with each other, love over- and underlying everything they did. Tina would no more have walked out on him after a quarrel, no matter how serious, than she would have run up thousands of pounds in debt.

He glanced at Fran again. In repose there was no doubt her face was troubled, but as soon as she caught his eye she responded with her usual almost joyous smile. Wanting to do far more, he reached for her hand, and on impulse lifted it to his lips in the old-fashioned but possessive gesture he knew she loved. If only Sammie would let Fran close enough to see what a decent woman she was.

'It's no good, you know. You'll have to tell me all about it. It's bloody Gates, isn't it?'

'OK. Since you ask . . .' She launched into an account.

'Return you to Uniform against your will?' Mark repeated a few minutes later. 'He can't do that, as well you know. And he knows too.'

'At least he didn't tell me — as he claims would have been within his remit — to have nothing at all to do with the Roper case,' she said, fastening her seat belt.

'So you have to squeeze a little hands-on crime investigation in between meetings and report writing?'

'I can squeeze quite a lot in. Provided the ACC (Crime) keeps schtum about my occasional unauthorised absences.'

'The ACC (Crime) is highly susceptible to bribes and blandishments,' he reported, not even bothering to keep a straight face.

'I'd better try a spot of both tonight.'

He wriggled in the seat. 'It may have to be quite late. I promised I'd pop round to Loose to have another go at Sammie's finances.'

She took a deep breath. 'Are you sure they're your responsibility? Mark, love, she's a woman of twenty-four. She's married. She ought to be turning to Lloyd, if to anyone, that is. Or one of the professionals you've put her in touch with. Or maybe', she ventured, 'a health professional.'

'Why on earth?'

'Because — if you think of it — spending three thousand pounds on shoes isn't exactly normal behaviour.'

'Not for our generation, it isn't. But maybe for hers.'

'All the same.'

'She's my daughter, Fran — of course I've got to help her.'

'Not if that help is counterproductive,' she insisted.

'I don't want to talk about this now,' he said, for good measure stabbing the radio's ON button and finding the signature tune of *The Archers*.

'Tell you what, why don't you go and do your parental duty, and I'll nip down to Jim Champion's for half an hour?'

'I thought you'd like to play with the children.'

'It disturbs their bedtime,' she said.

'Don't talk such rubbish,' he said. And then he flushed. He'd just recalled where he'd heard those words before. She'd fluently quoted Sammie.

* * *

'Corn in Egypt!' Maureen greeted her obscurely, but with obvious warmth, relief even. 'Come along in, Fran. Jim, I've got a visitor for you! He's in a lot of pain,' she added parenthetically, ushering Fran into the living room.

Jim might never have moved from the depths of his armchair, which was enisled in a sea of masculine detritus. A couple of beer cans, a bubble-pack of what looked like prescription painkillers, some videos, several paperbacks — Westerns — and a pile of red-tops. Two walking sticks rounded off the pile.

'I'm bored out of my skull,' Jim declared. Without waiting till his wife was out of the room, he continued, with a jerk of his head, 'And it's fuss, fuss, fuss from that one. Nag? She never stops. I'd offer you a beer but she says I've had my ration for today.'

'I'm driving,' Fran said, shaking her head and praying that Maureen wouldn't press strong tea on her. 'What I came for, Jim, apart from the doubtful pleasure of your company, you miserable old bugger, was to pick your brain.'

'But I've been sitting on the sidelines all these years.'

'Come on, there are loads of your old mates who've kept in touch, I'll bet my pension.'

'Well, one or two of the youngsters on the training course still regard me as a bit of a father confessor,' he conceded, as if ashamed of his justifiable pride.

'Like me. Except it's a long time since I was a youngster!'

'You'll always be a lovely young girl to me,' he said with mock gallantry. 'If I was ten years younger I'd have fought young Mark for you, pistols at dawn, ACC or no!'

'Thank you kindly, sir,' Fran replied in kind, dropping an ironic curtsey for good measure. In her normal voice she asked directly, 'Now, do you recall anything being said about the Roper and Barnes case?'

He stared into the past. 'Something about the corpse never being found? A MisPer case which turned into a murder inquiry?'

'The very same. It's coming up for appeal, and I want to make sure we don't get egg on our faces.'

'Quite right. Don't want all our good work undone because we've forgotten to cross a t and dot an i.' But he went quiet, as if he was recalling something he couldn't put his finger on. 'Funnily enough, one of the lads who kept in touch was on that case, as I recall. You may have seen him at my leaving do. Young Rob Venables. He's a bright lad. Mind you,' he added, as if it were a major criticism, 'he's not very tall — only five-eight. You'd be able to look down on his bald spot.'

'He can't be all that young,' she objected, laughing.

'He must have had a wearing life,' Jim said. 'Went thin on top in his twenties — before the days when it became trendy to shave it all off. Anyway, he was one of those high-fliers, very bright indeed. An inspector these days — traffic, I think, or whatever they call it this week. Chief inspector next year with luck, and him only thirty-four.'

What would she have given in her younger days for a bit of fast tracking? But she thought of Mark and smiled; perhaps things had a way of evening themselves out.

'And he had a real bad time with this case,' Jim continued. 'Fell out with all his mates. Nearly got a disciplinary, and then where would his high-flying have got him? I got him to go sick for a couple of weeks till it all blew over. But he ought to be telling you all this himself. Where's that bloody phone? I told her to leave it where I could reach it!'

'Don't you start giving Maureen a bad time just because your leg hurts,' she said with a sharp nod, passing him the handset. 'She's had to put up with your being married to the job all these years and she's entitled to a bit of respect.'

'She's entitled to a man with both legs.'

'She'll get one soon enough — and not you, either, if you don't watch your step,' she said. She leant to take his hand. When had he grown age spots? 'Come on, Jim, I know it's a rotten blow, but think of all those young footballers who've had knees as bad as yours and been playing in the Premier next season.'

'Aye, and more to the point some Test cricketers who've never played again. And they're young, Fran. Young. The NHS will do everything for them, all right, but they may reckon I'm too old for fancy surgery for free.'

'May they indeed? Who's your consultant?' If the NHS wouldn't fund the op, what about the Police Benevolent Fund?

Jim was evidently disappointed with the response from the other end, and cut the call abruptly. 'Says he's putting the kids to bed or some such. But I tell you, Fran, you want to talk to him if you can.'

'I believe you. Now why don't you phone him again, a bit more friendly, when he's had a chance to settle the kids, and invite him over here another night for a quiet drink? Would you do that for me?'

'So he'll tell you things he wouldn't want overheard by anyone? Right, Fran you're on.'

CHAPTER TWELVE

'I'd no idea you could get permission for prison visits this easily,' DC Sue Hall said, as she fastened her seat belt and started the car.

'Pat's doing. Pat Harper, my secretary. I didn't realise until she came on the scene that a good secretary's price is above rubies. Especially if, like Pat, she has a friend, it seems, with the Home Secretary's ear. Or whatever civil servant represents the Home Secretary on earth. And this person knows the precise time to get hold of the prison governor to expedite things his end. Who are we to argue, if we have the idea on Monday and everything's hunky-dory by Wednesday midday? What have you found out in the meantime, by the way?'

As if it were her fault, Hall bit her lip. 'By praying to St Anthony? Well, he's not been entirely helpful. I've been all through the paperwork with a fine-tooth comb and can't find anything more about Janine's books. But maybe it's St Anthony's doing that I've found a note that his sailing gear — wetsuits, aqualung, the lot — is up in the sailing club locker room in Whitstable.'

'That lot's diving, not sailing, isn't it?' Fran objected.

'There was no record of his having dived, though. And that sounds quite expert . . .'

'My sister might know . . . Hell, we've got our own Underwater Search and Recovery team — ask one of them, will you? We might even have a sailing club with members all too willing to share their knowledge. Meanwhile, why not ask Roper himself? We can park over there. Funny, I can never walk into a prison, especially an old one like this, without the hairs on the back of my neck creeping up the moment I step into the first airlock . . .'

* * *

'You and Janine met through the Internet!' Fran exclaimed. They were in an interview room that, try how it might — and she was not sure that it was making much effort — declared it was part of a prison, and an old one at that.

'Yes. Lots of people do,' Ken Roper said defensively. He was prison-pale and thin to the point of being anorexic. His standard-issue denims hung about him. He had a raw patch of eczema on his left wrist which he picked from time to time. 'And marry, too.'

'Of course they do.' Fran made a swift reappraisal of the few facts at her command. 'And was it a happy marriage, Ken?'

'We liked to think so. We didn't spend all our time in each other's pockets, of course. But we wanted the same things.'

'Which were?'

'A nice house. Company. Children, I suppose. You know . . .' Ken gestured lamely.

'Security?' Sue put in.

His smile transformed his face. 'Exactly. What more could anyone want?'

Fran could think of a very great deal more, but contented herself with an encouraging smile. 'You didn't live in each other's pockets. So would you say you saw much of each other?'

He seemed genuinely puzzled. 'We were at work all day. And she had to go into school in the evenings a lot.'

'She was a classroom assistant, wasn't she?' Were they as hard-pressed as teachers? She wouldn't have thought a lot of after-school work would be called for.

He continued as if she hadn't interrupted, 'And at weekends I had my sailing.'

'You don't think it helps keep a marriage together if you share each other's hobbies?'

'Poor Janine was frightened of water. Oh, she could swim, and at the start she used to go sailing with me once a month or so, but you could tell she wasn't enjoying it. So I stopped pressing her, eventually.' Sue raised a cynical eyebrow, which provoked him into adding, 'We weren't drifting apart or anything. It was just something we didn't share anymore.'

'So what did you share?' Sue asked. 'She liked reading, didn't she?'

'Not particularly, I don't think. The odd *Hello!* or *OK*. She watched a lot of TV, when I wasn't there, at least. We played Scrabble.'

Which wasn't in the file either. Whereas the love of reading was. How had that error come about?

'We used to buy a bar of chocolate every Sunday evening and play for it,' he continued, a gentle smile briefly lighting his face.

Fran and Mark had had games involving chocolate too, but not necessarily Scrabble. 'Every week?'

'Without fail. Cadbury's. One of those nice big bars.'

'Did you ever argue about who'd won?'

'Sometimes. It was often very close, and we'd say the other one had cheated tallying up their score.' He smiled reminiscently.

And innocently?

'So why did you kill her, Ken?'

She would have sworn his eyes filled with tears.

'I didn't. I told the policemen at the time I didn't. I explained everything, just like I'm explaining to you now. I got home one weekend after sailing with Moz—'

'That's Maurice Barnes?'

'That's right, Moz Barnes. I got home one Sunday night after a weekend's sailing and found she wasn't there. I phoned her friends—'

'Did she have many friends?' She couldn't imagine he had a wide circle.

'A few. Women friends, I mean. Because she and Moz were friends too.'

'How close?'

'Friends. You know, friends.'

'Sometimes it's hard for men and women to be friends and nothing more.'

She would have sworn he was genuinely puzzled.

'Janine and Moz were like brother and sister. I mean, Moz and I were like brothers, so why shouldn't she and he have been . . . ?'

'So how did you feel when she didn't come home?' Sue interrupted.

'How would you expect me to feel?' he responded, with more force than Fran would have expected. 'At first I was a bit irritated — she'd always had the supper on the table before, see. And then I got worried. Very worried, when her friends said they hadn't seen her. And then I called the police. Only they thought — yes, right from the start — that I'd done it and it was all my fault. But I swear to you I didn't hurt a hair on her head, ever.'

Sue pounced. 'But Moz — your friend and "brother" Moz — could have done it for you.'

'What do you mean, done it for me?'

'Tell me about Moz,' Fran said. One of her dictums was that wrong-footing was a useful interview technique. 'What's he like?'

'Very quiet. Like me, I suppose. Some weekends we could go for a whole day without needing to speak.'

'I suppose it's hard to speak when you're underwater.'

He flashed a pallid smile. 'Oh, my diving days are long past. I did it for a while after I'd left school. I'd really given up before I met Janine.'

'But you kept your gear.'

'For old time's sake, to be honest. Like other people keep tiny little footie cups they won when they were ten, or photos of weddings of friends they never see anymore.'

'Did Moz go to your wedding?'

'He was one of the witnesses. Ladies, he was a good . . . companion . . . And friend, of course. I'd trust him with my life.' His eyes flew to hers in apparent horror at what he'd said. His voice taking on a defiant note, he added, 'And with hers, too. With Janine's. When she had her migraines he was much better with her than I was. They said they found her DNA on his pillow, as if that was a bad thing. Last time we were there, he had to pick her up bodily and tuck her up in his bed, she was so bad.'

'He's strong enough to carry a grown woman?'

'Oh, yes. He's not like me, Chief Superintendent. Not a seven-stone weakling who gets sand kicked in his face. He's altogether stronger and fitter. I daresay while he's banged up he spends all the time he can in the gym.'

'And how do you spend your time, Ken?'

She thought his flicker of a smile was ironic. 'In the library. Yes, already. Shows you what a trusty I am. Or perhaps they don't like my cooking.'

She looked him straight in the eye. 'You don't look to me like the sort of man who'd spit or piss in someone's food.'

'Thank you. I'm not the sort to kill his wife and throw her body in the sea, either. And if I were, I wouldn't do it off that bit of coast — far too much risk of having her poor body washed up somewhere,' he added with a sudden gleam.

Sue asked swiftly, 'Where would you dump it then?'

He paused, as if trying to find a rational answer. '*If* I'd killed her — which I swear to God I haven't, nor Moz neither, then I wouldn't put her in the sea, Sergeant. Not knowing how she hated water. A nice quiet grave in a country churchyard, that's where I'd want her to lie. And me next to her.'

'And Moz?' Fran asked softly.

'He'd tend them for us — make sure there were always plenty of nice flowers.'

* * *

'What a brilliant actor,' Sue declared as soon as they were free from the prison environs.

'You think so?'

'Oh, yes. I wouldn't trust him as far as I could throw him.'

'He's a very slight man,' Fran said, as if considering the idea seriously.

'You mean you believed him? You certainly went very gently on him.' Sue sounded distinctly aggrieved.

'Yes, and I missed a lot of leads I should have pursued, which I'm sure you'll want to follow up next time.' When Sue didn't respond to the prompt, Fran said, 'Her friends: I don't recall a list in the file, do you? What sort of clothes she wore. Make-up.'

'You're right — there wasn't any in her bedroom or the bathroom, was there? And nothing in the evidence store, either.'

'Never mind. We can always pop round to see him again — he's practically a neighbour, and it'll break up his day a bit, won't it? And if I wanted to go any harder, I think I'd have insisted that his solicitor be there, just in case.'

Her mildness didn't deceive Sue, who blushed. 'Of course. Sorry.'

'No problem. Especially when I have a strong suspicion we've had an innocent man sent down.'

* * *

There didn't seem much doubt of Dale Drury's guilt, at least not in DCI Pearce's eyes. Fran popped down to see her before she returned to her own office, just, she said, to see if there was any help she could offer.

Pearce shook her head politely. 'We're certain he has a problem with women, guv.'

So what would he make of Joanne's plunging neckline? For herself, Fran had always found T-shirts adorned with the sort of lace she'd associated with slips and other underwear inappropriate for work. As for the high heels, Fran had some very similar for which she and Mark had an altogether different use.

'And we've had one or two outbursts his solicitor's had to rein in. But we're working away with the proposition that these days pleading guilty means his tariff is automatically reduced. And if he's going to go down for one murder, it might as well be for all he's committed.'

'He hasn't spotted that being a serial killer might carry a longer sentence than *just* doing your wife in?' Fran stressed the word slightly and ironically.

'So far he hasn't. Of course his solicitor has, hence things are a bit quieter today. But we'll get there, just you see.'

'There's one person you might mention. Janine Roper. She disappeared three years back, and her husband's case is up for appeal.'

Joanne Pearce digested the implications. 'Wasn't that one of QED Moreton's cases? And you think—?'

'Never mind what I think, Joanne. Just go digging.'

* * *

Mark replaced the phone handset with what he considered quite admirable calm. Why Lloyd should have considered it a good idea to phone him at work, when he was up to his eyes in urgent paperwork, just to complain about his part in Sammie's defection he didn't know. To be fair — which he didn't especially want to be — he conceded that Lloyd couldn't have known he had spent the whole morning wrestling with intransigent words, which, try how he might, refused to convey the nuances and subtleties he needed for a report that eventually the chief would have to put his signature to.

Perhaps the lad was right. Perhaps it would have been better all round if instead of offering his daughter a comfortable sanctuary, Mark had turned her round and sent her straight back home. Perhaps it would have been better if he hadn't offered to pay off all her credit card debts — the fact that Sammie was supposed to be paying her father week by week was irrelevant in her husband's eyes.

'Why the hell didn't you tell her to come back here where she belongs? It's my job to sort out all her problems,' he'd insisted.

The deadline for the report was getting steadily closer, and there was no time for a dialogue on the dynamics of modern marriage. 'Look, Lloyd, why don't you and I just have a drink together one night — tonight, if you like — and thrash this out. I'm far more on your side than you realise, you know.'

There was something curiously flat about Lloyd's response. Nonetheless, the date was made.

Hell and damnation, what had he let himself in for? Why the hell wasn't Tina here to help him sort it all out?

God, what was he thinking of? How could he resent Tina's death like that?

And how would Fran react to finding him spending yet another evening on private family affairs? And why on earth should they be private? He and Fran were a unit now. If anyone doubted it, they should look at their joint financial commitment in the Rectory. Although they didn't like to live in each other's pockets, since they'd come together, there'd been very few evenings that they hadn't chosen to spend in each other's company. Even if they both had to deal with paperwork after dinner, they preferred to work in the same room. And now, willy-nilly, his family was shattering the pattern.

If he felt resentful, what was Fran feeling?

* * *

True to her brief to discover what divisional CIDs really needed — it seemed to be like posing the age-old question of what women wanted most — Fran spent the next half-hour emailing divisional CID colleagues whom she knew to be computer literate or on the phone to some of the others, reminding each one that on top of all their other work they still had to prepare wish lists for her, and that she needed them pretty well yesterday. One old-stager, whom she rather thought had mistaken her for some office junior, was more honest than most, and told her he could give his answer there and then. 'And make sure you write down every word! I just wish HQ would stop asking sodding silly questions we're too sodding busy to answer.'

Instead of reminding him of the politeness due to senior officers, she said with mild innocence, 'The idea is to help you, Chief Inspector.'

'Well, help by finding me another fucking pair of hands, then. Three pairs preferably. Or, better still, four. I've got one officer on maternity leave, another on extended sick leave, two on bloody idiotic courses and one asking for a transfer to Devon. There's talk of me reopening an investigation we all thought was absolutely sodding watertight. And that bugger Henson's ticker is still supposed to be dicky, so I suppose we'll end up with some eighteen-year-old kid on the accelerated promotion scheme telling me how to run the case.' He paused, perhaps for breath.

'Which case would that be, Chief Inspector?'

'Roper and Barnes, of course.'

'How come you got landed with that?' Fran forgot she was a secretary.

'Oh, it's not official, not yet. But that smart-arsed new . . . Hang on, exactly who am I talking to?'

'Fran Harman, Doug.'

'Fucking hell, I took you for—'

'Doesn't matter. What's this about Gates asking you to take on Roper and Barnes?'

'He just happened to mention it when he dropped by, that's all.'

Did Gates ever 'just happen' to do anything? 'And when would that have been?'

'This morning. That's why I'm so pissed off.'

'And you told him what you told me?'

'Pretty well. Dressed it up a bit more polite, though — you know how it is.'

'One of these days, Doug, I'll get it into your thick skull that you should be as polite to the lowliest pen-pusher as to the chief. Understand? Meanwhile, I should stall as long as you can on the Roper case. I think they might find someone else.'

* * *

Mark was just contemplating another fat, glossy Home Office document and wondering how much it had cost to produce at a time when all police forces across the country were being told to tighten their belts in all departments except those dealing with organised crime and terrorism, while simultaneously improving, of course, all their results, when there was a tap on the door. It was a bit early for Fran, so his invitation to enter was a little on the curt side.

But Fran it was, carrying files and still wearing her reading-glasses; she looked, as she always did, very businesslike.

'Oh, is it time to go already?'

'I thought a cup of tea might be on offer.'

That was tantamount to conceding that something or someone had defeated her and she needed cheering up. But he'd have said that she was awash with adrenalin. Had she had another fight with Gates? He hoped not. They both knew that however much she had right on her side it put him in an awkward position.

'I'm sure it is. Do you want to take a pew while I brew up?'

She shook her head. 'I'm on my feet — I'll do it. Actually, if we did leave early, we could have another look at the Rectory — see what they've done to enhance security.'

He thought of the reading he still had to get through. 'Perhaps.' To his own ears that sounded a bit offhand.

'You know, you only ever say "perhaps" like that when you mean no and don't want to say it out loud.'

He'd risk a guilty smile. 'Perhaps I do.'

'No perhaps about it. The Rectory's clearly off the menu tonight, then. But since you're perhapsing, perhaps it was you who told Doug Kerr he's got to re-examine the Roper and Barnes files for the CPS.'

He looked at her sharply. 'And perhaps it wasn't! Doug's hideously under strength. How's he got that idea in his head?'

'Three guesses?' But she clearly wasn't joking.

He half stood in his anger. 'Are you sure?'

'According to Doug, Gates just happened to drop by this morning and told him it was a possibility.'

'Which pleased Doug no end, I should imagine.'

'He was certainly lacking intact and charm when we spoke on the phone ten minutes ago. But then, he didn't realise who he was talking to, the rude old bastard. So who made the decision? Hardly the chief, not from his terrorist conference.'

'I'd better find out. Officially, of course. Because whatever else is being rearranged in the interests of cost effectiveness, as far as I know, my job description isn't.'

She looked at him limpidly. 'I suspect that as far as the *chief* knows, it isn't.'

He uttered a few epithets she'd probably not heard from him before, apart from in the vilest of murder or assault cases. 'And what's been happening between you two that you haven't told me about?' he added more sharply than he meant.

He could see her efforts to relax. 'I didn't want to tell you quite everything — well, I wasn't proud of all of it. Yesterday, when Gates gave me that trimming, he suggested I resign — no, not just from the committees, but altogether! — while the chief wasn't here to talk me out of it.'

He wanted to make all sorts of lucid comments about Gates' lack of professionalism and especially lack of gratitude — after all, the man would never have reached his present position had it not been for Fran's constant encouragement. 'The fucking bastard.'

'So I told him that in no circumstances would I do anything like that behind the chief's back, and then we had an argument about something else. He was in the wrong that time, at least.' She rubbed her face. 'Actually, he's right about my committee work, Mark. I've been a complete arsehole. My behaviour might be excusable in a bored schoolgirl, but not in a woman of my age.'

Perhaps she was right. But he would never have loved a yes-woman. 'When did you ever suffer fools and their folly gladly? It's part of your charm. And God knows ninety per cent of those meetings — any meetings, I suspect — are a waste of everyone's time.'

'But I should have had the decency to take him on one side and tell him he was pissing us all off. It's not just me, you see.' She told him about the round robin she'd scotched.

He took her in his arms and gave a companionable hug. 'If I can shoehorn Lloyd and Sammie back together, we'll sell the Loose house and then you can tell him where to put his job.'

She shook her head. 'It'd get under his fingernails far worse if I signed an extended contract. But that apart, the sooner the youngsters are talking *to* each other, and not *at* you, the better for all concerned.'

'Which reminds me — I had a phone call from Lloyd earlier.' He felt like a schoolboy asking for the return of the ball that had just broken a greenhouse window. 'He and I are meeting up at a pub in Tonbridge at six-thirty. Just a drink, I said.'

She pushed him away and looked at him over her glasses. 'And you'd forgotten we'd only got one car here so either you need a lift and for me to wait for you in the car or you want me to hang on here for you.'

He nodded.

'And, of course, if you wanted to drink, you'd only be able to sniff the barmaid's apron if you wanted to stay within the limit.'

He nodded.

'And if I were sitting outside in the car, it would curtail the time you had to spend with him.'

'With luck,' he said fervently. 'From what he said on the phone he wants to spend an evening bollocking me for breaking up his marriage.'

She made a show of cupping her ear. 'I beg your pardon? On the contrary, I'd have thought that Sammie was trying to break up ours. Well, our relationship,' she added, biting back something and turning away slightly.

'What do you mean by that?' Despite himself, he fired up. She wasn't going to raise their unmarried status yet again, was she? He told himself that she had pulled back from whatever brink she'd seen herself on and that he must too. Taking a deep breath, he said, 'She's certainly grabbing as many hours of my time as she can. And now he's joining in.' He tried for a joke, which sounded off-key even as he made it. 'You don't think it's something deeply Freudian, do you?' What if it was?

She spread her hands, without much apparent amusement. 'What are you going to tell him?'

'That depends on what he asks. But I shall certainly say that our not being able to use my house doesn't help our domestic situation. And that the sooner they resolve their differences the better.'

'Do you think he could actually afford to pay all her debts?' she asked. 'I know he's got a good job, but the mortgage on that house of theirs must be astronomical. A four-bedroom detached in Tunbridge Wells, for heaven's sake.'

'You don't suppose you could come along too?' How supine was that? But if he'd miss Tina's advice this evening, her control of the emotional ebb and flow, he'd also miss Fran's astringent common sense and pertinent questions.

'In your dreams, Mark. I shall sit in the car park and catch up with my reading. But you'll owe me.' At least she grinned as she sat back, folding her arms.

'Another trip to France?'

* * *

'Sorry I've been so long,' he said, kissing her as he shifted the files she'd been working through from the passenger seat and settling down.

'No problem.' She permitted herself a glance at the clock — had he really been gone well over an hour?

'At least I phoned Sammie and persuaded her to let Lloyd go and talk to her over in Loose. He's on his way now, in fact. But he's very opaque, Fran. Will you join us next time? Please? I know there's something going on I can't understand and you don't miss much, do you?'

'Only my supper! What does the food look like in there?' She gestured to the pub, unwilling to commit herself one way or the other to a family meeting.

'No idea. Is there anything in the freezer?'

She snorted. 'Enough for an army at your place — remember that wet weekend and the new Kenwood?'

'Hell! I'd forgotten Sammie's taken possession of that too. Not that she'd ever use it. And all the meals you prepared, of course. Let's go and get them now.'

'Now? With Lloyd on his way there? No, let them get on with it, sweetheart. We shan't starve.'

CHAPTER THIRTEEN

One of the Pact team was already on site when Fran and Mark arrived at the Rectory at eight on Thursday morning. When they'd called Paula to arrange the hastiest of visits they'd suggested the more civilised hour of eight-thirty, but Paula assured them that Caffy Tyler would be in the building well before that.

'She may not necessarily be doing what you'd consider work, though. That doesn't start officially till eight-thirty. One of us always unobtrusively checks what time the subcontractors arrive and leave,' Paula explained. 'If they don't keep up to speed, we get held up and so do you.'

In fact, Caffy was in the old scullery, making coffee on a camping-gas stove. Her mug and a couple of paperbacks sat on the wooden draining board. Since alongside them lay a clipboard bearing a piece of paper headed *Schedule for the Day* neither protested, especially as she interrupted their conversation to log the arrival of some workmen who headed straight up onto the roof.

'Excellent,' Caffy said. 'They're ten minutes early again, all four of them. Paula had to Have a Word, and no one runs the risk of a second of Paula's Words. Can I offer you coffee? It's good Fair Trade stuff. I can't start the day without my fix, can you? Go on, try it. Fresh milk here and sugar in that tin.'

They found themselves clutching mugs. Mark's was *Sons and Lovers*, in the old Penguin livery, Fran's the National Portrait Gallery Shakespeare.

'Now, you wanted to talk about our security updates? First of all, did you notice the camera over the front door? Neat, isn't it?' Caffy said.

'Very. Now,' said Mark, who was clearly not in a mood to be charmed, 'has there been a specific threat or are you just taking general precautions?'

She hesitated, only for a beat, but long enough for Fran to reckon she was lying. 'So many places out in the back of beyond like this get robbed that we thought enhanced security was in order. Even if it's going to cost more.'

'So we noticed from the security firm's quote,' Mark confirmed, in his dourest morning voice.

Behind his shoulder, Fran pulled a conspiratorial face at the young woman — the silent message was that with another couple of sips of Caffy's excellent brew he'd show signs of rejoining the human race.

'Quite. But we thought — since you hear of so many security firms being bent — we'd go for belt and braces.' Removing her hands from her dungaree pockets, Caffy twanged the shoulder straps. 'Actually, hands in pockets too!' She replaced them with an impish grin. 'After all, one man and his dog can't be here all the time. And thank God for that. I loathe dogs.' Her shudder appeared genuine. 'So we thought we'd get mugshots of everyone coming onto the site. After all, it's not exactly as if there's a passing trade down here in the back of beyond. You have to try pretty hard to find your way. So there's one camera covering each entrance to the house. The others are better disguised than this.'

'Trouble is, if anyone just parked by the gate without attempting to come in, you wouldn't get photos of car number plates, would you?' Mark demanded, coming gradually out of his torpor.

'Oh, yes, we would! After all, what might seem to be someone pulling over to take a call on his mobile might be someone casing the joint — stealing architectural antiques to order's a popular pastime these days, as I'm sure Paula told you. Not that you wouldn't know anyway, would you? Anyway, there's a pair of cameras in the hedge, disguised as trees. A mate of mine from back in Brum makes the pretend trees for the Home Office, would you believe, and he's done some for us.'

'I don't think he's supposed to talk about covert government surveillance equipment,' Fran said dryly.

Caffy responded with a sunny smile. 'I wouldn't tell anyone else, but surely you're both important enough to be in on the secret! No? Well, he's never told me where these official cameras are sited, but I bet I could find out if you wanted.'

Fran shook her head. 'Lead us not into temptation, Caffy. But these of ours sound a brilliant idea.'

'Well, if you can't nick an idea from the Home Office, I don't see who you can nick one from.'

'Quite,' Mark said repressively.

Fran thought it better to change the subject. 'In fact, we're extra pleased to have the camera on the gates. Did Paula tell you we came the other night just to check the place was still here and saw a BMW driving away as we arrived? I gather it wasn't you driving it.'

Caffy looked ostentatiously heavenwards. 'Oink, oink! Oink, oink! Oh, it's a flying pig.' She became serious again. 'A Beamer can mean trouble, as I'm sure you know better than I. For some reason, people I'd rather not mix with drive big, flashy cars with tinted windows and alloys and such, which they fancy make them anonymous.'

'Or highly obvious,' Fran countered. She feared Mark was about to ask Caffy what gave her the idea that the BMW they had disturbed had tinted windows — it hadn't; she rather thought that the young woman was doing her utmost to help them protect a building they all seemed to love.

'Now, this here car you saw "loitering with intent" — do you want his number to run through your clever computer?' Caffy raised an engaging eyebrow as she used the old police cliché. 'Because it'll only take me a minute to check. We keep the gubbins out of sight in the cold pantry.'

Mark succumbed. 'Why not?'

'And I bet you both want to have another look at the inside of the house and give it a metaphorical hug. Hard hats, please. You'll find spares just inside the front door. Oh, and yellow jackets. Our insurance won't cover you otherwise. You ought to wear boots, but I won't tell if you won't.'

By the time they returned, Caffy was playing the video in an icy little room. 'Won't need a deep freeze, will you?' she flashed. But then she was serious again. 'I think we may need to adjust the angle of one of the cameras,' she said, 'to take in the driver's face. You see, the same car already appears twice on the video — yes, you can tell from the number.' She froze the frame.

'Which happens to coincide with the part of the number I jotted down the other day,' Mark said. 'Thanks for this, Caffy. Forgive me if I give you the advice I always give in situations like this. However important the property, human life is far more valuable. Don't take any risks, any of you. Promise me that.'

Caffy gave the sort of serious nod that told Fran she would carry on doing exactly what she thought fit

* * *

'What an extraordinary woman that Caffy is,' Fran began as she started the car and drove away, waving as if to an old friend. 'I've never heard a decorator talk about metaphorical hugs before.'

'You told Paula you wanted to hug the place better,' he objected.

'But I certainly didn't use the word metaphorical. And did you see the book beside her coffee? *Hard Times*. On top of *The Canterbury Tales*.'

'Well, there are plenty of post-graduates turned plumbers. Perhaps she found the atmosphere in the British Library reading room too rarefied.' Even the pleasure of seeing work in progress hadn't completely eradicated Mark's tendency to sound like Eeyore.

'She isn't old enough, surely, to have studied for a degree and then for all the technical qualifications Paula said she had. She can't be more than — what? — twenty-eight?' Fran countered.

'She might well have done — and we might be underestimating her age, of course.' He frowned. 'She's very edgy, isn't she? Too bright and chatty.'

'Perhaps she has a problem with mornings, too, and overcompensates.'

'She certainly seems to be overcompensating for something.'

'Paula wouldn't think it was good PR if one of the team was miserable when punters were around.'

'Hmm. I know you two entered into some women-versus-grumpy-old-men conspiracy, but there's something *knowing* about her. Didn't you spot it?'

Fran shook her head. 'I'd have said she was more vulnerable than knowing. But I see what you mean. Do you want me to ask Paula about her?'

He snorted. 'Question Paula's judgement? And have her march the entire team off the site in high dudgeon?'

'She would, wouldn't she? Maybe one day I'll get a chance to talk to Caffy on her own.'

'And find out what?'

'I don't know — just what makes her tick.' She got no response so she asked eventually, 'Are you going to see who owns that car?'

'I suppose so. You know, it seems vaguely familiar. The car and the number.'

'You always had difficulty with these new multi-letter ones.'

'Almost as much as you do!'

'Touché! If you're busy, I could.'

'No, it's all right. I'll try to make time.'

* * *

Pat greeted Fran with a pile of post and a broad smile. 'I'm terribly sorry but Mr Gates won't be in today. He's unwell.'

'Nothing too trivial, I hope,' Fran joked, astonished and appalled to find that she meant what she said. Was illness the reason he was so edgy? Hell, more than that — so downright unpleasant?

'And he's cancelled today's meeting.'

'The bugger won't trust me to chair it for him? Well, I'm blessed.'

She shared a smile with Pat. On a day like this it was good to make people smile.

And to make them jump a little. When had she last badgered Pete Webb down in Folkestone about the Minton case? He was getting all too adept at ignoring her demands for information, wasn't he? Her first phone call of the day would be to him.

'Hi, Pete. How's tricks?'

'Good morning, ma'am.' He sounded as if he was standing to attention.

'Guv. Unless you've no news for me.'

Now she could hear him stand at ease. 'Some. Only not much. Look, guv, strictly off the record, could I pick your brains?'

'I don't think you'll find much to pick, not these days. But they're all yours if you want them.'

'I feel such a fool, guv,' he began. 'This suicide business — there's still absolutely no suspicion of anyone else being involved, by the way, and I've double- and triple-checked it myself — is getting to me. Why should he do it, that's what I keep asking myself.'

'Good! OK, I'm sorry. It's my fault.'

'Yes. No. Maybe. I've gone through Alec Minton's things myself this time, and still can't find anything except a few out-of-date receipts and bills. Surely, even in these days of emails and mobiles, a man doesn't live entirely without paper.'

'What about his mobile and his computer, then?'

'There's no record he ever had a mobile,' he began bravely.

'A prepaid one?'

'Could have been.' He sounded increasingly hangdog.

'Come on, spit it out.'

'The computer's gone. I know, I know! I assumed it would be in that office-cupboard thing. I even told you it was in there. And the connections leading into the cupboard certainly were. But when we went to get it, the computer itself had gone.'

Well, well, well. 'Not stolen, by any chance?'

'Why should it have been?'

'His phone because that's what kids do. The computer because that's what burglars do.'

'But why didn't he report them as missing?'

It was obviously time to be brisk and inspiring. 'OK, let's look at this another way. You've got the CCTV from the Mondiale's reception area showing he went to his room alone. Have we any other CCTV from Hythe with him on?'

'Would it still be in the system? It's probably been recorded over by now.'

'Is it worth a shot? Grab a rookie constable—'

'Not a minion?' He was clearly feeling better, wasn't he?

'Anyone you can spare, Pete, to go and see. If there is anything, we could look at it together.'

'Would you really mind coming out all this way?'

'I'd welcome the sea breeze.'

'It's blowing half-bricks at the moment, so you'll get plenty of fresh air.'

* * *

Without needing Pat's advice this time, she took an unmarked car from the pool. If Pete was embarrassed about asking for help, there was no need to humiliate him further by turning up in a vehicle everyone knew was registered to Mark.

Pete Webb met her as she parked, something that confirmed her suspicions. Whom did he not want to know about her visit?

Like him she hunched her shoulders against the wind and shoved her hands into her pockets.

'As I feared,' Pete confessed, 'the CCTV footage from the relevant week was long gone, but young Tessa's brought back all footage shot since then.'

'Have you had time to run through it? OK, Pete, I've had enough fresh air. Let's go inside and have a morning at the movies.'

They peered at the screen together. Community policing — or the average age of the Hythe citizens — had obviously kept the street crime rate remarkably low. There was even very little unofficial dumping in the skip outside the house opposite the flats, as if decent retired people knew they should find their own means of disposing of waste. There was good stuff in there too, the sort that would have vanished immediately in a less affluent, law-abiding area.

'Is that a computer in there?' Pete asked, freezing the frame.

'My God, so it is.'

'Now that should have gone to a proper recycling depot. All that toxic stuff going to landfill.'

'The first minus point against Hythe,' she agreed with a grin, letting the tape roll again. 'And there's someone coming to liberate it.' She pointed and froze the frame.

Pete was entering the spirit of things. 'Do we arrest him for theft or congratulate him for services to the environment?'

She rocked back in her chair. 'Pete, you may want to call the men in white coats and the comfy van, but I've got a feeling about that computer. At the very least we should make sure that the hard disk's been removed to prevent any identity theft,' she said sanctimoniously. 'And if we strike gold we may find it's Alec Minton's machine.'

'It's a long shot. Very long.'

'And a complete waste of police resources. Unless we find some — er, minion — to do it, who'll think it's an honour to do our dirty work.'

He threw back his head and laughed. 'Guv, you're an education.'

'A bad one,' she said penitently. 'I should be encouraging you to give the coroner the straightforward information that Minton topped himself because he was temporarily depressed and then close the file.'

'Perhaps you should. But I'm glad you're not.'

'You may well regret that. Now, Pete, to the important things in life — is there any decent coffee anywhere?'

Before he could reply, her mobile told her a text had arrived. One from Mark.

Neither of them had mastered the shorthand of the young, so she wasn't surprised to see what looked like a standard email. *Phone ASAP re water. We're involved.* It took seconds to connect her to him.

'Invitaqua have contacted us,' he announced without preamble.

'Us as in the police?'

'In one. It seems they've just happened to notice something irregular in some water tests and they phoned to say, please can they borrow our divers? I just happened to overhear, you understand.'

Fran knew better than to ask for his source. 'What on earth would they want divers for?'

'A swim in some enclosed reservoir just down the road from us in Lenham. It seems they've found one of the reservoir covers unlocked — they have special keys, it seems — and they're shitting themselves in case someone has put something nasty inside.'

'And about time too.'

'We've got a DCI supervising, but I thought you might just want to be there.'

His tone might be casual, but there was a wealth of meaning behind it. The fact that Mark, as ACC (Crime), wanted her to be part of the investigating team meant he was tacitly backing her against his superior, the assistant chief constable. How would the chief react? They both knew that Mark enjoyed his respect, as did Fran when she wasn't being wilfully awkward.

'I might just,' she conceded, with a huge smile he'd certainly detect.

'Do you want the map coordinates? I believe there's a team already on its way.' Without waiting for a reply, he dictated them.

What about Henson? Was he still off sick? She dialled his number.

His secretary answered. 'I'm terribly sorry. DCS Henson's going to be off all week, Ms Harman.'

'With that cold he shouldn't have been in last Friday, should he?' Fran sympathised. More especially he shouldn't have been standing around outside without a coat on, participating in that foolish mothers' meeting. 'Has he left any instructions, Daphne?'

'Just to refer any problems to you.'

'That's his explicit instruction?'

Daphne laughed. 'It isn't like you to worry about that sort of detail, is it, Ms Harman?'

'Oh, you'd be surprised,' Fran declared.

* * *

It wasn't often Fran resorted to blues and twos and called on the skills once honed driving IRA informers and MPs alike briskly round the country. But when she did, once the panic had subsided that she could no longer trust her reflexes and the sweat on her palms had dried, she let rip. As she cleaved a way through the motorway traffic, she laughed aloud. What would her staid colleagues at tedious meetings make of her now?

The reservoir was not the sort of beauty spot that drew people like the open air ones in Wales or Yorkshire. Indeed, the uninitiated might not even know it was there. Any sightseers were firmly discouraged by locked gates and high fencing with a decorative topping of razor wire. It was next to a few acres of allotments, similarly fenced; today the allotment gates were wide open, and Fran could see a cluster of cars near the main track spoiling an otherwise perfect rural idyll. Clearly you didn't need to guard early vegetables as closely as drinking water, so no one could complain about the allotment tenants being relaxed about security. She'd guess, however, that any of the people digging away or tending little bonfires would have clocked a stranger from five hundred paces. And spades and forks would have made handy weapons. All the same, it was not impossible that whoever had tampered with the water supply gained access from the allotments by dint of wire cutters and a little brute force.

She, however, had to gain access a more legitimate way. There seemed to be someone inside a Portakabin just inside the gates, but a gentle toot on the horn failed to make him respond. Eventually a particularly loud and prolonged burst of the siren drew his reluctant attention, and he emerged to walk slowly towards her. Getting out of the car, she strode to the gates and rattled them.

'Hold on, hold on. You're not allowed in here.'

She flourished her ID and obviated any problems he might have with missing reading-glasses or inability to read with a loud declaration of who she was and what rank she held.

'I told you, we're not open. There's a bit of a problem and I can't allow anyone in. Specially a lady.' He sounded genuinely outraged at the thought.

'I'm not a lady, I'm a police officer and I'm in charge of the investigation.'

'Young lady like you? You're not in uniform. You don't want to get that nice suit muddy.'

'I'm a plain clothes officer — a detective! Open these gates, please.'

'Nah, you don't want to see what they're up to.'

'Indeed I do. Now, are you going to let me in or do I have to radio one of my colleagues down there to come and arrest you?'

'You don't want to do that.' He shuffled a little closer, producing an impressive-looking key from a sagging side pocket.

'Indeed, nothing would give me greater satisfaction. Unless,' she added silently, 'it would be to pop you in the reservoir yourself for a spell.'

Since the site was only now being set up, presumably her colleagues had had similar problems, despite their large official van brightly declaring it carried the Kent County Constabulary Underwater Search and Recovery team. The van even had some sort of boat on the roof, complete with impressive-looking outboard motor.

So all that haste and adrenalin had been a waste of time — worse, a risk to herself and others. She tore a strip off herself at least as vigorously as she would have dressed down a junior officer who had been as rash, and then settled down to observe real policing at first hand, as opposed to from the far side of a wide, wide desk.

'Didn't expect to see you here, ma'am,' said the DCI in charge of the operation, striding over and saluting. He was carrying a superfluous couple of stone, and had a tendency to puff. 'Dan Coveney, ma'am.'

Another one who knew she had problems with names. 'Guv,' she said with a smile. 'Well, I always like to be in on an inquiry right at the start, and Mr Henson can't cover everything at the moment. In fact, he's off sick this week.' Why did she need to justify herself? And to a colleague, who, judging by the look on his face, knew which of the two he preferred. Encouraged, she continued, 'Plus today, Dan, I've got this project for the deputy chief constable, checking what people on the ground — or in this case in the water — need to make them more efficient.'

'Get rid of another layer of top brass, for a start, begging your pardon, guv. The more chiefs, the less money for Indians' work.'

'Mark Turner apart, I wouldn't argue. But then I'm biased.'

'Now he's a good bloke, they say. A worker.' There was no higher praise. 'That's Sergeant Mills over there — he's the diving team leader — calling me over. Would you excuse me, guv?'

'Of course. Just ignore me and I'll watch.'

If her other colleagues were disconcerted by her presence there, they knew better than to query it, especially when she produced a clipboard. In her experience, whatever you were doing, a clipboard lent authority to it. Even if she didn't need a spurious token, since with luck she'd be running the investigation, she clutched it like an amulet. Perhaps it would ward off Gates' evil eye.

Everyone scuttled round obligingly, ostentatiously taking no notice of her.

At last, she spotted a familiar face among the lads in the diving team. She beckoned the young man over.

'How's things, Roo?' He'd acquired his nickname through his habit of running to work, burdened only by a bumbag that inevitably slipped round his waist. His colleagues thought this made him look like a marsupial; Fran had considered that since he was so tall and skinny him it made him more like a pregnant lamppost. He'd filled out in the five or six years since she'd known him and was rumoured to have turned his sporting sights on the triathlon.

'Fine, ma'am, thanks.'

'Guv. And Kanga?' Inevitably, Roo had met a young woman his opposite in build. Sharon was a constable who neither sought nor particularly deserved promotion, a rounded girl whose nickname, Kanga, bestowed by Roo's mates, was far more appropriate than Roo's had ever been. Fran could always imagine her doling out medicine.

'These days she actually looks more like a Roo than ever I used to — she's expecting. Due next month, ma'am. Guv.'

Hadn't she read somewhere that it could be harmful to carry too much weight while you were pregnant? 'And is she well?'

'Her blood pressure's up a bit, so it looks as if she may have to start her maternity leave earlier than we'd hoped.'

'And you're going to be present at the birth?' Fran hoped she sounded as if she knew about such things.

'You bet! We've been going to these classes together, guv.' All six-foot five of him demanded an approving pat on the head.

'Excellent. Don't forget to take your paternity leave, Roo, will you? All of it!'

She could have spouted about bonding and all the other buzzwords in the documentation she'd helped prepare for the policy, now standard in forces across the country, but she was all too aware that they were no more than words to her. Would she ever have made a good mother? She doubted it. But at least she hoped she had helped young people like Roo and his Kanga to be happier parents.

But now it was clearly time to don his diving suit, so she gave him a comradely pat on the arm to dismiss him. The atmosphere became perceptibly tense, the hum of the generator recharging the compressed air bottles taking over from conversation.

Soon Roo would be down there in an environment so totally alien to her that she couldn't imagine it. Hazel, her sister, had been born, according to her parents, with webbed feet. She'd certainly won medals at a number of school swimming galas. How would even Hazel feel about plunging through that ludicrously small manhole or whatever they called it into icy darkness? About groping for dead flesh, whether human or animal, and lugging it to the surface? All Fran knew was that, state-of-the-art underwater floodlights illuminating it or not, she couldn't do it.

Roo, now unrecognisable apart from his height, gave a cheery wave as he and two colleagues, all dressed like something from a nautical horror film, headed for the water. She waved back, a grin of encouragement strapped to her face. She hoped he wouldn't notice the finer details such as the fact it didn't reach her eyes and her teeth were clenched in a rictus, not a smile.

As soon as they lifted the hatch to the access hole there were yells. She didn't need Mills to beckon her over — she set off at a run. Junior officers parted like corn in the wind to let her through.

Immediately beneath the hatch, floating face down, was a fully dressed woman, her hair drifting around her as if she were a mermaid. As they watched, she moved a few inches, just out of sight.

Mills pointed. It was clear what the divers had to do. Roo was in first, and she could see him reach for the white hand and touch it. He would pull it back to the hatch where the others could grab it to heave it onto the grass. There. He was almost there. Fingers reached for fingers.

And hers came off in his. Huge flakes of skin and tissue, soft green-blue threads and fair hair exploded in slow motion around the corpse. And Roo's vomit filled his mask.

* * *

Fran did everything by the book, including offering a possible ID. That green-blue top — would that be the same colour as the thread in the Lenham woman's hand bowl? And the blonde hair the same as in the sinks of Mrs Green and even the unreliable Mrs Carter? Given the age of the young woman and her clothes, Fran wondered if she'd just looked at the remains of Janine Roper. She uttered a silent prayer of thanks to St Anthony — who else could have set this up? — that this had occurred in the middle of the case review, not after everything had been wrapped up. Then, without doubting his efficiency for one moment, she checked that Coveney had set up everything needed at what had clearly become a crime scene — one look at the remains of the body had convinced everyone that it had not been the young woman who had strung herself onto the concrete beam immediately above the water line. Meanwhile, the Home Office pathologist was on her way. All the mobile paraphernalia of modern crime detection would be lumbering past the unwilling gatekeeper within the hour.

Good. She had another job to do she couldn't see Coveney volunteering for. But first she called him over. 'This is clearly going to take a long time,' she said. 'And the fewer people tramping round here the better. So I'm going to take myself off. We'll use HQ's incident room since it's so close.' She rather thought that that would prevent any argument about who took on the case.

He nodded his understanding, if not total approval.

She was halfway to her car when she turned back to him. 'And I'd like a list of everyone who's ever used or had access to those manhole keys.'

He pulled a face, hands gesturing an object eight inches long. 'They're not the size you could slip into your back pocket, guv.' He stopped short. As people tended to do when they saw that glint in her eye. 'On your desk first thing, ma'am.'

* * *

Wearing nothing but a foil blanket, Roo was sitting dithering in the ambulance. Fran gripped his hands. 'It's all right. It's all right, Roo. We're taking you to hospital, and then I'm going to see Kanga and tell her what's going on.'

'This woman. Those fingers . . . I've seen bodies before, guv. Lots of them. I've seen them run over and crushed in a steel mill and dying in a cot at six weeks. So why am I like this?'

Fran couldn't tell him. She'd once shifted a man to give him mouth to mouth only to have the whole head come off in her hands. She was as well acquainted with maggots and blowflies as most. But there was something that made even her hardy gorge rise at the sight — now the memory — of the tissue that Roo had had to deal with.

'I could have shifted the whole corpse, no sweat. So why did just a few fingers . . . ? Have they got the rest out yet?' She could hear the effort in the question — he was desperate to return to normality, wasn't he? But maybe he'd never be able to return to diving again. At least, not until he'd had a huge amount of therapy.

'Yes. In some sort of plastic cradle-cum-stretcher thing — I'm sure you know the right term, Roo. They anchored her to it and then shoved the lot in a big polybag the fire service provided.'

He was silent.

Fran wanted to say all sorts of comforting rubbish, but waited, still holding his hands.

'What did I think I was doing?' He gulped convulsively. 'I emptied my mask in the rezzer, for goodness' sake. After I threw up.'

'That's it. Nice deep breaths through your mouth . . . What were you doing? Not choking to death, thank God. It'll all be sorted out. The water people will deal with everything.' She very much hoped so, as one intimately involved with the quality of the water round here.

'Everything. Christ, no! Oh, God!' He covered his face, but then pulled his hands away again. 'Fran, will it ever go away?'

More tears coursed down his face. She heard them splatter on the tin foil.

'Yes,' she said quietly, passing him tissues. 'Yes, I promise you it will.' Better to make a lying promise than to upset him with the truth. She put her arms round him and held him tighter.

* * *

She left Roo in A&E at William Harvey, Ashford, calling round herself to the section in Maidstone nick where Kanga was currently on light duties. Half of her had wanted to snap with some exasperation that a police station was no place for a woman in Kanga's condition, but she told herself off for being old-fashioned about pregnancy, for having views derived from male cops of the old school who made even period pains the butt of their doubtful humour. The other half wanted to smile at the sight of a young woman waddling determinedly round the office, more like a penguin than like a marsupial.

She briefed the duty FME, but made sure he was only hanging round in the wings, as it were. Then she ejected the resident sergeant from his little office and commandeered it for her own use, summoning a bemused Kanga, whom she seated comfortably. Since she was still flourishing her clip-board, she hoped to give the impression that the interview was routine, and not set off panic where none was necessary. After all, there was no earthly reason why Kanga should associate her with any problem with Roo.

But then she had to break it to this cheery young woman that certainly for weeks, probably for months and possibly even for years, she was going to have to mother not just her newborn baby but also the strapping man she'd waved goodbye to that morning. At least she could promise her that every expert going in post-traumatic stress would be consulted, that every aspect of best practice care would be extended to him. But while he might soon be ready to return to some sort of role in the police service, he might never rid his nightmares of that particular sight.

'Roo is perfectly fine, Kanga, I promise you.'

Kanga's eyes widened in fear. 'But—?'

'But there was an incident in a dive he was doing about an hour ago.'

'Incident?'

How stupid of her to have used the word everyone knew was synonymous with a disaster! She said quickly, 'He found a body — somewhat decayed. Not a nice thing to find when all you can think about is your new baby and your wife's health. He was a bit upset, so I packed him off to A&E. Just for a check-up — you know me!'

Kanga didn't look convinced by this confession of bossiness.

Fran came round the desk, squatted beside her and took her hand. 'I promise you he's not injured in any way. He's just had an unpleasant experience. In the old days we'd have sent him down to the pub and told him to drink himself silly and think no more about it. It's not like that these days.'

'So—?'

'He's still in A&E, Kanga,' Fran said, 'but I doubt if they'll want to keep him in. Now, I'm going to get one of your mates to run you home to pick up some warm things for him and I'll clear some compassionate leave for both of you — both, you understand? Not just him. No arguments. You've got your blood pressure to think about, he tells me, and it wouldn't do it any good at all if you're toiling away here worrying about him being on his own at home.'

The tightening about Kanga's mouth and eyes suggested she knew all the implications without being told. But her question was quite at odds with her grip on Fran's hand. 'Will he be well enough to paint the nursery, do you think?' She managed a smile meant to be cheerfully ironic but slipping painfully into distress.

Fran stroked the girl's hair back. 'I should imagine there's no finer therapy. But he'll have to be debriefed, I'm afraid. We'll need to know exactly where he found the corpse and anything else he noticed. It'll all be done under the supervision of the shrinks, I promise.' Was the young woman convinced? Fran released her hand the better to heave herself to her feet, using the desk to assist her.

'I was in the middle of—'

'Go, Kanga! I told you, I'll sort everything here.'

Which didn't take long, Kanga's sergeant knowing when simple obedience was best. As for Human Resources, they generally found themselves ready to concede defeat when Fran stuck her oar in. But she must remember to tell Cosmo — she didn't want to get his back up.

Surprising herself at her consideration she sank back behind the desk with a sigh. God, she was tired. And hungry, in whichever order.

'Are you all right, ma'am?' Someone was looming over her.

A hard blink and a stare confirmed it was the FME, a man of about her own age, disappointed, perhaps, that his skills had not been called upon to minister to Kanga.

'I'm fine. Had a busy day, that's all.'

'And quite a long one. You know it's nearly five?'

'What?' she squeaked. 'No, lunchtime, surely.' Not that she wanted to eat.

He shook his head emphatically.

'Well, I'll go to the bottom of our stairs, as one of my old sergeants used to say. I'd better head back to HQ, hadn't I?'

'Want a coffee before you go?'

'Caffeine at this time of day? I'd never sleep, doc.'

'Nor would I,' he conceded, withdrawing with a smile.

Would poor Roo? With or without caffeine?

CHAPTER FOURTEEN

'As crime scenes go, the reservoir and its environs are pretty corrupt, but that won't stop the entire site being cordoned off for the forensic scientists to have a nose round and then the old fingertip search going ahead,' Fran told Mark over a quick bite in the canteen. 'We've already got Janine Roper's DNA on record, of course, so if the body is hers the lab should be able to ID her pretty soon. I've managed to get the PM set up for tomorrow morning.'

'Will you want to be involved with that? Didn't you see enough—?' Not unreasonably he sounded disbelieving.

'You bet I want to be there.' She firmly suppressed the images that still floated like the detached skin before her inner eye. 'I shall go straight to the hospital. Apart from anything else, Ashford's a reasonable distance from HQ. If Gates is back I don't want him impeding me.'

From the quality of Mark's silence, she guessed immediately there was something wrong.

'I found a memo addressed to the chief on my desk this morning, copied to me anonymously,' he said at last. 'Look, perhaps we should talk about this in my office.'

'Don't worry — I shan't have a tantrum and I need to get back to the incident room in ten minutes. Let me guess: Gates has formally requested my return to Uniform? Knowing my opinion? The bastard. When I'm in the middle of a full-scale murder inquiry. Though I suppose if he sent the memo to the chief yesterday he wouldn't know that, would he? What will you do?'

He met her eye. 'There's only one thing for it — you'll have to tackle the chief himself. I don't think I can, since I wasn't supposed to get the memo.'

'But surely at the very least you should have been consulted? Crime's not his purview! Only professional standards, corporate communications, and organisation and development. Not to mention,' she added, relishing the polysyllabics, 'change management, strategic planning, delivering best value and service improvement, service inspection and performance analysis. Crime's still *your* bailiwick.'

He raised a warning finger as her voice rose. 'But he outranks me.'

'This is a classic case of empire-building at someone else's expense! Is he hoping to piss you off so much you retire too?'

'I'm not sure he wants to be rid of you. Or me, to do him justice. The thing is, you're popular and you're bright and hard-working, so he may want to keep you on his bloody committees.'

'I shall have to do something really bad, then, won't I? Like forget to turn up. Or fall asleep and snore.' She didn't joke any more. 'OK, the moment the chief gets back I shall be knocking on his door. Meanwhile, it's business as usual, as far as I'm concerned. After all, neither of us has heard the news officially. Not from Gates' mouth. Only from that memo. I wonder who leaked it . . .'

'One of your fans, sweetheart, trusting me to do the decent thing. Actually, perhaps it's no bad thing that Gates is off sick — if he'd been in the building I'd have shoved his damned note down his ungrateful little throat.'

'It's not his ingratitude that worries me,' Fran protested, 'but his incompetence and lousy priorities. I wonder what's the matter with him.'

'You mean in general or specifically?' He shook his head, falling silent, as if trying to find a neutral topic. At last he said, 'I wonder how long it'll take them to flush out the reservoir.'

'Long enough. But how they'll ever get it clean enough, after all that's gone into it—' To her horror she found herself shuddering. Maybe she'd shudder every time she thought of it.

He leant forward and clasped her hands.

'No, don't be kind or I shall cry. Lord, look at the time — I must be off. Don't wait for me. I can pick up a pound car and come home when I've done all I can here.' Disengaging her hands, she pushed away from the table.

He shook his head firmly. 'I've got plenty of reading here to catch up on. Just give me a bell when you're ready.'

And if that wasn't enough, he stood up too, and in full view of all their colleagues gave her a kiss and a hug. There could be no doubt, then, to whose mast he was nailing his colours.

* * *

According to plan, Friday morning saw Fran heading straight to Ashford and the William Harvey Hospital, to watch the post-mortem of what the media had promptly dubbed the Lady in the Lake and to discuss the findings with the new pathologist, about whom she knew nothing except the name, Dr Harris.

Dr Millward, Harris's predecessor, and Fran had been more or less contemporaries. Millward had had his own special way of involving the police presence at post-mortems, which consisted of getting the poor sap who was greenest to hold a vital instrument — worse, a vital organ — for him while he probed. His commentaries were equally idiosyncratic, full of outrageous blasphemy and a total denigration of the corpse's previous lifestyle. Whether the bile within had matched the bile he so constantly vented, or for some other reason, Millward had suddenly succumbed to cancer, from diagnosis to death in two short weeks. Fran rather thought he'd known exactly what he was suffering from and had deliberately avoided seeking assistance — not a cure, since he'd know all too well that there was none available.

Fran tapped at the half-open door of his replacement's office. She found a young woman attractive enough to star in that TV series about pathologists, wearing her wellies as if they were Jimmy Choos and her overalls as if they were — Fran had forgotten who was supposed to be the latest designer for the young and size eight.

Harris's smile included a couple of dimples and immaculate teeth. Fran prepared to hate her.

'Detective Chief Superintendent Harman? Come in. I'm Iona.'

'Fran.' They shook hands.

'Such a pain of a first name,' the younger woman said with a rueful smile.

Fran was taken aback, but smiled encouragingly.

'People always want to add something to it, instead of my surname. I own a bicycle; I own a car; I own a scalpel. Sometimes I think of abbreviating it to Ion, with a short O.'

'Which gives just as many opportunities for merry quips, I should think,' Fran said, starting, after all, to warm to her, 'beginning with filings. I shortened mine to Fran because so many people expected a male Francis to turn up and were disappointed when it was a female Frances.'

Issues of nomenclature out of the way, Fran and Iona turned to greet the new arrival, DCI Dan Coveney, who had just arrived, puffing slightly from the stairs.

'Sorry. It's been one of those mornings. First some prat had blocked me in, then the traffic was snarled up and then there were no parking slots left. Would anyone care for a mint? I know you always laugh,' he told Dr Harris, who had rather ostentatiously refused one, 'but I can't watch a PM without my peppermint!' He gave a nervous laugh.

Fran believed him, accepting one herself while they donned their protective finery.

At last Iona revealed their corpse, in all its pathetic glory. Normally Dan would have made all the notes the police considered necessary; today Fran augmented his with her own, jotting as Iona and her technician recorded each relevant observation.

'Do you have any ID on her yet?' Iona asked.

Dan jumped in. 'We're routinely checking the MisPer records,' he said. 'And running a DNA check. But the guv'nor here thinks she recognises the lady.'

'*Lady!*' Iona repeated scathingly. She seemed to think there was no need to explain why the word had offended her.

Fran, who rarely used it herself, said as if there had been no interruption, 'There's a chance she might be one Janine Roper, whose husband is currently in Maidstone Jail for her murder. Would two to three years ago fit your time frame?'

'Possibly. It depends on water and air temperature and so on.'

'I'm sorry — I could have nipped into HQ first for a photo to show you.' But she might have met the dreaded Gates.

Iona waved aside the apology; clearly such old-fashioned things were irrelevant in her hi-tech world.

'I'm hoping for an ID from her hubby,' Dan put in.

Even Fran winced.

Iona stared. 'Fucking hell! You want him to look at her? Like this?'

'It might just provoke him into confessing,' Fran said, 'horrible though it would be. In any case, we've not been able to run to earth any relatives at all, despite all my team's efforts last night. He'll be cuffed and brought here and cuffed and taken away.' And God knew what effect it would have on the poor grey little man.

'But if he didn't do it, think of the psychological trauma! Worse than being in jail for a crime he didn't commit!'

Fran nodded. Such an opinion from someone used to dealing in death must merit consideration.

'But shocking him into a confession would be nice,' Dan urged.

Somehow his enthusiasm made Fran's diminish. 'I'm going to have to do it, I'm afraid.'

'You'll do it yourself?'

Fran wasn't sure of the drift of the young woman's question. 'Yes. With a younger colleague who seems to have a rapport with Roper,' she added, lying through her teeth. If either of them had had a rapport with Roper, she thought it was herself. 'You see, you can get rusty, after being desk-bound. And every month psychologists come up with new techniques, new ideas for the best location for interviews, that sort of thing. Even the colour of the walls, would you believe. Amazing. And I wouldn't want to let anyone down because I'm out of date.'

It was clear none of this pleased Dan, who had no doubt registered that he was being pre-empted. So he made a little bid for power on his own account. 'Doctorarris,' he said, exposing another problem with her name the young woman was no doubt also aware of, 'you're probably more au fait with fashion than I am. Could you give a fair approximation of the date of her clothes?'

'I'm into Oxfam chic.' It was an unnecessarily firm put-down.

What was the history here? She'd never found anything actively to dislike in Coveney and had a very favourable impression of the young woman, but there was certainly a problem. It had better not interfere with their work together.

Fran said, 'I'd have thought the shoes might be helpful, Dan. Manufacturers change styles regularly, don't they? Especially fashion shoes like those.' Would she or Iona ever have sported such an extreme pair? Heels four inches high? Ankle-straps? And in lipstick red? And why had her killer not removed them?

They were stowed in an evidence bag.

'Clothes by Dorothy Perkins and Next,' Iona said. 'But — my goodness! — lingerie by Agent Provocateur. A set! What a mismatch, eh, Fran?'

Fran nodded.

'As a matter of fact, my mother always used to make my sisters put on their good undies when they went out in case they were run over. It didn't matter about the top clothes because they'd be ruined anyway,' Coveney said.

'But these aren't just good, they're very expensive and very sexy,' Iona said.

'What about you, Dan?' Fran asked idly, but registering Iona's point. What did such underwear say about a classroom assistant whose hobby was reading? Or not reading, if Roper was to be believed.

'In point of fact, Mum always confiscated my clothes at the end of every day, guv, or I'd have worn them till I became a public health risk.'

It was always like this at a PM. The coppers nattered rubbish, anything to distract themselves while the professionals got on with the business of cutting and sawing and taking intimate swabs. Nonetheless, at the end of the session, it would be amazing how much information had found its way into police notebooks.

* * *

Afterwards, in her office, when they were all back in civvies, Iona offered tea and a packet of chocolate digestives.

'I don't mind if I do,' Coveney said, taking two.

Fran limited herself to one but noted that Iona took none; even someone as young and lithe as she wouldn't stay that way if she celebrated the completion of each examination with calories. And why celebrate anyway, if corpses were your job?

'I know you'll give a most detailed report full of the appropriate jargon,' Fran said, 'and I'm sure you and Dan will know exactly what it means.' And no doubt the wordier it was the more Coveney would enjoy it. 'But for ages I've been trapped behind the biggest mound of paperwork in the Western world, and could do with a nice everywoman version.'

'It's been on the tip of my tongue to ask you what brought you here, guv,' Dan put in. 'Someone your level. I expected you to take an overview of the case, not to hobnob with corpses.'

'Since I was there when they found her, I thought I'd take a personal interest. It sure as hell beats a seminar on the delivery of best value and service improvement,' she added conspiratorially.

'It comes to something when you'd rather watch a stinking corpse getting cut about than go to a meeting,' Dan grunted. 'Mind you, I think you might be right, the number they lumber us with. And what gets me is it's all change Tuesday, change again Wednesday.'

Fran threw her head back and laughed. 'Believe it or not, that's a very useful contribution to the project I'm working on for the new DCC. Mind if I quote you? It's all right, Dan, not by name! Now,' she added with a brisk smile, 'since I'm out of touch with all this hands-on stuff, can I just check I've got everything right?'

Iona nodded, glancing with much more interest at her watch. Another punter in the lab? Or a lunch date? Fran suspected the latter. Well, she would just have to hang on three minutes: after all, if you were as young and lovely as Iona, it was more than likely that your lover would be patient.

Fran read through her jottings. 'About thirty-five. No children. Good health. Height, five-five. Weight, about a hundred and thirty pounds. Throttled. And then, judging from the verdigris marks on her skin and the deep indentations in her flesh, trussed with electric wire and slung up above the waterline.'

'Nicely refrigerated up there on that concrete beam, but not frozen,' Dan put in.

'So eventually the wire corroded and she plopped down into the reservoir and started polluting it. Now, Iona, if your report contains anything really viciously technical, you'll put a little footnote for me — OK?'

'I don't believe you, but if you insist I will.' She stood up. It was time for her visitors to leave.

Fran only took hints like that when she was ready, however. 'Thank you for letting me come along, Iona. Even with the very best path report, I find I don't get a feel for what the person was like. In fact,' she continued, smiling at the young woman despite the latter's now obvious urge to see them off, 'you probably did the PM on someone else I'm taking an interest in — Alec Minton.'

Harris looked puzzled. 'Straightforward suicide. He had all the injuries consistent with jumping from the fifth floor of a hotel onto the road below. Nothing interesting in the toxicology, no health problems.'

'Do you think—?'

But two phones cut short Fran's question, Harris's and her own. To judge from her reaction, Harris's was a personal and very exciting one, no doubt the reason she was eager for them to leave. Fran's was a text from Mark saying that he wanted her to front a press conference in the afternoon. Oh, and Gates had been sighted in the building. Heard, rather, giving someone verbal hell over the phone.

On consideration, Fran thought she'd rather be found at HQ, preferably in the incident room, than be caught out — in Gates' view — effectively truanting, especially if technically the Minton case was absolutely nothing to do with her. Gesturing thanks and farewell, she took herself off, holding the door for Coveney to follow in her wake.

They were already in the car park when Dan stopped, slapping his head. 'We never asked if she could get any DNA off her — the murderer's, I mean. There have been so many forensic science developments recently I can't keep up with them all.'

'Neither can I,' Fran confessed. 'But I'm sure Harris'll do all that's expected of her, and more. Now, I'm heading back to HQ. What about you?'

'I've got to stop off here in Ashford for half an hour. There's a court case coming up and I want to make sure everything's going along smoothly. But I'll be with you in the incident room as soon as I can.'

'With that list of reservoir hatch key-holders, don't forget.'

'And how about the key-holders to the surrounding area, guv?'

Trumped, eh? 'Well done, Dan.'

* * *

Fran had often in the past found ladies' loos excellent places for meetings, especially when she knew a man was, for whatever reason, hunting for her. So she was pleased to find DCI Joanne Pearce in front of the mirror, intent on reapplying all her make-up. Joining her, she dug for her own lipstick. One glance at the battered specimen, however, and she abandoned it as too pathetic compared with the full palette the DCI had at her disposal.

'How are you getting on with Drury?' Fran asked.

'Well, you know you suggested we got other forces involved? We decided to do that, only cast the net a bit wider. And we've got the French police wanting to come over to talk to him about a couple of murders in the red-light district of Marseilles.'

'So far afield?'

'Drury did a stint as an HGV driver.'

'So you could get interest from all over the place. Excellent. Do you want me to find some cash for an interpreter, just so there's no misunderstandings between you and them?'

Joanne shook her head, and concentrated very hard on her left eyelid. 'My first degree's in French, as it happens, guv.'

'Excellent.' Fran resisted the urge to ask sarcastically about her second one. She herself had had to leave the police in order to take her first degree, and her doctorate had come the hard way, too, via part-time study with the OU. 'You will keep me informed, won't you? Actually, if you could let me have precise details of his MO I'd be very grateful, especially if they involve wire or water. And in return I'll copy you in on our new corpse.'

'The Lady in the Lake?'

'The very same. Except with her choice of sexy undies and fuck-me shoes she may not have been a lady, and she was certainly not in a lake.' She'd need to talk to Roper about those clothes. And to find where Janine had stored the others, for Fran couldn't imagine that they were a one-off choice. Was there far more to his wife's evening activities than poor Roper guessed at? Or had he guessed and that was precisely the motive for his killing her? Another face-to-face interview was called for — not least to break it to him what was in store for him. She rather thought she should do that herself, even though it meant yet more hands-on work to irritate the likes of Gates. And she would certainly be there when Roper ID'd the body. One spontaneous gesture was worth a thousand words in an interview room. The trouble was, fitting it all in, especially as, for Mark's sake — and indeed her own — she must not miss any of the meetings Gates valued so highly.

Inevitably, while she was preoccupied, she ran into Gates, almost literally.

'Are you feeling better?' she asked, hoping she sounded as if she cared. A much more important enquiry would be into Roo's state of health this morning. And Kanga's.

Clearly he regarded her question as at best an irrelevance, at worst an impertinence. 'You weren't in earlier this morning,' he said.

'No. I was out on a case. The Lady in the Lake that the media are so interested in.' Her subtext was that if the media were sniffing round, it was incumbent on the CID to put up their most stalwart representatives. Fran had had more experience than most with fending off the wrong questions and seizing ones the police were more than happy to give answers to. She also seemed to have a TV-friendly face, though that always puzzled her, and presumed Mark would also want her to do a piece to camera for the regional news programmes going out at six-thirty.

'Really?' His face could not have conveyed less interest. 'Why you had to drop everything and scurry across country simply to watch divers in action defeats me. And then observe the autopsy this morning!' He flapped his hands in exasperation.

'You could say it was part of the project investigating the needs of divisional CIDs,' she suggested, tongue in cheek. 'I picked up some useful ideas.' He appeared never to have heard of the day-to-day needs of divisional CIDs, despite having delegated Fran to investigate them. 'But in fact, I was simply doing what any DCS should do. I was maintaining an active presence.'

'And of course you asked Henson?' The question was waspish.

'Of course. In the event I found he was off sick.' Should she tell him that Henson had left a message asking her to take responsibility for anything urgent or would that be to grass him up? Let Gates make his own deductions. 'I acted on my own initiative and informed the ACC (Crime) accordingly.'

'As if you couldn't twist Turner round your little finger. You know it's not considered good for staff morale to have two senior officers in a relationship working in the same area.'

Had no one told him that the chief had played a major part in bringing them together?

'I quite understand that, sir. But you will understand it's a view I don't share. Now, if you'll excuse me, sir, I have to go to the incident room to prepare for this afternoon's press conference.'

'You?'

The strength of his revulsion rocked her. It was all she could do to ask mildly, 'Who else would you suggest, sir? I'm sure the ACC is open to ideas.'

As he turned on his heel she regretted that particular shot. She had a feeling it might rebound.

The next person she came across was Cosmo Dix. He faced her, arms akimbo and head on one side. 'What shall we do with you, eh, Fran? Dishing out compassionate leave to constables as if it were in your gift.'

'You mean it isn't?' She rounded her eyes. 'And I always thought I could give out promotions and pay rises whenever I felt like it.'

'Well, you were right, of course. Morally. But it would have been nice if you'd warned me before I get some old buffer from Maidstone nick exploding down the phone at me. Seems the little pregnant lady hadn't finished her filing, or something.'

'Sorry, Cosmo. Of course I should have told you. Asked you, actually.'

He took a step backward, then peered at her. 'Are you sure you're all right?'

'Any reason why I shouldn't be?'

'Not your style, apologising, Fran. I wondered if you were going down with something.'

'Nope. Maybe just mellowing a little.'

Cosmo looked at her oddly. 'That's not like you either.' But his pager went before he could say any more and he had to toddle off.

* * *

However much pressure they were under, either in the incident room or elsewhere, Fran had always insisted that her colleagues take adequate meal breaks, getting away from computers and gruesome photos alike, in relays if necessary. Today was no different. So there were still a couple of latecomers dawdling back when they convened for a briefing before Fran moved on to her next task. She was glad to see they put on a sprint as soon as they saw she was in place.

'So what do I have to tell the press?' she began. 'What are they likely to bite and swallow? What's best kept away from them?'

* * *

'We're dealing with a killer who knew the district very well,' Fran told the TV camera, 'and concealed his victim with no regard to the health and safety of people living in the neighbourhood. But even in a remote part of the country like this, someone must have seen him dispose of the body. We're appealing particularly to anyone who had an allotment in this area, near Lenham, about three years ago to come forward. Every bit of information, no matter how trivial it may seem, could help solve this most unusual case. Thank you.' She smiled earnestly and stopped. There was no need to say that the police had already started to comb through council records and anyone who had rented an allotment at the salient time would be receiving a routine visit. It was better psychologically for Joe Public to feel important. 'I hope the wind didn't blow all that away.'

Dilly Pound, who always insisted she owed Fran a favour after a stalking case, gave a thumbs-up sign. 'Perfect. I don't know how you manage to get it right first time.'

'Years of practice,' Fran said. 'Maybe too many.'

'Have you got time for a drink, Fran? Daniel was only saying the other night how nice it would be to meet up again.'

Fran's mobile gave her the excuse she needed. 'After this case, Dilly, if you don't mind. You can see what it's like. My best to Daniel.' She turned away with more haste than courtesy to take the call.

It was Jim Champion. 'How are you fixed tonight, Fran? Because I've got young Rob coming round, remember.'

Why hadn't God put more hours in the day? 'I can't see myself making it before nine,' she said. 'And I'm afraid it may be later, and for a flying visit.'

'Don't tell me,' Jim said with great satisfaction, 'it's the Lady in the Lake case, isn't it?'

'Right. I'm just shooting a TV statement now,' she fibbed. 'Watch out for me at half six.'

'Watch out? I shall bloody wave!'

'And I'll try to wave back.'

* * *

Back at the office, she slapped her head. Despite Cosmo's equivocal rebuke, she'd not given any thought to how Roo and Kanga were today. She reached for the phone. Then stopped, as if someone had bitten her hand. Was she permitted in these days of litigation for damages for work-related stress to ask how he was, poor kid? Not to mention Kanga. She fancied that for some reason it would be permissible to phone her, but not him. After all, her being pregnant was scarcely Kent Constabulary's fault.

She started nibbling her pencil. She'd always thought that being brusque and bending a few rules were acceptable at her level. Clearly they hadn't been in QED, who had left behind a reputation she'd rather not share. What if she was going round causing similar offence? Getting up the nose of a cold fish like Simon Gates was one thing, irritating a benevolent man like Cosmo quite another. Perhaps she should run it past him. And even as she used the cliché, she cursed herself. What if Simon were right? What if she were becoming a liability?

* * *

'I'm sure your instinct is right, Fran,' Cosmo said, with his most winsome smile. He turned briefly to switch on his kettle. 'We're implementing all the correct duty of care procedures. Believe me, no one can fault us. But since you rather took young — what did you call her? Kanga! — under your wing, I'm sure a phone call wouldn't go amiss.'

Fran rubbed her face. 'I didn't want Roo's Police Federation rep scratching his head to see if he can detect any sinister plot behind the call.'

'I take your point. No, phone away — but perhaps you shouldn't ask about the incident itself.' Cosmo poured them China tea from a delicate pot with a wicker handle. How much more civilised than the quick dunk of a tea bag. He placed a translucent cup and saucer in front of her. 'There.'

'Thanks,' she said humbly, though half her mind wondered, as it always did, how much of his camp act was simply that — an act, a pose.

He looked at her sharply. 'Are you quite sure you're well? All this adherence to the rules stuff?'

'Must be my age, Cosmo.'

Shaking his head, he remonstrated, 'You know quite well that's something else we're not supposed to allude to. Tell you what, Fran, you call Kanga — let me just check the computer for her phone number . . . Yes, here we are — and I'll phone that Mark of yours and tell him to take you out for a nice romantic dinner tonight. You should wear that chic blue top of yours.'

'Dinner? We've got a murder on our hands, Cosmo.'

But the impact that that would have on her private life simply didn't register with him, did it? Rather than stop to explain, she blew him an exit kiss and headed back to her office. A short but friendly conversation established that Kanga's blood pressure was about the same, at least no worse, and Roo was throwing himself into plans to paint the nursery in between sessions with all the people the police had arranged for him to see.

'This leave,' Kanga ventured. 'We're ever so grateful.'

'Entitlement,' Fran lied cheerfully. 'Now, go and put your feet up.'

Had she achieved anything? Except for her own peace of mind? At least Kanga hadn't reported that her young husband was waking every night screaming and in a cold sweat. No doubt they'd have a little giggle at the thought of this grandmotherly old bat taking the trouble to phone. Well, let them. At least her conscience felt a bit better.

CHAPTER FIFTEEN

Fran joined the rest of the team in the incident room to watch the TV news. It took a gratifyingly short time for the phones to start ringing.

What Fran hadn't expected was to be waved at by one of the youngsters taking calls. The arm became quite frantic. Her brisk walk became a scuttle.

'It's from a guy called Ken Roper. He says you went to see him on Wednesday.'

Fran hoped the widening of her eyes would signify exactly how significant this might be and gave a curling thumbs-up of gratitude. Removing the headset, the young woman vacated her chair. Fran would have stood, but she wasn't going to argue about her comfort now.

'It's Fran Harman here, Ken. What can I do for you?'

'It's that body you've found. Is it my Janine's? I've got to know, Inspector. I've got to know.'

'Of course you have. All we know at the moment, though, Ken, is that the body—'

'Is it a woman? Is it?'

Maybe Sue Hall was right and Roper was a superb actor. On the basis of this, Fran would award him an Oscar.

'What makes you think it might be?' she countered.

'My fucking phone card's running out. Just tell me!'

'Ok, what I'm going to do is this. As soon as there's any sign it might be Janine', she crossed her fingers like a kid fibbing in the playground, 'I shall get straight on to the governor and ask permission to take you to see the body. If you're willing, that is. Because I have to tell you, Ken, she's not a pretty sight. You do understand that, don't you?'

A strangled sob might have been an affirmative.

'Very well. Now, I'm going to cut the call, Ken. And I promise that I shall do as I've said.'

* * *

'Good God, I've never heard of that before,' Mark admitted as she called into his office well after eight to update him. She'd tried to send him home, but he insisted that he too had work to do before he left. 'And the governor's already OK'd it? Well, it cuts the Gordian knot of whether you should ask him to do the ID, of course. Who'll you get to accompany you?' he asked ultra-casually. 'I know you rate him, but the grapevine tells me Coveney might not be the most subtle and tactful of men.'

Playing dense, she bit her lip in deliberation. 'I thought young Sue Hall, since she came to the prison with me. It'd be good experience for her. But it'd cut into her weekend something shocking, and it's a hell of a sight to expose a young officer to.'

'I know someone whose weekend's already been cut into,' he said brightly. 'And he's seen some pretty vile sights in his time.'

'Are you sure?' She genuinely was anxious, even though half her brain told her it was absurd to try to protect a man of his seniority.

'I can't see anyone arguing, can you?'

'I can. Gates. He doesn't like us working together anyway. He'd find it really offensive if we did something so unorthodox.'

'Would he know?'

'He'd find out. Hell, it'd be all over the building by noon.'

'Does it matter if he does find out? Because I happen to have found something out about him.'

She hated it when Mark drew out what was obviously a good story like that. 'Bloody hell, just spit it out, Mark. I'm due the far side of Ashford in half an hour.'

'Take a driver and do it in style. You're entitled.'

'Can't. I'm trying to get the inside story on the original Roper and Barnes case from one of Jim Champion's mates, and it's all strictly sub rosa. For God's sake, what are you smirking about? You look like the Cheshire Cat before it disappeared.'

'Purr. You know that car we disturbed outside the Rectory? The one the Pact camera caught twice? You'll never guess who it's registered to. None other than the deputy chief constable of Kent Constabulary, Simon Gates.'

'Simon? What the—?'

'I don't know. But before I leave I shall do some digging. Off you go — and remember, I want you back home in one piece.'

* * *

'Remember the Roper case? I do indeed. I was this close to getting a disciplinary while I was part of the team investigating,' Rob admitted, leaning forward as if he feared Jim's over-decorated, over-warm room were bugged. He held his thumb a millimetre from his index finger. He'd arrived at Jim's before Fran, and was well down a bottle of Beck's. He greeted Fran with what she fancied was a mixture of relief and apprehension. As Jim had said, he was small for the police, but his compact body suggested serious workouts.

'How come?' Fran asked. Despite herself, she too spoke softly, and hunched towards him like a fellow conspirator.

Ostentatiously Jim hooked a hand round his left ear.

'Because I wouldn't accept what the rest of the team agreed,' Rob said, at normal volume.

'The team as in QED Moreton,' she prompted.

'Quite. Anyway, he was convinced.'

'That was the trouble with old QED. He always was,' Jim put in. 'Plus he was one of the sort that believed that shouting speaks louder than words.'

'And the DPP were convinced, of course,' Fran pointed out gently. 'And then the judge and jury.'

'St Peter himself would be convinced by QED in full flood. It never bothered young Rob, though, swimming against the stream,' Jim noted with evident satisfaction. 'Same as you, Fran.'

He'd love to hear about her run-ins with Gates, wouldn't he? But she just said, 'If it had cost me my pension it would have bothered me a lot. And it might have cost you your career, Rob.' And thus a lot of money and soon a lot of status.

He nodded. 'That's what shut me up. I was getting married, needed the job to pay my mortgage, and instead of being on track for inspector at thirty or so, I'd be queuing up to become a security guard. I think that's why I ended up stuck in Road Management and Safety—'

'Told you it would have a fancy new name,' Jim said.

'To get me out of CID's hair for a bit.'

'Don't stay becalmed there too long. Mind you, it can be fun, can't it? All those nifty sets of wheels?' she added with a grin. 'But what did you disagree with? Off the record for now, though I can't promise I shan't come back to you more formally.'

The likelihood of any formal inquiry at this stage was remote in the extreme, the chief perpetrator of any misdemeanour being dead. In any case, how many senior officers could put their hands on their hearts and claim never to have cut the odd corner?

'You can trust our Fran, I promise you that,' Jim put in.

Did Rob need that reassurance? He gave Fran something like a complicitous grin, as if they were both indulging Jim. She hoped her body language and intent expression would convince him that this was nothing that she for one would joke about.

'You've got these two chaps,' he began, slowly at first, as if marshalling facts. 'One is Janine's husband — that's Ken Roper — and the other is Maurice Barnes, who's supposed to be her lover. And the theory is that the hubby finds out about their affair and kills her, then blackmails her lover into helping him dispose of the body out at sea. Right?'

'I admit it sounds a bit far-fetched,' Fran conceded, saying nothing yet about the latest developments, 'but people under stress often do strange things.'

'They do. But Lover Boy wouldn't have been having an affair with the wife, not in my book. If he was shagging anyone, it'd be the husband. Like this they were.' He crossed his fingers. 'That was the sense I got, anyway. Very strongly.'

Jim said, 'I suppose they couldn't have killed this Janine so they could continue their affair? She taunts one or both of them and one or both of them loses his cool and . . .'

'Didn't strike me as violent, either of them. All the evidence was circumstantial — er, ma'am.'

'Here I'm Fran.'

He glanced at Jim, who smiled encouragingly. 'Fran. The jury went bug-eyed with all the DNA stuff.'

'The blood in her bathroom and her hair on Barnes' pillow?'

'I'm sure a lot of people bleed in the privacy of their own bathroom! As for the hair, Barnes said she'd had a migraine and had had to lie down. You can imagine what prosecuting counsel made of that. And her DNA was all over her husband's things, of course, and over Lover Boy's — but he also claimed she used to give him a hug every time they met.'

'Wouldn't catch me hugging any queers,' Jim said.

'I don't doubt you for a minute,' said Fran with a broad grin. 'But I think you mean people who are gay. Rob, I have to ask you straight: do you have any hard evidence, even any strong rumours, that QED sat on stuff he shouldn't? Lied or cheated?'

'He just didn't look hard enough. There were great gaps in what we knew about all of them, Janine in particular, that we should have filled. We knew there was a major media campaign about poor clear-up rates across the country. The Home Secretary was jumping up and down. The old chief was putting huge pressure on us. And poor old QED rolled over.'

'*Poor?* I didn't get the impression that he was the most popular of bosses.'

'He had a heart attack three weeks after retiring. Whatever sort of bastard he was — and he was a bastard, no doubt about that, with his bullying and the rest of it — he deserved a bit better than that. I reckon the stress of the case drove him to it, as it happens.'

Fran was impressed. Rob should go far with such clear-sightedness. But then she yawned, not the little gasp that could be concealed modestly behind her hand. A great filling-exposing gape. 'I'm so sorry. I seem to have been on the go a bit today.'

'I bet you've not eaten either,' Jim said with an avuncular shake of the head. 'She's left a spot of cheese and a few biscuits in the kitchen.'

Fran flared before she could stop herself. 'And who's she? The cat's mother? Honestly, Jim,' she temporised, 'Maureen deserves better than that! She's a lovely, patient woman and she's had more than enough to put up with. Come on, admit it.'

'I wouldn't let anyone else but you speak to me like that and that's a fact,' he grumbled.

She got up and kissed him on the cheek. 'Come on, you know it's only 'cos I love you, you daft old bugger. Rob, if you think of anything I ought to know, because just at the moment I'm picking up the bits left lying around, promise me you'll be in touch. My home number if you prefer.' She flipped him her card. 'No, I'm sorry but I have to push off now because I've got a really early start tomorrow.'

'Come on, young Fran — you're top brass! You can have a lie-in at weekends!'

'I wish . . . And there's a problem I have to look at before I even hit the hay.'

'I can't see that bloke of yours putting up with that. Mark Turner,' he explained to Rob. 'Partner, they call it, as if he shared a Panda car with her. You tell him from me, young Fran, it's time he married you and made an honest woman of you.'

* * *

'So why should Gates be watching our house?' Fran asked as, still with her outdoor clothes on, she slumped onto the sofa, miraculously finding a glass of Glenfiddich in her hand. She was allowed to ponder the question now, after all. She was too tired to consider any new aspects of the apparently flawed Moreton investigation, and didn't want to think about her forthcoming Saturday morning treat, taking Roper to see his wife's corpse. If it *was* his wife, of course. Of course it was his wife. If it wasn't — no, she didn't want to think about the implications if it wasn't. 'Do you think we should tackle him about it?'

'And say what? Sweetheart, I've been turning this over and over in my mind, apart from one point when I was driving home and picked up *Any Questions*. At that point I sat and shouted at the panel as if they could hear me.'

'Don't tell me. Radio pundits always want more legislation and longer prison sentences.' She didn't bother to suppress her yawn; if anyone could distinguish fatigue from boredom, Mark would.

'Right. And this lot were so bloody stupid and reactionary — and that was just the Labour representative . . .' He laughed at himself. 'Anyway, what I did think was that we should mention this to Paula. After all, it was he who recommended them. He might simply be checking up on how they're doing.'

'Of course he might! How silly of me to think there might be something strange in his behaviour!'

'I'd like to talk to Paula face to face — to see how she reacts. But I'm not quite sure when. I'm not expecting to see much of you this weekend, frankly, not with this case rumbling on.'

'I know you're scared of Paula, but you surely don't need me to hold your hand while you talk to her.'

'Not to hold my hand. But maybe to be a witness. Who knows?'

Fran had an idea she was going to say, 'Let's sleep on it,' but since her next conscious moment was when Mark tried to carry her upstairs, she wasn't at all sure.

CHAPTER SIXTEEN

If the prison staff expected more police muscle than a couple of middle-aged senior officers, they did not say so. No doubt they too considered their convicted murderer remarkably low risk. Once inside the car, Mark dispensed with the handcuffs and settled on the back seat he shared with his fellow passenger, who needed no more than a gentle reminder to use his seat belt.

Many prison inmates regarded even the shortest trip as a Cook's Tour, eyes gobbling up every detail of the world they'd been denied. Some simply sat staring forward, having been institutionalised beyond the capacity to be interested in anything. Despite his comparatively short sojourn behind bars, Roper seemed one of the latter. Or was there another reason for his self-absorption? How would Mark himself feel if he were imprisoned for killing his beloved Fran and then had to identify a three-year-old corpse that might be hers?

Except he wouldn't, would he? It'd be the next of kin, in other words Fran's fiendish sister, Hazel, who would be called upon to do her that last service. Because live-in lovers they might be, sharers of a huge mortgage, but they weren't man and wife. Was that one reason for Fran's intermittent commercials for matrimony? Had she thought ahead to the point where one had to authorise medical care for the other — but was denied the right, because they lacked a simple piece of paper? And what about inheritance tax? When the Rectory was habitable, it would be worth enough to have the Treasury rubbing its collective hands in glee at the prospect of all that lovely income.

Fran was already parking, and in a consultant's slot, if he knew her. On this occasion she was right to do so; the shorter the journey to the morgue the better.

While they waited for the duty attendant, Fran turned to Roper. 'Are you quite sure about this? Remember you don't have to see the whole corpse, just any feature by which you could identify it.'

'She always had lovely hands,' he whispered.

How would Fran deal with that facer?

'I think the coroner would want something more specific than that. A scar, a birthmark, that sort of thing,' was her gentle but firm response.

'She had the most perfect body,' Roper added, almost to himself.

The announcement was so flat, so asexual, that Mark found himself glancing at Fran. Her body was no longer perfect, not in teen magazines' terms, but he would have swapped it for no other, and he hoped she knew it. She however was frowning slightly, concern more than anger, he thought, as if repelled by Roper's emotionless delivery. Or was she relieved by it? Probably they both were.

Both ought to be concentrating on Roper, he reminded himself. That was his excuse for being here, after all. But it took an effort to scrutinise the little man, grey-faced now and shaking in anticipation of what he must do. Had his worst nightmares prepared him?

At last they were in the viewing area and the sheet was pulled back, the attendant as reverent and gentle as if he were displaying a holy relic. He exposed the face only. The path had done a very good job putting her back together, Mark noted, realising that his habitual ability to dissociate himself at the moment of crisis had not deserted him.

Roper collapsed like a concertina, ankles, knees, hips in order — not onto the corpse, thank God, but onto the floor. By mutual consent, Fran and he left him there for a few moments, trying to close their ears to an animal wail of grief. But the keening stopped as abruptly as it had started, and he seemed glad of their hands hooked under his elbows, as if he were a pensioner having taken a slip on black ice. 'Yes, that's my Janine.'

Was he surprised or otherwise that the car journey back to the jail was equally silent? There was nothing like a traumatised corpse for reminding one of one's own last end.

Someone — was it Fran, or a sympathetic prison officer? — had arranged for the prison chaplain to be on hand once Roper was banged up again. But as they waited in the airlock, Fran would have been doing less than her duty had she not asked, so softly that she was barely audible, whether Roper wished to change his statement in any way.

An invisible string pulled Roper's spine straight. 'Not by so much as a word, Chief Superintendent. But I'll tell you this. Whatever questions you and your colleagues need to ask to find out the bastard who did that to her, I'll answer to the best of my ability.' Only when there was a slight splash on the newly swabbed floor did Mark realise that tears were streaming down the widower's face.

Fran touched him lightly on the arm. 'Just one thing today, Ken, and this is important. Did your wife ever wear really expensive underclothes — bras and pants?'

He stared. 'Never.'

'And what about high-heeled shoes — really high heels?' She held her thumb four or five inches from her finger.

'She was a teacher, near enough. A respectable woman.' His voice had recovered some strength.

'Of course. I'll be in touch again very soon, Ken.' She patted his arm again, as if suiting the word to the deed.

* * *

They had driven halfway back to HQ before she asked, 'Do you think he's guilty, then?'

'Apart from anything else, what about the logistics of a man his size trying to hoist a woman her size onto the beam in the reservoir? Not to mention getting access in the first place? Finding a key? Swimming round down there?'

'Bloody hell, he does have diving equipment, though. Did. It was logged. My God, have I been right royally deceived?'

'Wait to see what the path tests show up before you start panicking. And of course, you could see if any of her DNA was left on it, if Moreton hasn't already done that. But my impression was absolutely the same as yours. That unless he had an accomplice—'

'Who could have been his best friend Moz—'

'There was no way he could have done it, the hoisting part at least. And I didn't see any guilt in him, just absolute horror.'

'Which could have been at the results of what he'd done. It's no good, I must talk to Barnes. Budget or no budget, I shall have to nip up to Durham as soon as I can, Mark.'

'No, you won't.' He laughed as her face tightened with anger. 'I think you'll find — and you must promise to ask absolutely no questions — that Moz Barnes has been mysteriously and suddenly transferred to Lewes Jail.'

Now what was she doing? Instead of taking the obvious exit for HQ at the next island, she took the road that would lead ultimately to the Rectory.

'I'm sorry,' she said. 'I have to have a moment away from an institution. Jail; hospital; jail — I can't face HQ for a few minutes. Let me just get a breath of air and I'll be all right.'

He reached for his phone and dialled Pact's number.

'Paula Farmer's phone,' came a cautious voice, not Paula's.

'Could I speak to Paula, please?' He shot a sideways glance at Fran, who responded with a quizzical smile. 'It's Mark Turner.'

'Oh, hello, Mark. This is Caffy. For some reason Paula's left her phone here in the scullery and she's up the scaffolding at the moment so I don't like to disturb her.'

'You wouldn't be at the Rectory!' And charging double overtime, no doubt.

'We would. We got rained off yesterday and did a quick interior job elsewhere. So we're putting in an extra couple of hours. Don't worry — usual rate!' Mark felt an irritating blush rising. Had they got the measure of him already?

'Will you still be there in twenty minutes?'

'Want to give it another metaphorical hug, do you? No problem.'

'It's a police matter — of a sort,' he said by way of an excuse as Fran started laughing at him. He cut the call.

'So it is,' Fran agreed. 'But there's a briefing at two, Mark — I have to be back well before that to get all the updates and prepare my own. Which may take some doing.'

'You dictate, I'll make notes,' he said, obligingly reaching for his unofficial notebook.

* * *

Caffy greeted them in the former scullery that Pact used as their base camp. She was in her dungarees, but was remarkably free from paint splatters. In fact, now Mark came to think of it, she was always clean, as if she were in TV-land, where Costume and Make-up never got their heads round the dirt of the working world. Did she actually do anything? Or did she stand round looking decorative to increase their fees to male punters? For he had to admit she was a remarkably attractive young woman, despite his reservations about her vivacious loquacity.

'Golly, it isn't just the house that needs a hug,' she declared, grabbing a rag to wipe non-existent paint from her hands, 'it's you two.' She looked them up and down. 'I'm sorry. Have you just come from a funeral? I didn't know they had them on Saturdays. Or a death bed? On such a lovely day, too!'

Fran said curtly, 'Work clothes.'

'But they're surely not your "customary suits of solemn black"? You looked quite normal the other day.'

Mark dug into his school memory. He came up with a rejoinder he hoped the Shakespeare-loving chief would have been proud of. 'These are "the trappings and the suits of woe", Caffy. We had to escort someone to identify his late wife's body.'

That mobile face of hers showed she registered all the implications. 'No wonder you wanted to come out here then, where everything's coming alive. Have you seen the way everything's greening up, despite all the neglect? Maybe because of it. Now, can I make you a cup of tea or coffee while you look round? We've not made much internal progress, of course, because we wanted to make sure it was weatherproof, but you'll see the roof's looking very much better if you want to pop up the scaffolding and take a look.'

'Paula's Words worked, did they?' Fran asked, but her face looked too stiff to smile naturally. If only he could get her to sit down before she fell down.

'They usually do,' Caffy said, with a quick glance at her. 'Fran, we rescued this chair from the roof space. It may look flimsy and rickety, but believe me it's comfortable. We thought you ought to take it to get it valued, actually — it's clearly eighteenth century. The tea's twenty-first, though, and these biscuits are my attempts at shortbread — heart attack on a plate, in other words.'

Mark doubted if Fran realised how she was being organised, but, as she sat sipping the tea, colour returned to her face. What had gone wrong? He'd never known her react to a case like this.

There was a sound from outside.

'That'll be Paula. I'll swear she smells these biscuits from fifty feet.'

'Not the biscuits so much as the coffee,' Paula declared, coming in and smiling generally. She registered Fran's wan appearance, no doubt, but did not mention it. 'Have you come to check our security footage? We've got some good shots for you.'

'Anyone you have reason to be suspicious of?'

Fran laughed. 'God, doesn't he sound like a police officer! I hope you'll forgive him.'

'Not for having a preposition at the end of his sentence,' Caffy said. 'That's a capital offence.'

Paula said, 'I'll get the tapes, then you can make up your own mind.' She said it as if to prevent further discussion, Caffy shooting her a rather mutinous glance, he thought. 'Are you coming up the scaffolding to see what's been done?'

'I'm not very good at heights,' he admitted.

'I'll come,' Fran declared.

'Sorry, not in those shoes you won't. But come another day properly shod, and I'll take you up with pleasure.'

Fran didn't argue. Mark guessed she realised she'd pretty well met her match.

Paula smiled dismissively and took a call on her mobile. 'Very well. It sounds promising. I'm on my way.' And was.

Fran mouthed, 'Ask Caffy?'

But he shook his head gently. Cooperative the Pact team might be, but it seemed to him that Paula was very much the boss. In any case, Caffy was clearly anxious to leave too. And, whatever Fran would say later about it, painters and decorators were definitely entitled to their weekends.

* * *

Fran would have been the first to admit that the briefing was brisk. It was, after all, one thing to tell her cynical colleagues that she thought that another colleague might have got it wrong, quite another to do it on the basis of something like intuition. So she had compromised by saying that she had some doubts, sufficient to wish to interview Maurice Barnes as soon as she could get Home Office permission. With no Pat at weekends to expedite such niceties, she did not foresee that happening before Wednesday. They wouldn't get any forensic science results until early next week either, if then — she hadn't stretched the budget to give them the very highest priority.

Meanwhile, she wanted the house searched again for expensive shoes and underwear. She pointed to the photo of Janine on the mortuary slab. 'As expensive and come hither as those. And equally tarty shoes. OK? Anything that doesn't fit with her quiet, demure persona. I want someone down at the library now checking what books she borrowed and how many a week. She used a gym — find it and see if she had a permanent locker. Dan, has anyone checked whether Ken Roper's diving gear was tested for Janine's DNA?'

'I doubt it, guv. If it wasn't, it will be. The allotment holders, past and present, and any of their family and friends who might have had cause to visit the allotments are being questioned even as we speak. And we've found that the fence between the allotments and the reservoir was repaired last year, unfortunately, because it was in a pretty bad state all round. Someone's on to finding the contractor, and better still, the individual who did the work to see if they can recall any specific damage. It's a long shot, but I thought it was worth it.'

'Well done, Dan. Anything else ongoing?'

What passed for door-to-door inquiries in the thinly scattered houses of the countryside were in train, and the poor sods detailed to do their fingertip search were still on their knees.

'Excellent. Now, my inclination is to have the shortest briefing tomorrow, with only essential personnel involved. So some of you should get a bit of your weekend at least. Thank you all very much for your efforts so far. I'm sure we shall nail the right person in the end.'

Someone at the back raised his hand. 'Ma'am, you're speaking as if we haven't already got two men behind bars for this crime.'

There was a murmur of agreement, perhaps from Moreton's former colleagues, resenting that they were about to undo all the good he had done.

'The cases of both men are up for appeal. My feeling is that a good defence lawyer could run a coach and horses through the case now that the new evidence in the form of Janine's body and her clothing has turned up. And let's not forget', she added, 'that every time we imprison someone wrongly — in this case possibly two men — the real killer is roaming around free, possibly ready to strike again.'

Which thought took her round to DCI Pearce's office. She was about to bound in, cheerfully demanding the latest news on what could turn out to be a serial killer, when she realised Joanne was face down on her desk, her arms supporting her head. No, she wasn't crying, as at first Fran feared. She was deeply asleep. Fran stole away, found a piece of card on which to write, and returned as quietly as she knew how. At least when the younger woman awoke she'd find a written order staring her in the face. Signed with every detail of Fran's rank it said, 'Go Home Now!'

Her own cottage was beginning to call loudly, but she ought to make one more check of her desk before she phoned Mark to see if he had finished his self-appointed tasks. She was aware he was keeping an eye on her; half of her was mildly irritated, the other rather more grateful than she cared to admit.

She found what she least wanted to see — a reminder she'd written herself that she had a working party on Monday morning which she must not miss and for which she really ought to prepare. She would need to spend three hours in front of a computer screen running to earth more statistics than she could shake an asp at. The trouble was that statistics could prove anything Gates — and ultimately the Home Secretary — wanted. And no doubt would.

Hell, her brain wouldn't get round figures now, not the ones dancing in neat columns. Only on waterlogged ones in morgues. She took what she ironically described to herself as an executive decision. She would have to leave it till tomorrow, when Mark would in any case no doubt be visiting his grandchildren.

She was just about to pick up her phone when it rang. Or rather, her direct outside line phone rang. So it wasn't Mark, whoever it was.

It was Pete Webb, who now seemed to regard her as part of a conspiracy. She had a sense of him hunched over the phone, looking over his shoulder to check that he was unobserved. 'We've found the kid who walked off with the computer in the Hythe skip,' he said. 'We could press charges of course. Officially. Anyway, he says the hard disk had been wiped before the machine was dumped. We've borrowed it so that our forensic computer scientists can have a look.'

'"Borrowed"? Does that mean you'll let him have it back afterwards?'

'Why not? Come on, guv, it's a perfectly serviceable model, and should get him through university.'

'You're a man after my own heart, Pete. By the way, I never had a look at Alec Minton's body, did I?'

'Nope. Want me to fix it?'

Fran was quite capable of doing her own fixing, but didn't point this out. Instead she said, 'I'm up to my ears over here. Why don't you email the photos? I can manage without the morgue smell, can't I?'

'You must have got used to it after all your years in the service.'

'I never have, you know. I'd never let on to the macho youngsters, and certainly not to a pathologist, but I have to steel myself each time. And I haven't even got a very good sense of smell! How these forensic archaeologist folk go round digging up and identifying rotting corpses defeats me. So the photos will do, thanks very much. How's things, by the way, Pete?' She waited for a wail of righteous anger.

'I took your advice,' he said, his voice perceptibly tight, even over the phone. 'Which is why I'm toiling away here on a Saturday afternoon. My wife's taken the kids to her sister's for the weekend — there's some hideous children's birthday party but my sister-in-law can rise to not one but two au pairs. So they're in Esher and I thought I'd keep myself busy.'

Why all that information? But it was certain he wanted some sort of approval.

'I hope it works out for you,' she said. That was too cold. She said with a laugh, 'Of course, a truly heroic man would have gone to that party dressed as a clown,' adding seriously, 'but I really think you're doing the right thing, Pete. Well done.'

After that it was a session emailing her recalcitrant colleagues in divisional CIDs to remind them that she really did need their information post haste. Then, at long last, she popped into Mark's office to admit that she was ready to go home.

As if he'd been expecting her he had the video zapper in his hand. 'Sit yourself down and have a look at this,' he said, patting the arm of a chair he'd placed next to his. Tea or coffee?'

He busied himself with the kettle as she ran the video. Amongst a veritable convoy of delivery vehicles and workmen's vans — Paula must have put the fear of God into her suppliers and subcontractors — the black BMW Mark had already identified as Gates' appeared with some regularity. Once Gates had actually got out of the car; the camera caught his back as he apparently leant on the gate and looked over it. Sometimes — from the clock in the corner of each frame — he arrived during the working day; sometimes he arrived in the evening or even in the very early morning. Fran rewound the cassette. Yes, he'd even managed to get there several times when he'd claimed to be sick.

'Well, well, well,' she said, wishing her brain would come up with something more apposite and original.

'Precisely.' Mark put a mug of green tea in front of her. 'I couldn't have put it better myself.'

'Your brain's atrophying too, is it?'

'Withered almost to nothing. I'll put some of this lot away while you drink up, then we sign off for the day. OK?'

It was very OK.

* * *

When Fran had slung Mark the keys, she'd expected him to point the car straight for home. Instead, to her amazement, he pulled into a garden centre. Fran following in his wake, he pushed an enormous trolley through the alleyways heaving with whole families, the kids less rather than more under control. Eventually he stopped before a display of ready-planted tubs. He loaded three, then a fourth, in his trolley.

'Why?' she asked.

'Because sometime today spring seems to have sprung, and I thought we could do with some colour in our garden.'

'There's plenty of colour. At least when I last looked at it.' Which had probably been a week ago, now she came to think of it.

'No. Not that garden. The Rectory garden. Next time we go past I want to drop them off as a little present. An offering to the household gods, if you like.'

'I don't think you'd have those in a rectory. Just God,' she added as he looked blank.

'Of course. Well, I think He'll like them, don't you?'

She was too tired to argue. In any case, perhaps he was right.

CHAPTER SEVENTEEN

'I tell you, I find cooking therapeutic,' Mark insisted. 'And you must admit it's nice to be able to sit down knowing there'll be a bottle of fine wine on the table and that we don't have to drive home.'

She smiled and raised a pre-dinner glass to him. Even to her defective nostrils the chicken smelt wonderful, and she wouldn't spoil the moment by reminding him that although he cooked a mean roast, he'd never learnt how to clean an oven. 'And that we can have water from out of our own taps,' she agreed. 'Supposedly. We can believe those flyers saying it's OK, now?'

He pulled a face. 'Maybe if we boil it . . . And I'd rather shower at work, just for another couple of days. Now, Fran, I know this is almost shop, and we shouldn't be talking about it now we're home. But it is important. What are we going to do about Gates? Now we've seen for ourselves. They certainly installed some state-of-the-art stuff on our behalf,' he added, as if to give her thinking time.

'Which may prove to be worth every penny.' She was learning that it was better to anticipate his worries about money. 'My only worry is whether everything should be more obvious, to act as a deterrent.'

'You didn't raise that with Paula, I noticed,' he said dryly.

'Nor you, neither! And neither of us tried to stop her nipping off. But I still think that Paula's the one to talk to. After all, it was Gates who recommended her — perhaps there's something going on between them we've no need at all to know about. And fearsome though Paula is, I'd rather beard her than Gates about it. Imagine saying, "Stop nagging about your next meeting and tell me why you keep peering at my new home".'

'I'm not sure . . . OK, you couldn't, I agree. There's too much going on between you, and I wouldn't put it past the bugger to insinuate you were trying to blackmail him in some way.'

'He's not an ogre! Just Meetings Man!'

'He goes behind both our backs to the chief about moving you. He reduces two of the secretaries to tears — oh, yes, I'm surprised the jungle drums didn't get that gem to you. God knows how many noses he's shoved out of joint. Yes, I'm quite sure he's a man of delightful, albeit well-hidden, charm. Actually, until that's sorted out, I think you're right after all. It is best to deal with Paula in the first instance.'

'And we take our cue from her?'

'Exactly. OK. Decision made. Can I top up your glass? I'll just check that the butternut squash is cooked . . .'

'Hang on. There's one other thing to decide. Who speaks to Paula and when?'

He looked shifty in the extreme.

'I knew it! You're too scared of her! So when do *we* do it, Mark? It can't be Monday morning because I shall have to be in at the crack of dawn to finish a report in time for a nine o'clock meeting. And I'm afraid you won't see much of me tomorrow for the same reason — though you'll be off to Loose to catch up with the kids, won't you?' She hoped she did not sound bitter. If she did, he didn't remark on it, but applied himself to basting the chicken.

* * *

As she'd promised, Sunday's briefing was short and to the point. All the points she'd raised the previous day were being dealt with. She added one more. She wanted the Ropers' neighbours to be questioned again. Were they sure that when Roper and Barnes waved goodbye, there was no answering wave from the house? Absolutely sure? Sue Hall said she'd get on to it, since it was on her route home.

Fran dismissed everyone briskly, though with a warning that she expected a great deal more of them all by noon the next day. Again she popped down to DCI Pearce's office, this time to find her very much awake and looking pleased with herself. Since Pearce had her hand on the phone as if about to dial, Fran was able to believe her claim that she was just about to contact her with the latest development in the Dale Drury case.

'His DNA ties him in with two other cases, guv. One in Manchester, the other in Burton on Trent. We've still got to talk to him about these, as it happens, but I'm saving them up till West Midlands have called back. Wolverhampton and Oldbury, wherever that might be.'

'They call it the Black Country, on account of the smoke the factories generated during the nineteenth century. Did you know Queen Victoria thought the place was so awful she had the blinds of her railway carriage pulled down so she didn't have to soil her eyes with the sight?' Fran asked, slightly alarmed that her mind, which should have been preoccupied with far more momentous thoughts, should have produced such trivia.

If she was alarmed, Joanne Pearce was clearly puzzled but joined in what she perhaps thought was Fran's game. 'Queen Victoria wouldn't have wanted to soil her eyes with what he did to the toms there,' she replied. 'In fact, she would not have been amused. Here you are.' She laid a set of particularly graphic photos for Fran's inspection. 'Alas, though I understand the Midlands have more canals than Venice, guv, the murderer's MO doesn't seem to include water in any form. Nor good old-fashioned throttling either, more's the pity.'

'Even so, if he doesn't have an alibi for the weekend in question, it'd be worth pressing him. Is he still singing?'

'Not anymore. His solicitor's obviously warned him.'

'Bugger. I may still want to have a word with him, though, Joanne, if I can lay my hands on a few more bits of evidence.'

'He's yours whenever you want him. He'll be charged tomorrow with the offences he's admitted to and I can't see even the most passionate brief getting him bail.'

'Don't you bet on it.'

'I won't.'

As Fran turned for the door, Joanne added, 'By the way, guv, thanks for — for yesterday.'

'Ah, you got my orders, then. I trust you acted on them?'

Joanne sprang to satirical attention. 'To the letter, guv. I feel much better today,' she added in her usual tone.

'Good. Make sure the rest of your team has breaks, too — OK?' Fran left with a smile. But she popped her head back round the door immediately. 'I suppose you haven't heard when Dave Henson's likely to be back?'

Joanne pulled a face. 'Tomorrow, I'm afraid, guv.'

* * *

Despite all Sunday's efforts to pull together the material she needed, she was in by seven on Monday to finish her report. When the door opened without a knock, she assumed it was Mark, raising an admonitory finger lest he interrupt her in mid-sentence.

'You're in early, Fran,' the chief declared.

Bugger and blast him. She managed a polite but not very warm smile as she got to her feet. 'Sorry, sir. I wasn't expecting you.'

'Always a lot to catch up on when you've been on these conferences. Everything going well?'

She thought she knew him well enough to give the hint of an ironic smile as she gestured at the printer, busily delivering her report.

Wrong.

'It's not like you to make such a fuss about obeying orders, Fran.'

'I beg your pardon, sir?'

'You heard me. If you're given an important job to do, I expect you to do it, without question. Understand?'

'Sir,' she said, wilfully misunderstanding him, 'I've been doing this job to the utmost of my ability ever since you appointed me to it. You've had no reason to complain, I trust? We've had good results in all the cases you've allocated to me.'

'You know what I mean, Fran. You're supposed to be showing young Gates the ropes—'

'Sir, I am as unaware of that as I'm sure he is. I've continued with every aspect of my CID work, and have joined his committees and working parties as appropriate. Heavens, you can see, sir,' by now the printer had run out of space for the pages it had produced and was spewing material willy-nilly onto the floor, 'I've been burning the midnight oil for this one.' She stooped to pick everything up. Her knee cracked audibly, but she would not reach for the desk to lever herself upright. She willed herself vertical.

'It's always hard when someone one knew as a rookie officer overtakes one,' he said, in tones presumably meant to soothe. 'But I did assume you might be generous spirited enough not to resent Gates' promotion.'

What an extraordinary thing to say! Was he accusing her of jealousy? Was he pleading for forgiveness and understanding for their colleague? Both? Fran seethed. She'd pushed off the careers of many fine young men and women, watching them float off into the promotional sunset as she stood and waved, metaphorically singing 'Aloha' as they went. Surely he couldn't think she was resentful that Gates' career had outstripped hers. He might as well accuse her of resenting Mark's superior rank.

She said nothing. How could one tell a man whose life was bound up in paperwork and decision-making that they were simply not for her? For more years than she cared to remember, they'd been an adjunct of her career, but never been its entirety.

The chief wasn't used to the silent treatment. Was some synapse of his mind, one that should years ago have been interrupted by equal opportunities training, trying to insist that Fran was simply suffering women's troubles? Or was he genuinely concerned that this hitherto loyal officer, whose life had been devoted to the force, should be in obvious, if tacit, mutiny?

At last she said, 'Sir, in recent years I've tried to be both an administrator — and, I liked to think, a reasonably efficient one, one whose work had reached forces nationwide — and a practising CID officer. Actually, I'm in the middle of a murder inquiry even as we speak — that's why I'm in now, so that as soon as this morning's meeting is over I can return to it.'

'I believe DCS Henson is back today.'

'Sir, you can't order me to hand everything over to him at this stage! Damn it, the man's not well. Remember he's only on seventy-five per cent of his programme at the moment anyway.' Did she detect a softening of his expression? 'It was Dave himself who asked me to take this on, sir, since it's been getting huge — and quite spurious — media coverage.'

'"Dave", Fran? You and Henson on what we're no longer supposed to call Christian name terms? I don't believe it.'

'We've been getting on better recently, sir. Acting more professionally, you might say.'

He did not respond to her wry smile. 'I might, if I hadn't heard that you two were responsible for some sort of palace revolution.'

'The Peasants' Revolt, more like. It's absolute rubbish, sir, if I might say so. I won't deny that there is unhappiness in some quarters over the number of meetings that senior officers are summoned to these days, but I absolutely and flatly deny that I was involved in any rebellion. Come on, sir, you've known me long enough to know that I would tackle anyone I disagreed with face to face.'

He gave a crack of laughter. 'I see you've got your coffee machine on already.'

'Would you like a cup, sir? No biscuits, I'm afraid. I've been a bit busy on this Roper and Barnes case.'

'You've let it keep you out of the kitchen! Shame on you, Fran. Thanks.' He sipped and sat down, motioning her at last to do the same. 'You think there's a real problem with the previous inquiry?'

How fortunate she was used to his sudden changes of tack. 'Yes,' she said flatly. 'The trouble now is that the media have got their claws into what they will insist on calling the Lady in the Lake case.'

'I suppose that nice girl Dilly Pound's reporting it, is she?'

The chief had taken a huge shine to the local TV crime reporter, a victim of a stalker. Fran had run the investigation into her case. As a result, Pound was more cooperative than most reporters in conveying the information the police thought the public ought to know, and sitting on anything that would positively hinder an investigation.

'She is. We'll be having dinner with her and her fiancé Daniel as soon as we've sorted out the current investigation, sir,' Fran said, upgrading a tentative drink arrangement to a positive commitment. 'Maybe you and your wife would care to join us.'

He was far too bright not to see that he was being manipulated. 'I'm sure we would. But you still have to work with other people, Fran. And it's not always possible for the status quo to be maintained indefinitely: you can't make an omelette without breaking eggs.'

'Oh, come on, sir — lives are not eggs! A cliché like that and you an Orwell scholar, too!' She shook her head, more in apparent sorrow than anger, but realised with a jolt that she'd gone too far. 'Seriously, sir,' she continued, trying to retrieve her mistake, 'the middle of a sensitive case is surely not the moment to pull me off it. I seem to have a rapport with Roper, the man currently doing time for the murder of his wife. Only the more evidence we acquire, the more convinced I am that he's innocent. As soon as Pat Harper's in, I shall get her on to her mate in the Home Office to authorise a prison visit to Barnes, the other man sent down for it. There may also be a tie in with a case Dave Henson's got in hand.' She preferred that expression to 'supervising' — it implied, she thought that Henson had everything totally under control and that they were truly collaborating, admittedly for the first time in their acquaintance.

'What case might that be?'

'Dale Drury, sir. Henson got him when a domestic went wrong, and then managed to tie him up with the death of at least one and possibly several prostitutes here and abroad. He's involved Interpol and I gather the Sureté are coming over this week.' She crossed her fingers behind her back.

'So it would be a shame to interrupt his investigations. Especially while you're making progress on yours.' He set his cup down on the only four square inches of desk visible under her paperwork. 'Shame about the biscuits, Fran.'

'I'll get Mark on to them. He's a wonderful cook — as you'll find out, sir.'

'As indeed I will.' He made it sound more like a threat than a promise. 'So long as you don't neglect other things, Fran.'

'Sir.'

She listened carefully as he walked along the corridor. Did she hear the subtle sound of Gates' note being screwed up and slung into a bin? On reflection, the chief was more likely to shred it, wasn't he? Or consign it to some secret file for future reference.

* * *

There was never any need to supervise anything that Pat might be doing, so all Fran needed to do was ask her to fix the appointment with Barnes and scoot off to Gates' meeting. What she wanted to do was stand arms akimbo and publicly challenge

Gates' visits to the Rectory. What she had to do was become a model committee member, eager to share her information and absorb others'. She and the chief might have a tacit understanding but underlying it was a bargain, equally unspoken. If she failed to deliver on committees part-time, she would sure as hell lose her CID brief and learn to administrate full time.

She polished her halo and sat as upright as she could after two hours on the computer. And realised a whole section of her dratted report had got itself into the wrong order, no doubt while it was leaping about the floor.

* * *

The meeting finished earlier than she dared expect.

Gates had been perceptibly more efficient, sticking absolutely to the agenda and summing up each point well. To her discomfort, however, he fell into step with her was they left the seminar room she was coming to loathe.

'How are Paula Farmer and her girls getting on with your new house?' he asked with what might have been a smile.

What an opening! Dared she jump straight in? Despising herself for insisting she move slowly, she kept her voice neutral as she remarked, 'They seem to be very efficient.'

He bowed as if she was complimenting him, not the women.

'I was wondering how you came across them, actually,' she fished. She'd had him down as much more a man to buy new property with a view to improving and selling it at a swift and excessive profit.

'In one of my earlier incarnations,' he said, with no smile at all. It was clear he thought the conversation closed.

'He wouldn't admit it, but Mark's terrified of Paula,' she fibbed, possibly, raising the stakes a little.

'She's a pussy cat really.' Conveniently, his pager prevented any further questions. Why on earth should he head off at something approaching a trot? It wasn't as if he was pursuing a major criminal.

But here was DCI Pearce, exposing rather less bosom but more leg than usual, through the medium of a deeply gored skirt stitched only halfway down the thigh. She also sported distractingly dangly earrings and a huge grin.

'The Sureté have been delayed, guv — they seem to have found yet more cases to discuss with him. But he's languishing in Maidstone Jail for the time being, and we've got clearance for any number of interviews with him.'

'Maybe he'd like a welcome party,' Fran said. 'Could you contact his lawyer and fix it for early this afternoon?' With a smile she turned on her heel and went to have lunch with Mark feeling, though she couldn't have explained why, that the morning hadn't been a total waste of time after all.

* * *

With no sense of déjà vu at all, accompanied by Sue Hall, Fran sat in an interview room facing a man accused of murdering his wife — plus, in this case, possibly half a dozen prostitutes. Unlike Roper, Dale Drury looked more than capable of physical violence. If she wasn't careful, he might dominate the room with his size — at forty, he must have weighed in at seventeen stone and been something like six feet one. He had a couple of tattoos, neither particularly offensive, just visible on his neck. His nails were surprisingly well manicured.

Why should she feel sorrier for a puny specimen like Roper than for this man? After all, Drury hadn't even been to court yet, let alone sent down for life. Had his wife been the only victim, he might even, disgracefully, have got away with manslaughter, arguing he'd hit her under provocation. Counsel would certainly make much of the fact that he'd made no attempt to run away when the police arrived and had shown every sign of distress at momentary loss of control.

Had he wept for the others he would be accused of killing? All those prostitutes?

Suddenly she realised that she had the thinnest, the most tenuous of reasons to question him. Janine wouldn't fit his pattern, would she? Fran grasped at intellectual straws. Had Janine become a part-time prostitute, like far too many young women, to service debts or a drug habit? She wanted to discount the first motive: Janine didn't have huge student loans to pay off, and the contents of the house had suggested expenditure well within the Ropers' income. All the same, something danced tantalisingly at the back of Fran's brain — those red shoes and the bra set, no doubt.

In any case, she hadn't been interviewing suspects without a shred of evidence all these years to let the lack of it inhibit her now. 'Have a look at this, Dale,' she said, casually passing across Janine's photo in its evidence bag. 'Do you know this girl?'

He looked, to do him justice, but, with a glance at his solicitor, shook his head. 'Not my type at all.'

'Have another look. Tell me what you make of her.'

Shrugging, he picked it up and made a show of holding it this way and that, the better to peer at it through its polythene covering. At last he stuck out his lower lip. 'Looks a bit of a goer on the quiet, don't she?'

'How do you mean?'

'Meet her at the pub, she'd have her knickers off before you could say shag.'

She shook her head and wrinkled her forehead in puzzlement. 'I'm a woman — explain how a man can tell something like that from a photo.'

She didn't like the look he gave her before staring at Sue.

'Put you two together, now. Which would I rather fuck? Not her — she's as tight-arsed as they come. But I reckon you'd screw all right, love.'

Fran didn't so much as glance at poor Sue, confining herself to kicking her foot lightly to register sisterly offence and also to prevent her speaking out. Should she snarl at the bugger? Nine-tenths of her wanted to. The other tenth insisted she say ironically, 'Thank you kindly, Dale. But I'm afraid neither my colleague nor I need your sexual evaluation. It's this woman here we're interested in.' She touched the photo.

'Meet her on a street corner and I'd ask if she was doing business. And probably give her one anyway. Only joking,' he added, as his solicitor hissed him down.

'Of course,' Fran agreed, with a gracious smile at the poor sap landed with the idiot as client. 'You're saying she looks like a tom?'

'Doesn't have to make a living by shagging. And all these shrinks say toms don't actually enjoy it, don't they?' he added, surprising her.

'Good point,' Fran said. She really ought to have shed some of her preconceptions after all these years, shouldn't she?

'So she might be just a housewife not getting enough and asking for it from someone else. Not me, though, love.'

'What if she was prettied up a bit — you know, big hair, eye make-up, shiny lips?'

He narrowed his eyes, as if trying to be helpful. 'You want to ask some of the local girls. You know, wherever she lived.'

'You said "lived".' Sue pounced.

''Course I did, sweetheart.'

Fran's toes curled at his easy use of one of Mark's endearments.

'You wouldn't be showing me a mugshot of her if she was alive, would you now? I know you want to pin it on me, but I tell you, I didn't kill her. Didn't even poke her.'

'You've poked a lot of prostitutes, Dale?' Sue asked.

'A few.'

'A good few?'

'Suppose.'

'So you might not recall one among so many.'

'Never forget a face, not me. Nor a place. Photographic memory they call it.'

'Wow. You don't meet many people like that,' Fran said. 'So if my colleague and I walked out of the room, you'd be able to describe us in detail to your solicitor next week.'

The solicitor looked as if it was a delight he would not press for.

'Sure,' Dale declared. 'Try me, mate — it's a date.'

* * *

'So we might push harder on this idea that Janine might have led a secret life,' Fran said, to break a seething silence as she drove back to HQ. She could understand Sue being furious, not just with Drury but also with her, for failing to make a stand against such personal observations.

'You don't have to take the suggestion of a psychopath, surely, ma'am.'

'Lord, no. No more than his nasty little innuendoes against us.'

'Why didn't you . . . ?' Sue's voice cracked.

'Because I wanted him on our side, as much as a man like that can be, even more than to lecture him on the politics of gender. Believe me, Sue, you'll hear far worse than that — and often from our colleagues, I'm sorry to say.'

'But—'

'But the interesting thing was that we hadn't mentioned to him those anomalous undies and shoes,' Fran overrode her, wanting progress not polemic. 'There's more to Janine Roper than met the eye, Sue. And I'd like you to find out what it is. In fact, what I'd like you to do is get on to the snappers. I want this image digitally enhanced with make-up and a tarty wig.'

'But, guv—'

'The moment we arrive. Get it? And then I want plain clothes officers, preferably those working with the women, to ask around. And not just the poor girls on the street. Lap dancers, pole dancers, belly dancers, any bloody dancers you can think of. OK?'

As for Fran, all she wanted was to make a cup of tea and metaphorically put her feet up. She would never, however great the need, do it literally, not when anyone might catch her doing it. She permitted herself the tea, at least, and checked her emails. None. *No emails?*

She padded out to her secretary's office, where Pat held up her hands in exculpation. 'The whole system's been down all afternoon, Fran. But I did have a phone call from DI Pete Webb. He said he'd put the PM photos in the internal post for you.'

'Thanks. I suppose tomorrow's another day. I might as well go and pick up Mark, then — we're off to see how things are moving on the Rectory. But if anyone wants me, I shall be back by six for another briefing.'

'Have fun. But Fran,' Pat added as Fran left the room, 'you might want to put your shoes on before you go.'

CHAPTER EIGHTEEN

'It's a good job it's been so dry,' Caffy said, 'or the garden would be like a jungle. Mind you, we do need the rain — they say we're going to have standpipes in the streets unless we have a wet summer. Which is a bugger when you're painting exteriors, of course. At least with a site this big we can all nip indoors and carry on there when it rains.'

'All? I must say I thought there'd be more of you.'

'There are. The rest of the team are finishing smaller projects until everyone else is off site. Then you'll find the place crawling with us. Meanwhile, I get on with specialist stuff like stripping paint and restoring plasterwork in rooms you don't propose to change. All the plasterwork that's been chipped and scuffed — I'm looking after that. My special project's the ceiling in the old drawing room — have you seen what I've discovered under all that gloss paint?'

They could scarcely decline the implicit invitation. And Fran for one was pleased they had followed the young woman. What had been an ugly indeterminate lump of peeling gloss paint was now a delicate piece of plasterwork.

Caffy's face glowed with the sort of delight that Fran had seen when new mothers looked at their babies. 'I've had to rebuild that edge — you can see it's still not quite the same as the rest. And then I shall work on that beautiful section over the door. Didn't our ancestors do a wonderful job of their domestic architecture?'

'And you're doing a wonderful job, bringing it back to life,' Mark said, his voice full of more admiration than even Fran would have expected. He traced a curve with his finger. 'Look at that . . .'

* * *

They left Caffy perched on a stepladder, her work lit by a sort of miner's light strapped to her forehead, to find Paula scrubbing her hands in the scullery sink.

'Those shoes are better but you really need lace-ups,' she informed them.

It took Fran a second to register the problem. 'No, I'm not here to shin up the scaffolding. Isn't it a bit windy?'

Paula clearly thought such an excuse beneath contempt.

'We're actually here because of the security footage,' Fran continued. 'There's one particular car—'

'Yes, that black Beamer. Rather a regular visitor, isn't it?' Paula leant back against the sink, crossing her arms. 'Should we be worried?' It was clear she meant all three of them.

Mark, however, showed an unnatural interest in his shoes. At least he managed to say, 'I don't know. I don't think it's anyone going to strip lead off the roof or rip out fireplaces. At least, I'd be very surprised if he did. You see, the driver's a police officer, Paula.'

Her eyes narrowed. 'It's not that bloody copper that fancies Caffy? Shit! I think way back she might have found him attractive — for half an hour or so — but he was absolutely smitten. What was his name now?' She clicked her fingers in irritation. 'Dawes? Gates! Worked for Police Standards or something — you know, fuzz checking up on other fuzz. Do you know him?'

'It was he who recommended you, remember,' Fran said, weak with relief that their conversation was going so easily.

'Shit, so it was. I thought it was out of the kindness of his heart. And all the time it was because he could sneak over and ogle poor Caffy whenever he felt like it. The poor bastard.'

'Except it's called stalking,' Fran said quietly, 'if the woman doesn't want to be ogled. Don't get me wrong, Paula. There's no law against some lovelorn bloke — or woman — leaning against a gate in the hope of seeing his beloved. It's if he does it against the woman's will or starts doing other things that the law takes an interest.'

'Which would be a bit of a problem if he's a policeman himself,' Paula reflected. 'Do you want me to talk to Caffy or would you rather do it?'

This was blissfully easy. All the same, Fran wrinkled her nose, as if in doubt. 'It might sound a bit official, a bit intimidating, if we did — at this stage.'

'I can't think of anything that would intimidate our Caffy,' Paula declared. 'Not after what she's been through. Tell you what, to spare her the trouble of telling you all about it, you check up a guy called Clive Granville in your records. Caffy's surname's Tyler, in case she hasn't told you. And if you read carefully you'll work out why she always wears dungarees when she's working. Meanwhile,' she continued, overriding Fran's obvious question, 'I'll ask her what she thinks about the visits from this here mate of yours.'

'Colleague, not mate,' Fran said with too much emphasis.

Paula's eyes narrowed. 'You mean he's your boss? Well, I can quite see why you'd rather do nothing.' Her voice oozed scorn.

Mark stepped forward. 'If the chief constable himself was breaking the law, the Home Secretary, even, I'd want him dealt with.'

Paula looked him in the eye. 'I believe you. But I'd guess,' she added shrewdly, 'that you'd rather it was the Home Secretary — someone nice and remote, not someone you know and presumably trust.'

'If someone steals your lead, you'd rather it was someone nice and remote, not someone you know and trust.'

'Touché! OK, I'll trust you,' she said, leaning lightly on the word, 'to do the right thing, if doing anything is necessary, of course. Caffy might be quite touched. She might even want to go out to dinner with him occasionally. He was quite a nice-looking bloke, I thought. But I do recall her saying she didn't like his eyes. Like granite or something.'

Fran nodded. 'I know what she means,' she said softly. And wished she hadn't.

Paula quietly patted her on the arm, as if praising her for her honesty. 'Bring those shoes next time,' she said. 'You'll regret it if you don't,' she added, clearly dismissing them.

* * *

With Mark at the wheel, they were returning to work, Fran for the latest Lady in the Lake briefing and Mark to check out this Clive Granville's connection with Caffy. Fran's phone rang. She'd have been tempted to let the caller leave a message, but it was Maeve Burton, to whom she undoubtedly owed a favour.

'Fran, I was wondering if Bill and I could come and see you both this evening,' Maeve said, the preliminaries out of the way. 'Unless you're tied up in some high-profile case?'

'I can untie myself,' Fran said equably. 'But if you'd like to join us for a meal, it'll have to be a takeaway, I'm afraid. We won't be back much before nine.'

Mark groaned.

'Nine and just a drink would be fine. See you then!'

'Which scuppers our chance of a leisurely meal,' Mark grumbled.

'So it does. But who has leisurely meals in the middle of a murder case?'

'Someone who isn't running it? Sorry. Only joking. Why didn't you put her off?'

'Because of our history, Maeve and me. She wouldn't ask if it weren't important. Anyway, I don't expect the briefing to run for long — it's just a matter of collating updates, after all — and it won't take you five minutes to check on the guy who did whatever it was to Caffy.' Bloody names.

'Clive Granville. OK. See you at seven-thirty. Though that isn't half tempting Providence. I bet your team have come up with vital evidence and you have to go out and make an arrest.'

* * *

In the event, Mark got grabbed by the chief, who demanded to be talked through the document he had delegated to Mark to prepare. Fran's meeting went on longer than she would have liked, but it wasn't very productive, with only nil returns coming in from the team that had been working at the reservoir site itself, and she sent her colleagues off with the instruction to have an early night and come back with a few brain cells ready for action. 'I might have some myself', she added, 'by then.'

* * *

'Buy my cottage? Our cottage. You mean now? Just like that?' Fran put down her glass very carefully. Now Bill's thorough inspection of the place on his previous visit was making sense.

'If everything works out, yes, just like that,' Maeve said. 'You know, have a couple of independent valuations for a start, and if we agree a price, subject to all the usual surveys and searches. And we'd be paying cash — did I mention that?'

'The only thing is', Bill said, 'that we don't want to hang around. We'd want to be in here by July.'

Mark said, 'You'll excuse us if we don't make a decision tonight? After all, it's Fran's home—'

'But you've got the new place, haven't you? And don't tell me conservation and restoration don't cost an arm and a leg,' Maeve declared.

'And take time,' Fran said quietly. 'The Rectory doesn't have an operative bathroom or kitchen at the moment. Mark's right, I'm afraid. We'd need to give it some thought.'

Which included, when their guests had finally left, the possibility of moving to Mark's house in Loose, whether on their own or with Sammie and her children still *in situ*.

'Because that's the obvious thing to do,' Mark reflected, watching in the mirror as Fran took off her make-up. 'Especially if Lloyd's overtures the other night worked.'

'Didn't you ask her? When you saw the kids?' Fran's voice was sharp with a mixture of disbelief and accusation. She turned for a moment to face him, but then resumed her task.

To his own ears he sounded defensive. 'Of course I did. But I didn't want to put her under pressure and start asking awkward questions. Not in front of the children, anyway. In any case, it's not really our business, Fran. Or,' he conceded, in the face of her continued silence, 'it wasn't until this offer came up. Do you really want to sell? The original idea was that we should rent it out to provide an income for our old age,' he added, in a quavery voice.

'Circumstances change.' She got up and came to sit on the side of the bed. 'The longer we're here the more obvious it becomes that you're not going to grow any shorter, so I foresee permanent scars on your forehead and on that bathroom beam you never see. Selling this to pay for Pact's work and living in Loose would be the obvious solution. And Loose can pay for our old age.'

'So we put everything in train? You're sure you don't want to sleep on it?'

'Whoever said anything about sleep?'

* * *

The photographic section had come up with what looked like cracking shots of an attractive young woman, dolled up for a night out. In some she was blonde, in others brunette and in yet more she was a stunning redhead. It wasn't just her hair that had received attention; she might have been in the hands of a professional make-up artist, not someone with a digital touch-up programme. Someone had arranged the details like a halo round the original penny-plain photo.

'Monday's a dead quiet night in the clubs and pubs,' Coveney complained on Tuesday morning, 'so we got zero take-up. But we'll push on with it.'

'The trouble is, people who were the right age for clubs three years ago may have moved on — got babies and mortgages,' Fran said.

'Not some of the clubs I have in mind. If she was a pole dancer or stripper, or even a high-class call girl, she might have been operating in gentlemen's clubs—'

'What a misnomer!' Sue snarled.

'So we'll be concentrating our efforts there until Friday. If that's OK with you, guv?'

'Sounds good to me.'

Sue's hand shot up. 'Will there be men and women on this particular team?'

Dan looked to Fran for help.

'Volunteers, I'd have thought,' she said crisply, though her heart sank. Of course, Sue was right — hadn't Fran and her generation fought for just such opportunities? Except the older she got, the more Fran thought about compromise. 'So long as the team members bear in mind that they're there to elicit information about what the men involved may think is of a delicate nature, not make political points themselves.' Damn, that had been really heavy-handed. 'But I can trust you all on that count, can't I?' Worse and worse. Time to rush on. 'Any news of the reservoir key-holders? Not the gates, but the manhole cover thingies.' At least people were laughing at her now.

'There's no record of any having gone missing in the last five years, guv,' another young woman put in, only to earn a glare from Sue. 'And we've interviewed all the blokes entitled to use them. Nothing suspicious in any of their statements at all, though of course we'll double check. They've all got completely unblemished records to date, anyway.' She threw the last sentence down as a challenge, rather foolishly, Fran thought.

But no one took her up on it.

'OK, the perimeter fence, with special reference to the side facing the allotments?'

'We're still checking that, ma'am. But it's a bit of a no-hoper, I'd have thought. A lot of families go up every weekend, and you know what kids are like. The new one's already sagging in places, and little tunnels run under it in others.'

'OK. And what about the plot-holders themselves?'

Coveney said, 'We're about halfway through the list, so far. As you say, they all seem to know each other by sight, even though they all insist they keep themselves to themselves. Trouble is, some of them are very elderly indeed, and it's always possible several have died since the relevant date.'

'Tell you what, Dan,' Fran said, 'why don't you check on those who've given up their allotment but not pegged it? Just in case.'

'What about the ones who have pegged it?' some wag asked.

'You could send someone to heaven to question them there.'

'Or "seek him i' th' other place yourself,"' another voice concluded.

The chief!

He nodded pleasantly to his surprised colleagues, and especially at Fran and Coveney. 'I understand what you're doing may expose the weaknesses in the performance of one of our former colleagues,' he said. 'This is unfortunate, but shouldn't inhibit you in any way. The truth is sometimes inconvenient, I'm afraid.'

Would he say the same if they ever had to talk to him about Gates and Caffy?

Pat, whom the chief would probably describe as twice blessed, greeted her on her return to her office with the news that she could visit Maurice Barnes the following day, and that the internal post had arrived, bringing, amongst other mail, a packet from Folkestone. She handed it over with a smile.

Fran opened it like a child expecting a Christmas present.

Before her eyes was a selection of shots of the suicide victim, all with a ruler to show the measurements. Where on earth had she got the idea that Alec Minton was a poor, weak old pensioner? He was over six feet tall and strapping with it. He might have been a member of the bowls club, but she'd wager her pension that he weight-trained too, and probably went on regular runs. You certainly didn't get a torso and a set of quads like that without a great deal of purposeful effort.

'Not what you wanted, Fran?'

'Not what I expected, certainly!' She chose one showing the least obvious injuries, which in any case she covered over with her thumb. 'What do you make of this guy?'

'Quite a hunk. But a dead hunk, I'd guess?'

'Like that parrot. And once it could talk, too. And I wish it had spoken before it topped itself.'

She phoned Pete Webb immediately. 'I thought Alec Minton was a little old pensioner given to playing bowls!'

'He was.'

'I should guess he played very well, then. On the days when he didn't work out in the gym.'

'The gym? You're joking!'

'You have another look at those photos, Pete, and tell me what you think. They may not be the pecs of a young man like you, but pecs they are. He's got quads, too. I want to know about that gym, Pete, and anything else you can unearth. And — just as a sweetener — I'll authorise you the funds to prioritise the investigation of his computer. Bring it off the back burner, please, and raise the heat a little.'

'You sound like a woman who's scented blood, guv.'

'Do I? I don't think I mean to. Or maybe I do. Tell you what, Pete, I know you're up to your ears in things that won't wait, but I want you to depute someone really reliable to check the contents of that parish magazine of his again. As a matter of urgency, right?'

'Right, guv.'

'Oh, and Pete — are you still there?'

'Yes, guv.'

She almost laughed at the misery and resignation in his voice. 'I want a photo or an e-fit of how he may have looked in real life. Absolute priority.'

* * *

'I had to leave a message,' Mark confessed over lunch. 'Do you know, Sammie's actually re-recorded my answerphone greeting?' That had really annoyed and hurt him more than he would admit, even to Fran. Not that he knew why. It made eminent sense in one way. But some part of him insisted that she should have asked him — even told him, knowing Sammie — that that was her intention.

She said nothing but reached for his hand and squeezed it. 'Did you say why you needed to speak to her?'

'I thought it might come as a bit of a shock. So I just said it was important and would she get back to me immediately. Do you remember those communication exercises we had to do as rookies? How to you break the news of someone's death? "Leave a message on the widow's desk?"'

'Or "all those with a husband stand up? No, not you, Mrs Briggs. In any case, you ought to sit down 'cos I've got bad news for you."'

Through their laughter, he confessed, 'I rather thought mine might match those. "I thought you ought to know Fran and I are moving back this weekend. You can stay if you want." No, it'll have to be face to face, won't it?'

'Do you think it might be worth phoning Lloyd to find out how his overtures were received?' she asked with that tentativeness she only used when she spoke of his family. 'I know it wasn't our business before but now it just might be.'

'Good idea. I'll get on to it after this afternoon's meeting. "How long do we want to detain terrorist suspects before they have to be charged?"'

'Why do I get the feeling that whatever you say and for whatever reasons the politicians have their own agenda and will decide accordingly?'

'I think you're telling me I'm wasting my time.'

'Who's to say we all aren't? But at least I'm going to be able to talk to Maurice Barnes tomorrow.' She gave a complicitous smile. This was one thing she never asked about, and he sure as hell wasn't going to divulge, even to Fran.

CHAPTER NINETEEN

If anything, Lewes was an even more depressing prison than Maidstone. Fran let Sue Hall drive this time, all too aware that the young woman still hadn't forgiven her for her lapses in sisterhood. As if she and her contemporaries hadn't invented the whole thing, investing time and effort and even marches to secure the opportunities women like Sue now enjoyed as of legal right. She wanted to tell Sue not to be years out of date, not to waste her energies over battles long since won. But she couldn't, because Sue was right. There were all too many areas where the police was still a man's world, and there were women — like Fran herself — who had to connive with the prevailing culture to get results.

'Why don't you take the lead on this one?' Fran asked.

'Because you don't think it's so important?'

Stupid child. 'Because you don't think it's so important, *ma'am*!'

'Sorry, ma'am.'

'Sorry, *guv*. OK, let's forget it. But don't go down that road with me again, Sue. I want you to lead on this interview because I've seen you in action and I know you're shrewd and intelligent. I don't think you'll let me down.' She added frankly, 'And you've got me there if you need rescuing.'

Sue had the grace to blush. 'Thanks, ma'am. Thanks, *guv*.'

* * *

As Ken Roper had said, Maurice Barnes was an altogether bigger man, perhaps five inches taller and at least three stone heavier. He had clearly benefited from time in the prison gym, however, he wasn't as muscle-bound as Drury, nor did he have anything like the physical presence.

'You're a scientist by training, Mr Barnes,' Sue began, startling certainly Fran and possibly Barnes.

'That's right. A biochemist. I got my degree at Sheffield.'

'How do you keep your brain ticking over now?'

He pulled a face. 'I *was* trying to do an OU course. But every time I'm moved, things like my books and coursework disappear and no one notifies the OU tutors and so I doubt if I'll ever finish it. Up in Durham, while I was waiting for my books to catch up with me, I was trying to fathom sudoku and to teach some of the inmates to read and write.'

Sue nodded as if it were leading somewhere. 'And the rest of the time?'

'I read. I use the gym. I do press-ups.'

'Not a very fulfilling life.'

'No. Oh, and of course, I'm helping you with your inquiries. Into what, might I ask?'

'Into the murder of a friend of yours. Janine Roper.'

His face lit up. 'You've realised poor Ken's innocent! Excellent.'

So why didn't he include himself? But Sue didn't pick up on the point.

'I didn't say that, Mr Barnes. But new evidence has emerged.'

Secretly, ironically, Fran applauded the verb.

'Now we want to discuss it with you,' Sue continued.

'And what might that evidence be?'

'Janine's body,' was the brutal response.

His hands flat on the table between them, he bowed his head in what could have been prayer or equally a desire not to show his face. Certainly it was carefully blank when he raised his head again. 'Might one ask where?'

'You might want to tell us where.'

'If I were a mind-reader perhaps I would. As it is, you'll have to tell me.'

'I'm still waiting for an answer, Mr Barnes.'

'Then you'll have to wait till kingdom come.' He got to his feet in an easy movement.

Fran was desperate to dive to the rescue, but wanted Sue to have one more chance to redeem herself. It didn't take long to realise that she waited in vain.

'Mr Barnes, you might as well sit down again, you know,' Fran said. 'From what I know of HMP Lewes, this is one of the better rooms, and believe it or not we're better company than some of your colleagues.'

'Not much to boast about, Inspector, when most of the inmates are illiterate drug users whose only occupations seem to be self-abuse or buggery.'

'I told you, it's Det—'

Fran overrode her. 'Quite, Mr Barnes.' She allowed her voice to become conversational. 'You've put your finger on a major problem with the present prison system. I wish you could have a word with our beloved leaders, most of whom clearly haven't spent so much as a day in a nick, let alone weeks, months and years. How have you kept your sanity?'

'Believe it or not, Inspector, by staying angry. The system has deprived me not only of my career but also of my ambition. I wanted to put something back into society. To make a difference. I was standing for the town council. I don't see me getting so much as a nomination when I get out, do you? And no amount of your playing around trying to get me to tell you the whereabouts of a woman I emphatically did not kill is going to help that.'

Fran nodded. 'Very well. Let me come straight out with the information. Mrs Roper's body was found in a covered reservoir. She had been strangled and trussed to a beam inside the reservoir roof. To have put her there you would need to know about diving — swimming at the very least — and to have no mean physique. However kind one wants to be to Ken Roper, one can't imagine his being able to string her up that way. You were always perceived as his accomplice, and I have to tell you that in my view you'd be capable of lifting Janine and—'

'Of course I was capable of lifting the poor woman. I gave evidence that I had carried her upstairs to my bedroom. She had a severe migraine and couldn't see to walk. Your colleagues, not surprisingly, found her DNA on my clothes and on my bedclothes. Their deduction was that I had helped kill her.'

'And the deduction of the jury,' Sue put in.

'As you were kind enough to observe, Constable, I'm a scientist, and, believe me, people are taken in by anything a man in a white coat tells them. Even if they know he's an actor in a white coat, they still get taken in.'

'And you're trying to take me in now.'

He snorted. 'The philosopher said, all men are liars. He was a man. Therefore he was lying. Therefore all men tell the truth. Surely, Constable, you can do better than that.'

Fran said, 'Well, you've given us a lesson in logic, Mr Barnes. How about giving us your unprejudiced opinions of Janine and her untimely death?'

'I thought you'd never ask.' He settled down in the manner of a man about to share a chinwag over a pint.

Fran mirrored him, though Sue still sat aloof. 'Janine first. Make me see the living woman,' Fran urged.

'She and Ken were the mistakes in each other's lives. Oh, Ken will tell you how happy they were—'

'He has,' Fran agreed. 'Why are you telling me different?'

'One of your colleagues' insinuations was that because Ken and I were friends and enjoyed sailing we were in a gay relationship. We were not. We were friends from our schooldays, and liked sailing. That was it. I had my own private life, which involved all sorts of things Ken had no interest in. Alas, he did not have a life, private or otherwise. And then, God help him, he got the idea that he could meet his heart's desire on the Internet. Janine was on the rebound, I suspect, and he had never fancied himself in love before. Because it was undeniably cheaper for them to live together, they chose to do so. Janine even had her big white dress day. But to their friends — and I really liked the woman, don't get me wrong — the marriage was hollow. Six months of living with Ken and she was bored out of her not very large skull — any fool could see that. She fed Ken a stream of lies about having to work late at school — as if she were a teacher, for God's sake! — and went off and did . . . whatever she did. She didn't tell me and I didn't ask, for everyone's sake. I reasoned that what the eye didn't see, the heart didn't grieve over.'

'Surely you had a duty to tell your friend that his wife was two-timing him!' Sue declared.

'If I'd *known*, yes, perhaps I would have had a duty. I took great care not to know. If Ken had ever told me he was unhappy, then I would have had a duty. But he was genuinely happier than I'd ever known him, so proud of his lovely wife.'

'Was she lovely? In appearance, I mean,' Fran asked, hoping her question would drown the sound of Sue's derisive snort.

'She could be, no doubt about it. One of Ken's gifts to her was a portrait. The sitter goes along to some photographic studio with several changes of clothing. A make-up artist transforms her. She's photographed in a variety of poses and outfits. The result is a soft-focus fraud which costs the buyer far more than it's worth. Anyway, Janine looked very good indeed in her photograph.'

Fran leant forward, stroking her chin. 'The funny thing is, Ken, we've never come across any photo like that.'

'You wouldn't have, not unless you've had access to my house.'

'Not yet,' Fran was forced to admit.

It was, of course, a serious omission, one he was quick to seize on, shaking his head in ironic sadness. 'I'd have thought you'd be more thorough than that. But I suppose you've been focusing on Ken.'

She tried to regroup. 'So what will I find at your house, Maurice?'

'You do these searches yourself? Don't you delegate?' Then he looked meaningfully at Sue. 'Perhaps not.'

'Tell me what to look for when I go. Janine's portrait apart.'

'Don't you want to know why I should have it?'

'If you want to tell me I'm more than happy to listen. But I shall make up my own mind, remember.'

'It upset Ken to see her tricked out with such glamour.'

'Come, now—'

'He liked his wife as he saw her every day,' he insisted. 'Loved her. He was a simple soul — still is, I should imagine. And it suited me to have the photo on my wall.'

'Was she your beard, Maurice?'

He acknowledged the term with a lift of one eyebrow. 'Oh, I'm not gay. The funny thing is I believe I'm asexual. I've never had the privilege — or perhaps the opposite, though the antonym escapes me for the moment — of a grand passion. And curiously Janine's portrait kept predatory people of both sexes at bay. I stress I was fond of the girl, in a strictly fraternal way. I liked her as if I were her brother, Constable,' he enunciated very slowly.

'Don't try to patronise my colleague, please, Mr Barnes,' Fran said crisply. 'And while we're at it, I'm a detective chief superintendent, not an inspector. But please call me Ms Harman.'

'They *are* sending in the heavy guns!' he mocked.

'We've got them — we might as well use them. Now, what do you think Janine got up to when she wasn't with Ken?'

'I can only speculate. Janine was the opposite to me, Ms Harman. Oversexed, I would say. And basically, Ken wasn't delivering. And I suspect she took risks. And drugs. Hence her insomnia.'

'And she took these drugs where?'

'Clubs? But she was a bit old to go to discos, and there were times I wondered . . . there were times I saw someone looking remarkably like her — oh, she was dressed up to the nines and heavily made up — picking up delegates to conferences in hotels in the area.'

'Might she have looked like this, Mr Barnes?' Fran fanned the doctored photos on the table.

With a slight, sad laugh he touched one. 'This is remarkably similar to how she looks in the portrait in my living room.'

Fran made a little rewinding gesture. 'You imply she was a part-time prostitute. What did she do with the money she earned?'

'I would say she probably spent some on drugs. The rest — who knows?'

'And where would she keep the glamorous clothes and wigs?'

He spread his hands. 'I could scarcely ask her, could I? Certainly, before you ask, not in my apartment. And although she must have had some women friends, I never heard her allude to them — certainly never met them.'

'How long before her death did you see her apparently picking up men?'

'Six months? After that, I had no sightings. I reckoned that she had found herself, to use an old-fashioned phrase, a fancy-man. Find the man, find the clothes?' He stood, not overtly stretching, certainly not displaying, but very much a man in control of himself and — now — the situation. 'If you need to see me again, I will cooperate in any way I can. I would like to see poor little Janine's killer rotting in jail — preferably for life.' As he raised his hand to knock for the prison officer to take him away, he added with a charming smile and a slight bow, 'Actually, Ms Harman, I've been teasing you. I only rented my apartment. All my belongings have been packed away and put in storage. Every last book, every last CD. But at least they'll be safe for when I come out.' He paused. 'If you want to see them my solicitor will furnish you with the details of the self-storage warehouse. But promise me one thing. There's valuable antique china and glass in the packing cases. Don't let a plod get his — or her — hands on them.' Very carefully he did not glance at Sue.

* * *

Sue Hall took Fran's few but pithy observations about her interview style very badly, and Fran suspected she'd spent long minutes in the ladies' loo bathing her eyes and applying fresh make-up. The best way, Fran decided, to repair her dented ego would be for her to take the lead during the afternoon's briefing session. Suspecting the girl would get the jitters if she had an advance warning, Fran simply told the group that Sue would do the business. And she did it very well, after a rocky start.

'So you two believe the guy?' Dan Coveney asked.

''Fraid so. He's cocky, likes long words — I should imagine he put the jury's back up,' Sue said, though she had the sense not to add that she spoke from experience.

'Well,' Coveney continued, 'that fits in rather with our other hope — the diving gear stowed in Roper's locker at the yacht club. The DNA on it, to be precise. There's loads of Roper's, as you'd expect. And that of several so far unidentified people. But of Janine's and indeed Barnes' there is none. And no, I'm not joking,' he snarled to a couple of lads at the back. 'So just as it looks as if we're getting closer, it all slips away again.'

'Like a mirage in the desert,' Sue muttered, surprising Fran.

'So we're back in the desert without a camel,' Fran summed up. 'We had great hopes that Dale Drury — Dave Henson and Joanne Pearce's serial killer — might have done the biz for us. But he swears he didn't and, bar making him take a polygraph test, I tend to believe him. If I were a juror, I'd certainly have let Roper and Barnes walk, and I'm certain the Appeal Court will now. So where do we go from here?' It was a genuine, not a rhetorical question. 'What have the local door-to-doors thrown up?'

Dan Coveney spread his hands. 'Not a lot. Any bank holiday weekend there's a lot of activity on the roads. Even when people live in the countryside, and there's a lot of that round Lenham, they tend to hunt for another bit of countryside. Or the seaside. Whatever. The result is that very few locals were around anyway, and no one registered anything unusual. Except one guy — blind as a bat, I'd have thought — was out exercising his dog and swears he saw a guy parked up in a lay-by in tears.'

'He's sure?'

'That's the trouble, guv. He isn't. It could have been last year, or the year before that or the year before that — you get the picture. Imagine what defence counsel would make of him. Assuming he's still alive by the time a trial comes round.' He was as downbeat as if he were announcing an outbreak of avian flu in the next office. Was that why he irritated Iona Harris so much?

'Of course, it's always possible that he'll lead us to such conclusive evidence that we wouldn't need him as a witness,' Fran said crisply. 'Who's good and patient with old-stagers? Sue, how do you get on with your granddad? OK? Tell you what, why don't you see if young Tom's got a spare hour when this briefing's over? He's good with old folk, too.' In fact, he'd be far better than Sue herself, but there was no need to tell anyone that.

It seemed that nil returns were to be the order of the day thereafter. It was time to inject some more pace. Once a team stopped believing in itself, the painstaking routine work would become deadly.

'Dan, has Iona come back yet with any reports on the tests she must have run?'

He shook a miserable head. 'Do you want me to have a quiet word with the young lady?'

'I'll have a loud one, thanks, Dan. Come on — *nil carborundum illegitimi*, as my first desk sergeant used to say. *Don't let the buggers grind you down*,' she translated loosely.

CHAPTER TWENTY

'Why not go and talk to this Dr Harris in person?' Pat asked, dropping into Fran's office with a pile of paperwork for checking and signature. 'It's lovely out there now — all those clouds seem to have lifted and a bit of sun does us all good. And nothing beats a woman-to-woman talk without a helpful man around. I'll tell Mark's secretary you're nipping out. And I'll tell Mr Gates' secretary you're out following a vital lead.'

Fran shook her head emphatically. 'Tell her I'm at a top-level meeting — that'll impress Gates far more.'

Once on the road, however, she asked herself what she was doing, wasting time, not to mention all that fuel, when an email or a phone call would have done just as well. She was being stupid and irresponsible — but she wasn't going to turn back.

Dr Harris was obviously surprised to see her, as she might well be.

'I was just passing,' Fran lied, 'so I thought I'd pop in to see if you've got any test results for me.'

'The Lady in the Lake case.' Harris's sneer was audible.

'Cliché it may be, but maybe the media will elicit a response from the public,' Fran parried. 'And we need all the help we can get, don't we? Hence I'm here now — time is of the essence, and all that.'

'I was just going to check today's emails,' Harris said.

Fran had to stop herself pointing out that it was nearly four, a time most people thought was a little late for a first scan. 'Please, go ahead.'

Harris seemed to take what remained of the day. And certainly she had a huge incoming mail. But at last she pointed. 'There we are. They've been very quick.'

'And . . . ?'

'That vaginal swab — did I mention I was taking one, although I didn't expect to get anything? She'd had recent sexual activity, and they've actually got some DNA. No record of it on file, unfortunately, so that doesn't get us any further forward.

'Traces of cannabis in her blood. And cocaine. There was too much tissue damage to her nostrils for me to remark on that when I examined her,' Harris added defensively.

'Of course. Anything else I should know?'

'Nope. Nothing I didn't put in my report.'

'Which I've not received yet.'

Harris started. 'I sent it through as soon as I'd completed it.'

'To me?'

Eyes heavenwards, Harris checked her sent mails. 'Sorry. God knows what I was doing. I sent it to Mr Coveney, copied to DI Webb. Who the hell's he? Ah, the bloke who was interested in Alec Minton.'

'Finger trouble,' Fran said lightly, adding *or love*, under her breath. 'So long as someone in the team's got it, that's fine.'

But Harris had already found another screen; her printer whispered into action and the report emerged even more quickly than Fran's printer would have managed.

'Thanks. Speaking of Minton, has anyone been along to organise a facial reconstruction yet?'

'Here? No, should they have been?'

Fran nodded. 'As long as he's in your morgue, where else would they go?'

'Good point.'

To hell with the morgue smell, to hell with the fact she'd already seen the photos. 'While I'm here, I'd like a look at him, please. No, I'm not joking.' As Harris held the door open for her, she added, 'Have you put Minton's DNA on file yet? Because I rather think it's vital it should be. And I'd like a crossmatch with that found on Janine.'

'You're joking! An old guy like him,' Harris said dismissively.

Fran waited until they were both looking down on the body before she said, 'As old guys go, I'd say he was doing pretty well, wouldn't you? And three years ago, he might have been doing even better. You said he had no major illnesses. Any minor ones? Anything that might have made him subject to great fits of fury?'

'No. Not that I can remember. Do you want me to email you the report on him too?' She managed a sudden smile. 'With the hard bits in lay person's language?'

Fran felt an awful pun coming on. Dared she risk it? 'Speaking of hard bits, would you be able to tell if a man were impotent? That would make him lose his temper in a sexual situation, wouldn't it?'

'There's too much damage to the genitals for me to tell you that. He landed with considerable force on a concrete bollard or something similar. In any case, you'd be better looking between his ears, surely, Fran. That's the origin of most impotence.'

'Of course.'

'Your theory is that this guy got involved in a sexual situation with Janine down there,' she pointed at another drawer, as casually as if it were a neighbour's house, 'couldn't perform, and killed her in a frustrated rage.'

Fran nodded slowly.

'But she'd had sex. And you think with him. There's something that doesn't hold water there, if you don't mind my saying so.' They grimaced amicably at each other.

'I don't. On the contrary, I'm grateful. You've saved me saying the same thing to a roomful of people who'd be a lot less polite than you. My brain must be turning to pulp. God, what if I'm turning senile?' She was afraid her sudden panic made her voice crack.

Harris scrutinised her. 'I'd say you were just tired. But I know a very good gerontologist if you need one. Meanwhile, I'll double-check the notes I have on both Roper and Minton, and see what I might have missed. I'll let you know if there's anything you might find useful.'

'Me personally, if you don't mind.'

* * *

She got through to Pete Webb first ring. She cut across his pleasantries. 'Pete, two questions: why didn't you forward a report by Dr Harris you must have noticed was meant for me, and why the hell hasn't anyone been along to do the photo-fit or whatever of Alec Minton?' Fran leant against her car bonnet, pleasantly warm in the sun, and surveyed all the other cars in the hospital car park as she made the call. Two or three young men seemed to be doing exactly the same thing. She just hoped she wouldn't see some idiot trying to break into a vehicle — she didn't want to be interrupted for a few moments.

'Sorry, guv. It's been frantic here. Some survey for you folk at HQ. All leave suspended till we come up with the stuff.'

'You're sure it isn't security for some royal visit or something?' she asked dryly.

'Absolutely. The photo-fit's right at the top of my list of things to do when I'm allowed to breathe.'

'Take it from me now, Pete — you can breathe. So long as you give that reconstruction absolute priority. On my personal orders. Would it help if I spoke to your super direct?'

The pause was long enough to show he was giving it more thought than it deserved.

'Oh, just get on to it, Pete. Now. I need the best you can do on my desk tomorrow. Understand? And if you haven't got the staff to check that parish magazine, just let me know the date of the issue and I'll check it my bloody self.'

The youths were still lolling around. She looked upwards. At least one CCTV camera, possibly two, had a beady eye on them. So at least something was someone else's problem. She got into the car and headed back to Maidstone.

* * *

'Since when did gathering figures take precedence over fighting crime?' Fran demanded, trying not to pace round Mark's office.

'Sit down, Fran. And give me the time and date. I'll look into it. But you must give me some nice official reason. After all, a suicide isn't usually regarded as a major crime for which all else must stop. Indeed, the superintendent at Folkestone's a little concerned that you should regard it as such, and overrule his direct instruction to Webb.'

'Of course he is. I tried to phone him to explain and apologise, but it's hard to grovel to an answering machine.'

'They're not very forgiving beasts, are they? And they tend to cut one off in mid-sentence. Promise me one thing, Fran — you won't sound off to Gates, will you? Or the chief? Let any complaints go through the proper channels.'

'In other words, you. The chief's been giving you a hard time, has he? I'm sorry, Mark—'

'I didn't say that. I may have to have a word with him on my own account. After all, I'm still technically in charge of crime, and I do wonder about priorities! But, you see, this government directive . . .' He looked at his watch. 'Is there anything else you need to get off your desk — or indeed, off your chest? Because it occurs to me that we've not delivered those tubs to our new home, and it's just the evening to do it.'

'So it is.' She blew him a kiss and left. She hoped making her feel better hadn't left him feeling worse. As she closed the door, an idea came to her, so she opened it again and called, 'I'll phone Paula Farmer to let her know.'

Gates and the chief were passing, deep in conversation. But she would have sworn that something made him blush right up his neck, then go equally pale. She was still wondering what that something might be — surely he hadn't overheard her and surely he wouldn't have reacted like a sixteen-year-old even if he had — when she reached her office to find a note on her desk. Sue was trying to earn a brownie point or two, no doubt.

Sorry, guv

Went to see the old guy who says he saw a guy weeping at the relevant time. No joy. He says he often sees a man weeping in a car. But he can't give a description of the man or the car — not even colour or shape — and he's so frail it wouldn't be fair to put him in the witness box.

Sue

Drat. Well, it had been a long shot anyway. There'd always be blind alleys and cops to crawl up them — and back again.

* * *

As Fran put the car into gear, Mark said, 'I've just done what Paula told us to do — I looked up the Clive Granville case.'

She shot him a look. It wasn't often a phlegmatic professional cop allowed himself to sound so angry or so upset.

'Granville started out as a fairly petty criminal in Birmingham — drugs, prostitution, that sort of thing. Later he gravitated — as so many lowlifes seem to do! — down here to Kent, where he got involved in a spot of people smuggling too. By this time he'd got some of our people in his pocket — that might have been when you were on secondment, Fran, and I was on that infernal management course — and this is where Gates came on the scene.'

'Rubber-heeling, right?'

'Exactly. He met Caffy because it was her evidence that had helped net Granville and indeed the bent cops.'

'I'm missing something here. Why Caffy?'

'Because she was working high up on a house and saw things you wouldn't see from ground level. And did her public duty and reported them. It's a long story. Anyway, I'm glad to report that Clive Granville got himself killed — nothing to do with Caffy — and so everything was nicely wrapped up. She picked up a sum from the Criminal Injuries Authority — nothing like enough, of course — for what he'd done to her.'

'She looks OK,' she objected. 'Though I suppose you can't see psychological scars.'

'It seems to me she may have dealt with the psychological ones quite well — I know I find her a bit OTT, but that's a matter of taste.'

'You're saying she's got physical scars? Didn't Paula say something about her always wearing dungarees?'

'Exactly. She doesn't want a gap between her tops and her trousers, I'd guess.'

Fran could feel herself growing cold. 'What did the bastard do?'

'Slashed her abdomen. Left a scar.'

'Dear God. But why?'

'Because at one time he was her pimp. He'd forced her into a life of drugs and prostitution so when she escaped and tried to make something of her life he objected. When she did it a second time, he took his revenge. Apparently, after her final escape his mission was to run her to earth and send her to the morgue with her intestines wrapped round her neck.'

* * *

'Sorry to be a little later than we hoped — we wanted to pick these up and install them in their new home,' Fran apologised.

Paula dismissed the poor tubs with a nod. They'd looked good in the garden centre, but there was no doubt that against the grander backdrop of the Rectory, they were pitifully small. But then, Mark wouldn't have been able to lift an empty tub large enough to look in proportion, let alone a ready-planted one.

'Thank goodness the house is in the hands of people who know what they're doing,' Mark said, by way of apology. 'And I've an idea that they're going to be in your way wherever I put them,' he added, looking helplessly round.

'Don't worry. Just leave them there, by the front steps. We can move them as and when.' Paula smiled forgiveness. 'And your being late isn't a problem. Caffy's only just finishing one of the corbels in the hall. It was too dark for her to work in the drawing room this morning so she decamped to where there was more natural light. I wouldn't have the patience, I tell you. I believe she uses a dental burr for some of the finest detail. Anyway, here she is.'

Fran turned, aware for the first time how small Caffy was compared with the rest of them. What was life like for someone who had to go round looking up into other people's faces? More to the point, what was life like for someone who had had to look over her shoulder in case her ex-pimp turned up, ready to deal the most horrible death? How did the girl manage to be so positive all the time? And how dared life deal her another bad hand in the form of Gates?

'Hi, there!' she greeted them all, sunny as usual. 'Paula tells me you've identified the man who keeps parking here — Simon Gates, is that right?'

'I'm afraid he's a colleague of ours,' Mark said, contriving all the same to leave no one in any doubt that in a dispute he would back Caffy.

'Oh, I know that. He's a pretty big cheese, isn't he? But such a cold fish. Whoops! I didn't half mix my metaphors there, did I? He passed out at my feet once, in the morgue.' She produced an impish grin. 'Which I thought was a bit ironic, since he was supposed to be looking after me.'

'You're not worried about him stalking you like this?' Mark asked. Again, he had exactly the right tone — a blend of compassion, interest, possible anger.

Caffy blinked, as if taken aback. 'Stalking's a very serious term, isn't it? I suppose he is, come to think of it. It's a good job I never let anyone have my mobile number or he could have been on to me all the time. I suppose I hoped he was more like Gabriel Oak, really. Doing a spot of yearning. Except yearning implies a strongly beating heart and warm glances.'

'Warm! Gates!' Paula snorted.

Caffy ignored her. 'Not that I see myself as a Hardy heroine anyway.'

'Not Jude?' Fran asked, adding in a cod-rustic voice. 'All your book learning?'

'That's one book I just can't reread,' Caffy said seriously. 'I can't get past the hangings. Any road up, as we said in Brum, what I'll do is try and catch him at his yearning or stalking or whatever it is — quite by accident, you understand.'

'You're sure?'

She burrowed in one of her dungaree pockets and produced a screamer. 'We all carry these,' she said flatly, 'on a project like this. You know, thieves, tramps, that sort of interloper. One peep out of them and they get more than a peep from this. And the rest of the team materialising from nowhere.'

'You promise you won't attempt this when you're on your own?' Fran asked.

'Sacking offence,' Paula said briefly.

'So you're all right here. What if he turns up at your home?'

Paula and Caffy exchanged a glance Fran couldn't read.

'I'm doubly safe there. I live with a family that's more or less adopted me,' Caffy said at last.

Fran had a vision of a vulnerable ex-council house. 'Security?' she ventured.

Paula snorted with laughter. 'Think Fort Knox. Todd Dawes is — used to be — a pop singer.'

Fran's eyes rounded despite herself. 'Not *the* Todd Dawes? I had a crush on him once.'

Caffy smiled with a warmth and tenderness way beyond Gates' range. 'He and his wife Jan are my family now.'

Fran said no more. You couldn't talk about someone's dad in those terms, could you?

Perhaps Caffy picked up on her embarrassment. 'Wherever I meet Simon, what could he do to me? Swear undying love? In which case he's going to be a lot more upset than me.'

'Some men turn nasty when they're upset,' Paula snapped.

Fran recalled her theory about Minton and suppressed a shudder. She dug out her card. 'Phone me, please, day or night, on this number, if there's a problem. You won't have to battle your way through a switchboard. And we'll be there.'

'Thanks.' Caffy took the card and stowed it. 'But it might be he just wants to ask me out for a date or something.' She sounded less certain about this theory.

'And would you go?'

'By taxi,' she nodded. 'If he took me somewhere posh enough.' As if to reassure herself as much as them, she said briskly, 'Oh, come on, people, this is not the Yorkshire Ripper we're talking about. It's a highly respectable middle-aged policeman. Who once fainted at my feet, remember.'

Fran couldn't stop herself asking, 'What made him pass out when — presumably — you didn't? It must have been a pretty nasty sight.'

'Only this.' Caffy wriggled out of the dungaree straps and pulled down the bib to hip level. Then she hitched up her T-shirt.

'I think I might have passed out too,' Mark said, staring not at some abstract scar but at the pinkish-purple puckered flesh of the initials, CG.

CHAPTER TWENTY-ONE

'What's so frustrating now is sitting around waiting for other people to come up with the goods,' Fran said, loading the last plate into the dishwasher and switching it on. 'And though I can prioritise lab tests, I can't wave a magic wand and make them take less time. What we really need is what they've got in other parts of the country, mobile labs that go to scenes of crime as soon as the crime's been detected, before the scene's been corrupted.'

'Put it in your next report for Gates,' Mark suggested. 'He wants a wish list — let him have one that'll make his eyes water. Enough shop-talk! Come and have your feet massaged and another glass of wine.'

She stood in front of him, arms akimbo. 'Not until you've phoned Sammie. Come on, Mark, she's had all day to contact you. You're going to have to have another go. Meanwhile, I shall go online and see if I can find someone to value our house. But I might as well take some wine with me,' she conceded.

If there was one thing he hated it was being railroaded into something, especially where his family was concerned. But she was right. Sammie should have responded, if not to last night's message then to the half a dozen other ones that he'd left during the day and that Fran didn't need to worry about.

The answerphone yet again. No, he wouldn't leave yet another bloody message! He slung the handset down with more passion than accuracy and had to scrabble on the floor for it, hoping to God he hadn't broken it. He lifted it to his ear. It was working. Replacing it more gently, he stood staring it, as if willing Sammie to respond.

He didn't know how long he stood there. Eventually, however, he realised that there was no sign of Fran; if anyone might have a sensible rather than a panicky reaction to the news, it was surely she.

He found her in the room she used as her office, poring over the computer with an expression on her face halfway between puzzled and anxious. Putting his hands on her shoulders, he peered at the screen.

She whipped off her reading-glasses. 'Here, put these on and sit here and tell me what I'm seeing on this property website.'

'I can tell you what you're seeing. You're seeing Sammie and Lloyd's house in Tunbridge Wells. With a For Sale board in front of it. That's what you're seeing.'

'And, if you read on,' she scrolled down, 'you'll see the magic words, No Chain.'

She left it to him to ask the obvious question, so he did. 'What the hell's going on?'

'It looks as if what you hoped would be a helpful little chat the other night didn't work, doesn't it? They're breaking up and going their separate ways. Oh, Mark, I'm so sorry. For them all. And especially the kids.'

And for the Loose house. How long would Sammie need to stay? Would this put their deal with Bill and Maeve at risk? The way the Rectory costs were mounting, they dared not renege on the deal. Hoping his voice sounded calm and reasonable, he asked, 'But why won't she pick up the phone and tell me?'

She spread her hands. 'Perhaps she's so upset she can't talk about it yet. Perhaps she's taken refuge with a friend to see her through the crisis.'

'But the Loose house is supposed to be her place of refuge.'

'Yes, but only as a place. Perhaps she needs to be with a confidante.'

'Would you?'

Fran pulled a face. 'I've never been solely responsible for the twenty-four-hour care of two demanding babies. I've never been in the middle of a marriage breakdown. I don't think I'm qualified to say.' She checked her watch. 'I know it's getting late, but why don't you pop round to the house to see if she's still there but too miserable to pick up the phone?'

How could he explain the anxiety cramping his stomach? 'Please — come too.'

She took his hand, only partly using it to pull herself up. 'If you want me to, of course I will.' Which meant, in view of her previous refusals, she must feel something was seriously wrong. 'In fact,' she added, pointing to the untouched wine, 'I'll drive, shall I? Have you got your house keys?'

'What would I need them for?' Did she imagine Sammie lying ill, with only two howling babies for company? A glance at her serious face gave nothing away.

'I don't know . . . But take them anyway.'

* * *

'That's Lloyd's car,' Mark declared, as Fran pulled onto the drive, to find curtains drawn and lights on all over the house. 'My God, what's he doing to her?'

He was out of the car, pounding on the front door, before she'd even cut the engine. She wanted to shout at him to be careful, to remember that he wasn't a young man. He might have passed his annual physical with flying colours, but factor stress into a situation and that way might lie heart attacks.

Now wasn't the moment to voice her fears. She must simply support him in whatever way he wanted. If she had had a standard-issue ram she believed that she would have forced the door in person.

At last, however, the door opened, but only enough for her to see it was held on the chain.

'What the hell's going on?' But it wasn't Mark furiously asking the question. It was Sammie.

'That's exactly what I want to know!' he thundered. She'd seen him perfectly calm in the face of armed sieges and other critical situations. Now he was almost incoherent with a potent mixture of anxiety and anger.

She stepped forward herself. 'Your father's been trying to reach you all day, Sammie—'

'Who rattled your cage?' Sammie asked.

She overrode the insolence. '—and has grown very concerned. Is Lloyd with you?'

Sammie pointed at her. 'Tell her to fuck off.'

'Don't you dare speak to her like that!'

Fran laid a restraining hand on Mark's sleeve. 'All you need to know is that she's all right,' she murmured. 'And that it's OK for Lloyd to be here.' Taking a step back, she put her hand in the small of his back and pressed him gently forward.

She didn't know when she'd ever been so angry. But this wasn't her show. As she'd said, they had one priority, the second, she supposed, being not to disturb the children. How they could have slept through Mark's onslaught she had no idea. She made a great show of walking back to the car. A glance in the door mirror showed that the front door was now fully open, with Lloyd and Sammie side by side. Their arms were firmly folded. It was clear that Mark wasn't going to be invited into his own home. Alarm bells rang very loudly in her head.

At last he stepped forward. Grudgingly, she guessed, they stepped aside. She got in the car and watched more overtly. The conversation continued in the hall for several minutes. Then Mark turned on his heel and returned to the car.

'There's something up,' Mark said, 'and I've no idea what it is.'

'Do you want us to go back in together? Or would that simply make things worse?'

'Let's leave it for tonight. I'll talk to her again tomorrow, when we've had a few hours to calm down.'

She didn't argue, despite a profound and inexplicable unease that tomorrow would not bring the improvement he hoped for. Instead, she put the car into gear and took the long way home, hoping that the sight of the Rectory, now illuminated by a fitful moon, would help to bring him calm.

'Are you sure we're doing the right thing, letting Caffy talk to Gates?' he demanded suddenly.

Perhaps it was better to let him worry about something other than his family. 'We didn't have much choice in the matter, did we? And I can't see Paula allowing her to take any risks. It's certainly preferable to us sailing in and demanding that he unhand our decorator.'

'Do you think we should talk to the chief?'

'Not unless Caffy asks us to.'

'Yes, I suppose we must trust her judgement. After all, she's no more a helpless under-educated victim than you're a PC Plod.'

'The fact that she's intelligent and articulate is neither here nor there,' she said, rather more firmly than she'd intended. 'If she's being stalked she's a victim. Think of the high-profile men who've been stalked. They certainly weren't helpless in the world's terms, but they were certainly victims.' She could have added that though he himself was scarcely helpless, she had a nasty feeling that he was going to find out what it was like to be a victim in his conflict with his daughter. Now she had seen Lloyd with the woman they had supposed he was separating from she was very alarmed.

'But I wonder if we should have her wired before she talks to him. And certainly if she goes out for dinner or whatever with him.'

'Wired! That's a bit heavy!'

He sighed. 'He's beginning to get a reputation for losing that famous cool of his. Didn't Pat tell you that he reduced his own secretary to tears the other day? She swears it was only because he couldn't reach across her desk that he didn't hit her.'

'You're joking! Why on earth hasn't Pat—?'

'Because the woman was sworn to secrecy, I suppose. I was. The chief said it was so confidential I wasn't even to tell you. Sorry. And of course Gates' version of events is somewhat different.'

She grimaced. 'And we can't mention this to Caffy, of course? Hell. OK, that wiring—'

'I shall have to talk to the chief . . .'

'It'd be protection. For her. And, you never know, maybe for him.'

He shook his head. 'If it comes to that, I shall have to talk to the chief first. I have no option.'

* * *

The following morning, Fran was just about to settle down to collate some of the information she'd gathered on the needs of divisional CIDs when her phone rang. Of all the voices she might have expected to hear, Roo's was probably the last. But Roo's it was. And it was a good job she could place it, because he was too excited to give his name.

'She's had the baby, ma'am. We've got a little girl!'

'That's wonderful. How is she? And how's Kanga?'

He told her all about the birth — which he assured her was natural, with him holding Kanga's hand throughout — and assured her than the birth-weight was perfect and that Kanga was already breastfeeding her.

As much to interrupt the flow as anything, Fran asked, 'And what are you going to call her?'

'That's why I'm phoning, guv. Because we were wondering if you'd mind if we named her after you.'

'Fran's not all that much of a name,' she parried joyfully.

'Francesca is, though. And actually we were wondering . . . well, if you'd be her godmother, too.'

'Me? Roo, why on earth? I mean I'd be delighted, but—'

'You were there when we needed you, guv. Both of us.'

'But I was only . . . Yes, please, Roo. I'd be more than honoured. Just let me have the details as soon as you have them.' Young Kanga would have the christening gift to end all christening gifts. 'And how are you?'

'Fine, guv.'

'How fine?' And bother the lawyers for making this a dangerous question.

'Fine fine. The shrink seems pretty good. And to be honest, I've not had time to sit and worry, not with painting the nursery and that. And there's little Fran, of course. I'm a bit gutted about the news, though.'

'And what news would that be?'

'Haven't you heard, guv? Darren Mills was saying—'

'He's the guy running you Underwater Search and Recovery people, yes?'

'That's him. Anyway, he was saying that we're likely to be axed. The budget, guv. He says someone's doing the figures and it'll be cheaper to buy in a team from another force whenever one's needed.'

'I hadn't heard,' she said, hoping to sound as if such a move were the remotest of possibilities, but knowing — with a jolt in her stomach — that it was all too likely.

'It doesn't mean we'll be out of jobs altogether, does it, guv?' he asked tentatively.

Over her dead body. 'Of course it doesn't! Hell, Roo, you've all got other jobs, haven't you — "day jobs"? I can't imagine the streets of Tonbridge without you.'

All that expertise being discarded! She was ready to scream.

'You're sure? Because they say it'll be Sussex that takes over, and I don't really want a transfer — I don't want to move house, not with the baby and everything.'

'You give little Fran a big kiss from me — and Kanga, mind! — and tell her not to worry her new woolly bootees about anything. You'll all be sure of jobs as long as I'm here, Roo.'

Fran put her head on her desk and cried. She didn't care to ask why or for whom.

At last footsteps outside brought her to her senses.

What if someone came in? She mustn't be found like this. Especially as she wouldn't know how to explain if anyone cared enough to ask. What she needed was a bit of action — preferably the sort that would upset someone else. What she must do, however, was find out if the future of the Underwater team was indeed at risk, and, if it was, on whose authority.

Every one of her mental fingers pointed at Gates, of course. Him and his bloody committees.

Of which she was a member. Many of them, if not all.

Had some motion been passed when she'd been away with the fairies, sitting doodling and fizzing with resentment? What if she and her attitude had let down her young colleagues? She surged out of her office.

Pat handed over the sets of minutes for each committee without a word, but with a definitely raised eyebrow.

'All our decisions have to be minuted, don't they, Pat? Absolutely all?' Fran asked as she leafed through them. No, nothing so far.

'Of course.' The other woman was shocked either at Fran's ignorance or at the suggestion that they might not have been. 'What are you looking for, Fran? It may be that I typed up the minutes, in which case I can scan through for the item you're after. That'd save you hours. And a few points on your blood pressure scale.'

'Can you search for Underwater Search and Recovery team?'

'Shall I look while you nip off to the ladies? Your mascara's run a bit,' Pat added, as if it were perfectly normal.

* * *

'That's better. You don't look like a panda now,' Pat declared five minutes later. 'No, there's no mention of the Underwater team in any of the minutes that I typed up, or in any that have been put on the network. So I think it's fair to say that it's not been mentioned officially at any of them.'

'But nothing could be implemented without an official record?'

'In theory, no. But you know what these mothers' meetings outside are like.' She gestured with a curling thumb in the general direction of the erstwhile smokers' corner. 'They could decide to secede from Europe and not tell anyone till we were being towed across the Atlantic.'

'So if I want to make sure no one gets rid of this team, I need to make it official that nothing can happen.'

'It's a high-risk strategy, because half the members will have forgotten it exists, and if they remember they might decide it's something we can indeed do without. What you need, Fran,' Pat whispered, hunching forward conspiratorially, 'is a little preparation. Gather together your mates beforehand and explain why you want something to happen — or not — and agree that it should be an item on the appropriate agenda. Then you can vote it through. All these years in the police, Fran,' she added, shaking her head, 'and you're still such an innocent.'

Was that praise? Was it accusation? Fran couldn't work it out. But since she was eliciting sympathy for her ignorance, she would ask something else. Did Pat know anyone who might value her cottage?

'As it happens, I do. Do you want me to phone him for you?'

'Pat, you're my secretary, not my serf. Just give me the number and I'll sort it, bless you.'

As Pat wrote down a number, Fran's phone rang. Grabbing the piece of paper with a smile of thanks, she took the call in her office; it was from Pete Webb, sounding remarkably perky.

'We've found the gym where Alec Minton worked out. Seems he came regularly, guv. And he came the day of his death to empty his locker.'

'Can you imagine, Pete, being so systematic about killing yourself? It makes you feel ill just to think about it, doesn't it? Anyway,' she continued, pulling herself together, 'it's a bit of a bugger for us, him leaving no trace.'

'Ah, but he was seen, guv. One of the cleaners was in the locker room. And what she couldn't understand was why this quiet, polite guy should be stowing ladies' underwear into a black sack. Real snazzy stuff, to quote her. Most of it still in the original cellophane wrappers.'

'So you're hunting the sack and its contents?'

'Hunting? We've found it, guv! In the cleaner's house.'

'I don't believe it. Why on earth did she admit it?' In her experience people were remarkably coy about liberating such goods, let alone confessing to having done so.

'Because she didn't take it for herself, and she figured if he didn't want it anyway, her daughter and her friends might as well make use of it. We have lift-off, guv.'

'Lift off as in DNA?'

'The lab's on to it now, even as we speak. Not to mention the prints on the wrappers.'

A surge of disappointment washed over her. She should have been in there at the kill, seeing what looked like evidence, assessing it. But she must ride it — it was no worse than all the other occasions when she'd been in charge of a case and one of her team had had the privilege if supplying a missing piece of the evidence jigsaw.

But Pete was saying something else. 'Seems she'd seen in the local rag about Minton topping himself and she panicked and stowed it all in the back of her garage. And at long last her conscience gets into gear and she calls us. Nowt so queer as folk.'

'Nowt indeed.'

'So now my super — who thinks he's just invented the whole theory of detection — is urging me to do everything I can to help you. You haven't been on to him, have you, guv?'

Had a soft phone message turned away wrath? But she wasn't about to confess to abject grovelling, so she said, innocently or even, she hoped, enigmatically, 'Me? Have a word?

So you've got someone checking the contents of that parish magazine?'

'I have indeed. And I've been on to the forensic computer lab. They should have a report on the hard disk ready for tomorrow midday.'

'Tell them today midday, with my compliments. Well done, Pete — you're doing an excellent job.'

* * *

Mark was having less success. Once again Sammie was locked into answerphone mode. He tried a firm approach. 'Sammie, love, I really need to talk to you, you know, about your future in the house. So I'll come over at ten on Saturday morning.' There. Was that firm enough?

On reflection, he wished he hadn't explained why he wanted to see her, but he couldn't unsay the words now.

* * *

It was a good job Fran had taken Pat's advice about her mascara because there was a knock on the office door and Dan Coveney appeared. He was so full of something, however, that he might not even had noticed anything was wrong.

'Sit before you fall and tell me everything,' Fran said.

'It's Roper's old neighbour,' he began.

'Old as in former or old as in aged?'

'Both. I got the lads to visit them again, as you suggested, to ask whether anyone had seen Janine waving goodbye when the two men set out with their boat. Now, the prosecution case, as you recall, was that no one did. But we now have a witness, who turns out to have been in hospital when Moreton's investigations were taking place. And he is prepared to swear that she was standing on the doorstep waving them goodbye. Wearing some sort of towelling housecoat, he said, and mules. And, guess what, they exactly match some of the clothes in the evidence store.'

'And those poor buggers have endured God knows what because Moreton's team couldn't run him to earth. Please tell me he was flat on his back for six months and didn't know what was going on.' She pointed to a chair.

Laughing grimly, he sat down. 'Pretty well. He had a spell of two weeks or more in hospital, then he went straight off to North Wales to stay with his sister while he convalesced. And then, would you believe, he went to stay with his other sister — this one lives in New Zealand! — for six months. So you can't really fault old QED there.'

'I would if I were defence counsel. Did he say if Janine ever wore unusual clothes? Glamorous ones? Or had very glamorous girlfriends visiting the house?'

He frowned. 'And who might they be?'

She managed not to sigh in exasperation. 'Janine in disguise maybe. Could you get someone to take those enhanced photos along and see if he recognises any of the make-overs?'

'I'll get right on to it.'

'I suppose last night's clubbing and pubbing didn't have any results?'

'The youngsters were on duty till three, guv. I thought I'd debrief them in about an hour, when they've had their beauty sleep.'

She bit back an observation that at their age she had worked round the clock without so much as a whinge. But things were better now that the police recognised that their officers were human beings with human needs.

'When you've done that, Dan, how do you fancy a trip across to the prison? I took young Sue Hall with me last time, and the trouble is our friend Dale Drury fancies his chances with women. He might react differently to a man. He might not, but it's worth a try. Take another bloke with you. Someone pretty unshockable — he's a confessed serial killer, remember.'

'Any particular line you'd like me to take?'

Since when had she had to spell such things out? 'Just push him as hard as you can on those rehashed photos of

Janine. And remember, even if the clubbing didn't work last night, flood the clubs and hotel bars this weekend.'

As he left, it dawned on her there was someone else who should see the photos — the residents of Alec Minton's block of flats. She was on her feet ready to nip out herself — surely she deserved that treat — when she realised what a fool she was being. Any decent young copper could doorstep, and deserved the boost of a successful inquiry. But he or she wouldn't be able to do what Fran could do: save the Underwater team. She'd start lining up her cronies now. What was Pete Webb's number?

CHAPTER TWENTY-TWO

'The trouble with this Underwater team is,' Dave Henson said, still smelling pungently of herbal cough cures and looking as if another day or so under the duvet would do him no harm, 'much as I'd like to poke Gates in the eye, and valuable as the team is on its day, the figures might not add up. You've got to balance the needs of the force against the costs of equipment, maintenance and regular training.' Unasked, he removed a pile of paperwork from a chair so that she could sit down. He even made her a cup of instant coffee. 'Here, take the weight off your feet.'

She smiled her thanks. 'You can't just send lads underwater into potentially dangerous situations without regular training updates, I suppose. And those take them away from their everyday duties. But they're all so keen — and it seems a wicked waste not to use the expertise they've built up over the years.'

'What does your old man say?' He put his feet on the desk, but the effort made him cough painfully, and he took them down again.

'I haven't discussed it with him yet,' she admitted. 'I wanted to see that the consensus at our level might be.'

'And what do the others feel?'

'Some of the old-stagers like me don't like change at any price, do they? Do you know, there are still some who won't read their emails? Or if they do, they don't respond to them.' And she wouldn't want to rank alongside them. 'And there are things we desperately need — mobile labs, for instance, and those natty little instant fingerprint machines. Oh, and I thought of equipping community officers with those miniature cameras you can attach to their helmets, so they can photograph antisocial behaviour as it happens. Plus we really ought to do something for the rural parts of our patch. There's no getting away from the fact that our response times are decidedly poor once you get out of built-up areas.'

'Sounds to me as if you're talking the Underwater lads way down your budget,' Henson said, coughing till tears ran down his face. 'Hell, Fran, I've never been like this in my life,' he gasped at last. 'I had myself down as fit and healthy. Now I'm hacking and hawking like some old geezer in a spit-and-sawdust pub.'

She frowned sympathetically. 'What's your GP say?'

'You know doctors — says I need another week off, maybe more. But I told him, we've got criminals to catch.'

'Quite right. But the thing is, Dave, if you don't take a little time off now, how much are you going to need when you have to admit he's right?'

'Six months ago I'd have said you just wanted to get me out of the building.' Even now he sounded suspicious that she still might.

'Six months ago you might have been right, Dave. Water under the bridge, eh?' They exchanged a wary grin. She stood. 'Anyway, thanks for letting me bend your ear. I don't know that it's sorted everything out for me, but it's saved me making a fool of myself in front of Gates.'

'Rule number one: never make a fool of yourself in front of management. Even if you're married to the ACC (Crime).'

'I shall remember that.' When they were married, that is. If they ever were. Her phone beeped. A text message from Pete Webb about Minton's computer, ending 'CU here,

2ish?' Yes! 'I've got to go, Dave. But remember what I said. And remember there aren't too many headstones saying, "I wish I'd spent more time at work".'

They exchanged an ironic smile, and she left.

'Ah, the unholy alliance,' Gates observed, as she closed the door behind her.

Drat him for making her jump. ''Morning, sir.' She had nearly called him Simon.

He flicked a glance at an expensive watch. 'I think you'll find it's afternoon.'

'But before lunch,' she countered, as if indulging in light chat, not scrabbling for a conversational foothold. The only thing she really wanted to ask him was about his intentions towards and feelings for Caffy, but even in her most blunderbuss moments she would have dismissed that as inappropriate.

'Still in cahoots with Henson, I see?'

She pulled herself to attention — or the nearest she got to it for anyone except the chief. 'Still consulting a colleague about a matter of mutual importance, sir.'

'Which might be?'

She balled her fists and took a deep breath. She said evenly, 'It might be about all sorts of things, but included, in fact, emergency response times in rural areas.'

'Of course it did.' Sarcasm dripped from his voice.

'Of course it did. Didn't you hear DCS Harman tell you it fucking did?' Henson erupted from his office, veins bulging.

'How dare you!' Gates exploded.

'I'm not standing by when a colleague's honesty is being fucking called into question.'

She put a firm hand on his arm. 'Leave it, Dave, for God's sake.'

'No, the bastard's got it coming—' Was he really going to hit Gates?

'Dave!' She pulled him away. He was gasping alarmingly, clawing the air for breath. 'Dave! Here, lean on me.'

Henson's knees buckled. He clutched his chest.

Fran turned to Gates. 'Call a bloody ambulance, for God's sake.'

Henson made a huge effort. 'I'm all right.'

'Oh, fuck off and have another heart attack,' Gates hissed.

* * *

'Pneumonia, sir. Not his heart this time, they say,' Fran, very much to attention as she stood before his desk, told the chief.

'Brawling like children, Fran! Whatever were you thinking of?' His voice was icy.

'I believe that you may have been misinformed, sir. No brawling took place. I believe that Mr Henson may have taken exception to something Mr Gates was saying. He came out of his office too quickly and started to choke. While we waited for an ambulance, the first-aiders took over. He had some oxygen, and was fully conscious when he was taken to hospital.'

'And why should Henson have taken exception to anything? How would he have heard?'

'That's something you'll have to ask him when he's well enough to return, sir.'

'Stop messing me around, Harman. Had you and Henson had another of your rows? Is that it?'

'Dave and I have more or less apologised to each other for the ill-will that originally arose between us, sir. We were quite literally talking about budgets. As a matter of fact he talked me out of adopting a quixotic stance about an item likely to be cut.'

'So how did the deputy chief constable get involved?'

'As I told you, he and I ran into each other just outside DCS Henson's office.'

The chief waved her to a chair. 'Fran, Fran, what's going on? And don't for a moment imagine that you're grassing anyone up.'

'Exactly what I just said, sir. I'd finished picking Henson's brains, took a text from Folkestone CID — I think there's been a significant development in the Roper and Barnes case, by the way — and left his office. I bumped into DCC Gates, who demanded to know what we'd been talking about. When he seemed to . . . disbelieve . . . me, before I knew it, Dave Henson erupted from his office — perhaps he'd been coming out anyway; I don't know — and started yelling.'

'At Simon?'

'And Simon responded.'

'Actual words?'

'I'm sure he'll tell you himself, sir. Then Dave collapsed, and Simon called an ambulance.' Bemused, she held up her still-shaking hands. 'It was all a bit stressful, come to think of it.'

'Intimations of mortality, eh? Come on, Fran, what were you two old reprobates really talking about?'

Since he poured her a glass of whisky, she could scarcely refuse to answer. But she left the tumbler on his desk, untouched. 'Budgets, sir. Truthfully. How they wouldn't run to everything. How a pet project of mine looks likely for the chop.'

'Which would be—?'

'The Underwater Search and Recovery team, sir.'

'And why would you be trying to defend them?'

'Because the members are afraid of losing their jobs altogether. And they're a really excellent team.'

'I know. But they'll all be excellent in their usual roles if the unit has to be disbanded — which I emphatically don't want.'

'Could you make sure their leader knows? A Sergeant Mills, I think.'

'I'll make sure the information filters down. And I'll break the news myself it if turns out to be bad. OK?' His smile was very dry. How many chief constables would tolerate such badgering, it asked. 'Come on, Fran. Drink up.'

'Sorry, sir. I can't. I've got to be on the road in ten minutes, with your permission, that is. Folkestone.'

'Of course.' He removed the glass. 'Carry on from where I interrupted.'

She nodded. 'At some point while I was talking to Dave, I realised there are things we need even more than the USRT. And much as I want to keep them operational, I can see reasons why they may have to be disbanded.'

'Are you quite sure you don't want that whisky? Because I have to tell you, Fran, you don't sound at all yourself. Now, you've been very loyal, and I appreciate that, but what I can't get my head round, as the young will insist on saying these days, is why Simon should want to cross-question you about a private conversation.'

'That's something you'll have to ask him, sir. In fact—' Cursing herself, she bit back what she was going to say. Now was emphatically not the time to introduce the subject of Caffy and the possible stalking.

'Go on.'

She got to her feet, shaking her head. 'The mutual . . . ill-feeling . . . has put me in what may be a very awkward position, sir. With your permission, though, I'd rather say nothing until the situation actually presents itself. With luck, it may not.'

She was aware of his scrutiny. She let neither her eyes nor her head drop.

'I know that look of yours, Fran. Mulish doesn't begin to describe it, does it? Very well, I'll let you go now. But nothing — not misplaced loyalty, nor resentment, nothing — will stop you doing your job properly. Do you understand?'

'Sir.'

'Because if it does, I shall have to recommend that one of you is transferred — or retired. Do I make myself clear?'

'Eminently, sir.'

Since having a full-scale tantrum about the unfairness of life was off the menu, she made what she hoped was a dignified exit — though it might have appeared to him as merely stiff-necked. She'd better tell Pat where she was going, and phone Mark to let him know, in the most general terms, of the latest developments.

Pat made a sideways gesture with her head. Someone was waiting in her office.

Mark.

She couldn't read his expression. But he held open his arms and she stepped straight into them. 'I promise you it wasn't my fault. Henson heard Gates ripping into me and rode to the rescue. He wasn't well — in fact, I'd told him only five minutes before he should take himself off home,' she added.

He snorted.

'Come on, Mark — six months ago I'd have told him to take himself off and stay there. What I said this time was that if he didn't look after himself he'd have to take even more sick leave. The quarrel was between him and Gates. Do they have history too?'

'I believe words have been exchanged, involving the reduced hours Henson's working, and his recent sick leave. But I don't think anything would justify Gates' telling a man who's just had a triple bypass to go and have another heart attack.'

'I never told the chief that.'

'I know. But walls have a great many ears in a place like this.'

'Simon's wheels are coming off, Mark. What are we going to do?'

'You, absolutely nothing. Me, very little. Cosmo and the chief, a lot, I hope. You looked as if you were in mid-flight — do you have time for a bite?'

She looked at her watch. 'Barely. And I'd better phone Pete Webb to tell him I shall be late. He might be relieved — it'll give him time for a break himself.'

'True. And the public lunch is policy, Fran. I don't want any gossip about people being made to retire.' As she called Pete on her mobile, he ushered her out, patting her bottom as they went.

* * *

Fran was halfway down the M20 when a call came through for her. Even though she had a hands-free set-up, she usually preferred not to use her mobile when driving. But when she saw the caller was Coveney, she broke her rule.

'Nil returns on Dale Drury, I'm afraid, guv. The French police are talking to him today, and the news on the street is that he's now clammed up, big time.'

Why did he never use plain English? 'Thanks for letting me know, Dan.'

'And just for your information the Froggies seem to think he was busy killing a couple of their toms when you hoped he'd been killing Janine.'

'It was more whether he recognised Janine as a prostitute than actually killing her,' she pointed out. 'But what about your debriefing, Dan? Did the pub and club crawl throw up anything useful?'

'Nil returns there, too, guv. But I told them we'd do the same tonight, tomorrow and Saturday — OK?'

'Please. And talk to lobby staff in hotels used by businessmen.'

'It's a very long shot, guv, given how long ago it was.'

'Just to humour me, Dan. And now I've got another call waiting. Sorry!' she lied.

No wonder young Iona Harris didn't have time for him. And what results had Harris come up with? No. Absolutely not. She would not make a call while driving at seventy in the outside lane.

* * *

Pete Webb greeted her as if she were a guest at a party, hurrying her upstairs to the CID corridor.

At last, as he took her jacket and hung it up for her, he said with a huge grin, 'I know I could have emailed everything, guv, but knowing you I thought you'd like to see it for yourself.'

And being in Folkestone had the merit of making her unavailable in Maidstone, should the chief want to question her further.

'I would indeed. Thanks, Pete. I take it that Minton had deleted everything but not actually wiped the hard disk.'

'You do indeed. But you did need a password to get onto the system, and the lad who found it didn't have the skills to hack in. It didn't pose too many problems to our people, though.'

'Good. Now, what have we got? Pornography? "Adult" chat rooms?'

'Plenty of both. And some photos, guv. Cup of tea before you look?'

'I wouldn't mind one *while* I look, if you don't mind.' She fished in her bag, and then her pocket. 'Damn, I've forgotten my reading-glasses. You know, if God had meant us to grow older, he'd have given us longer arms. I'd better nip out to Boots or somewhere and buy another pair.'

He coughed with embarrassment. 'I bet we could find a pair in Lost Property, guv.'

* * *

'Reading-glasses? What I really need for these images is sunglasses! My God, they don't leave much to the imagination, do they?' She gestured with her mug of tea. 'I hope poor Roper doesn't have to see all these. They wouldn't half shatter his image of his wife. I wonder how many men perv away from the far side of a camera, pretending they're taking artistic nude studies.'

'These would be more what they call glamour shots, though, guv.'

'Glamour! They're bloody pornographic. Which makes me wonder,' she continued, peering over her borrowed spectacles, 'how many other nasty little snappers got a view of what only a midwife should see.'

'You don't want it to be Minton who killed her, do you, guv?'

'I don't want us to *assume* he killed her. Because if we do, and close the case, him being unable to answer our questions, as it were, then we'll be letting the real killer walk free. Now,

I wonder how long it will be before young Iona Harris's tests come through.'

'Piece-of-string time, isn't it?'

'I'd like to say another couple of days won't matter because Minton won't be going anywhere. But it's Roper and Barnes whom I'm worried about. It's a pity we can't just phone up the prison governors and tell them to let them out till further notice.'

'What shall we do about chasing other photographers?'

'Until we find her address book we're stalled, aren't we? Unless it's worth tracing other users of those chat rooms and adult porn sites. Tell you what,' she said, almost thinking out loud as she leant back and stretched, 'there's no point in reinventing highly expensive wheels. Pass everything on to a specialised unit — when we've got as far as we can, that is — and see what they can make of it. Maybe a lot, maybe absolute zero.'

'Right.' He made a note. 'What else do we need to make a case?'

She stood and found a working white board marker. 'A hell of a lot. All we know is that he had a lot of pictures of her on his computer, filed, appropriately enough, in My Pictures. We don't have the camera, of course — can we assume that if it was digital it was small and if it was small he could smash it up and dump it in that skip?'

'Or even the sea.'

'Quite. We know Janine had sex before she died — we're just awaiting further DNA tests on the semen and on those clothes found in his locker. If we've got a match, it looks very good.'

'Big if,' he sighed.

'Don't lose heart yet. We've got even bigger ifs to worry about.'

'Such as why he should kill her. How he got access to the reservoir — both through the gates and into the reservoir itself. At least we've got a suspect big enough to have lifted her.'

Fran rubbed her face. How could she have forgotten? 'Didn't he work for a water company once?'

'Of course he did! Bloody hell, how could I have forgotten that?'

'It may have something to do with all those piles of files on your desk,' Fran suggested quietly.

But he was full of energy now. 'Are those big key thingies standard issue? It'd be very nice if they were.'

'Wouldn't it just?'

His face alight, he already had his hand on his phone and was asking someone to check. 'And chase that facial reconstruction geek as well,' he added. 'I want Minton's face on my desk by six tonight — latest.' He cut the call and turned to Fran. 'The bad news is that none of the residents at his block of flats admits to knowing that he ever had visitors back to the flat. There's a great cult of keeping oneself respectably to oneself.'

'No concomitant nosy-parkering?'

'They say he was a perfect neighbour.'

'Just like the Ropers. We don't know if they ever saw Janine dolled up, by the way. What have I said?'

He was choking back silly giggles. 'It's been at the back of my mind ever since you mentioned Ken. I wanted to call her Barbie!'

By now she was convulsed too. 'Oh, my God, yes. Ken and Barbie.' But she'd better keep laughing or she might end up in tears.

CHAPTER TWENTY-THREE

Fran guessed that HQ would be a-buzz with rumour when she got back late that afternoon, and that it would be almost impossible not to get sucked into the gossip-mongering. Accordingly, she arranged to meet Mark in the car park.

'I had a phone call from little Bill and Maeve,' Mark announced. 'Their valuer can be at your cottage—'

'Our cottage.'

'At nine tomorrow. What about our man?'

'Do you know, I can't even recall phoning him! I know Pat gave me the number of a mate of hers, but I've a nasty idea it got no further than my desk. Shit.'

'No problem. Knowing what your desk looks like in a crisis,' he explained, his eyes twinkling, 'I got on to an estate agent myself, who will be there at ten. I've arranged with the chief to take some time off in lieu so I can be there.'

'You mean I've got to go in and beard Gates on my own?' She feigned a wail of horror.

'I suspect Gates'll be late in himself tomorrow,' he said meaningfully. 'If at all.'

'I suppose you don't know what the chief said to him?'

'I really don't. Whatever it was, it would be to the point. Which takes me on to young Caffy. I really don't think she should be letting him chat her up, either at the Rectory gate — it does sound wonderfully rustic, doesn't it? — or in a more formal situation. Do you mind going home via the Rectory? I know it's late, but we may just catch them.'

'By them you mean Paula? I should imagine she'd be the only one capable of stopping Caffy doing anything she's decided to do.'

* * *

'A breakdown? Already?' Paula wasn't a woman to squeak, but she came near.

'We're not sure that it is that. All we know is that Gates . . . isn't . . . himself,' Mark temporised.

'Assuming it is, what's driven him to it?' Paula asked, passing round mugs of tea. Far from being standard builders', it was a fine lapsang souchong. Mark knew better than to comment.

'It must be very hard coming into a new job and trying to reorganise a whole group of people desperate to cling on to the status quo,' Fran said, almost apologetically. 'You don't make a lot of allies, let alone friends.'

Caffy shook her head. 'When I first came across Simon he already had a lot of anger seething round inside him. A lot. That was one of the reasons I wouldn't go out with him the first time he suggested it. Years ago, I mean. That and the age difference, of course. He's got to be forty-seven, forty-eight?' Fran nodded. 'And I was only twenty-five. Plus he's very highly educated—'

'Come on, Caffy! I've never known anyone as well read as you,' Paula said.

'But that wouldn't count with Simon, would it? He's a formal-qualifications man. Which would mean you could never have an equal relationship. Not like you two.' Caffy grinned at Fran and then at Mark, who found himself grinning back.

'No, I'm her boss,' he declared, taking Fran's hand. 'She does as she's told.'

'See what I mean?' Caffy said. 'Now, I know you don't weigh up every date as a potential partner for life, but you must hope you'll want to see each other again, at least as a friend, or what's the point? I don't see one anyway. I'd rather spend my time trying to make sense of Chaucer — my God, he's making my brains squeak.'

'That's because you insist on reading him in the original,' Paula said.

'So why did you tell us you were thinking of going out with Simon now?' Mark asked, desperate to get back on track.

'Because I've come on a bit since then. I've got some paper qualifications of my own, and Todd and Jan have taught me never to let anyone patronise me. And — I'm not very proud of this, mind — there's something intriguing about having someone so smitten with you that ages after you turned him down, he's still carrying a torch for you.'

'Hardy would approve,' Paula mused. 'Yes, Caffy's got me on him now. None of the team dares read the red tops either. And I tell you ours are the most grammatical and best-spelt quotations and invoices you ever saw.'

'They were before I came on the scene. And it was Meg who made us listen to Radio Four in our lunch breaks.'

'But now you know Simon's not himself '

'Or even more himself than usual,' Paula interjected.

'You'll forget about this scheme of bearding him at the gate and agreeing to a date?' Mark said.

'Too late. He was round here at about five. I said I'd see him at the new Tunbridge Mondiale on Saturday — a gourmet meal in the most elegant surroundings.'

'For God's sake, Caffy!' Even Paula sounded exasperated.

Caffy held up a hand with surprising authority. 'What else could I have done? He was edgy, I suppose. Yes, very edgy, and very intense. But he didn't pose any immediate threat so there was no point in letting off my screamer. I didn't know what effect telling him to push off might have. You know, as in, "What a noble mind is here o'erthrown . . ." And here I am, consulting you people. All of you.' She nodded at each in turn.

Paula wheeled away, staring over the scullery sink into the poor tattered garden at the empty skip that had replaced a full one. Fran did something that surprised Mark; she put her arms round Caffy and hugged her.

Mark once again tried to get a grip on the situation. 'In other words, you've bought yourself time. Well done. Now, will you let us consult our colleagues? Simon's our boss, after all — we can't do anything . . . to protect you . . . without letting the chief constable know.'

'Of course. And you can tell him I'll cooperate in any way I can. But I won't be party to entrapment, Mark. If — big if — Simon's ill, he needs care, not a police bust.'

'I'm not sure we do busts,' he said, finding himself smiling. 'And I'm equally sure that our duty of care extends as much to psychiatric illness as to injuries incurred in the course of duty.'

'I blame myself,' Fran said. 'I should have realised that something was wrong. When I knew him first he was quiet, serious, even, but always ready to join in with his mates. And he seemed to take my advice in good part.'

'Apart from that coldness, he was charm personified when I first met him,' Caffy agreed. 'A veritable pattern card.'

'And at our welcome-to-the job dinner party. Well, mostly.' Fran recalled his shocked, if silent, reaction to one of her comments. 'But not since,' she added with some emphasis.

'Did you find his criticism got very personal?' Caffy asked. 'Just something he was saying this afternoon . . . And he was already telling me what I should and should not wear on Saturday. If I go. Over to you people.' Her smile was both sad and gracious.

Fran seemed close to tears. 'You know, he was like a son to me at one point. I thought he was, at least. But now he seems to resent all the help I tried to give. It seems he must have hated me even then.'

Why could she say that to those women, comparative strangers, and not to him?

* * *

Fran was still subdued the following morning, though she reported a minor success when Mark, who'd waited in for their valuers, popped into her office to tell her he'd arrived. 'I've just had a call from Pete Webb. The Lenham magazine they found in Alec Minton's flat was the one that first highlighted our water problems. The edition before the one I found. Why he should have a copy is still a mystery. I've told them I'm going to show Mr Patel the e-fit Pete Webb's organised, just in case he recognises him. He may just have popped in en route from somewhere, spotted the stuff in the mag and drawn the obvious conclusion. And then started his preparations.' She spread her hands sadly.

'If anyone could recognise him it'd be Mr Patel,' Mark said, with a reassuring grin.

But she didn't even return his smile. 'We'd better go and talk to the chief. He told me he'd expect us the moment you arrived.'

* * *

There would be other meetings, no doubt, involving Cosmo and medical advisers, but for the moment the three of them sat as something like friends and equals, worrying over the fate of another friend.

'He's not at home, and his mobile phone is switched off,' the chief reported. 'So even if she wanted to cancel the date this Caffy — what a name, what a name! — would be unable to do so.'

'She was quoting *Hamlet* earlier, sir, to describe Simon's illness.'

His face lit up. 'Ophelia? "Woe is me, To have seen what I have seen, to see what I see"?'

'Possibly, sir.'

'A very unusual woman, then. I must make her acquaintance, despite her name. But to return to poor Simon: there have been no ATM transactions, no car movement to give away his whereabouts. I'm very worried about him. And I feel very guilty. I should have realised from some of his — let us say, vindictive — outbursts, that he was not a well man.'

'Presumably he passed his medical with flying colours, so I don't think you should blame yourself,' Mark said briskly. 'Caffy's worried what effect it may have on him if she stands him up tomorrow. But she'll accept whatever advice she's given.'

'Within reason,' Fran muttered. Responding to the chief's raised eyebrow, she said, 'Caffy's a very determined young woman, and also a very moral one.'

'So all the records show. Yes, I know all about her past, Fran, and also about her part in cleansing our Augean stable. I'm inclined to say that the tryst, if so it may be described, should go ahead — with the proviso that the young lady be wired up, and that some of our colleagues are on hand.'

'To do what, sir? They can't arrest him for anything. Having a mental illness is not a disciplinary offence. Treating a colleague as he treated Henson yesterday might be, but even then we can scarcely apprehend him. I don't even like the idea of suspending him. Without his colleagues he'll be totally on his own. Isolated.' Again Fran was near to tears.

'My view is that both those lives are equally valuable,' Mark said. 'We can sacrifice neither for the other. Let's leave it to the shrinks to make the decision.'

But his suggestion didn't end the meeting. Fran coughed. 'Before I go, may I present a problem I've got in the Roper and Barnes case? We've enough evidence to cast very real doubt on the original case. We believe that the real killer may in fact be a man who topped himself a few weeks back. We've not got conclusive evidence yet, and since he's systematically destroyed all traces of his life, the chances are we won't. How much further do you need me to dig, bearing in mind the budgetary constraints under which we all operate?'

The chief threw back his head and laughed. 'Fran, I never thought I'd hear you acknowledge that proviso. Seriously, once it's beyond all reasonable doubt that Roper and Barnes were wrongly convicted, tell the CPS your findings. They'll take it from there. As for your suicide, tie that case up as best you can, then we can issue a statement saying that we believe we have found the individual responsible for the killing but that no further action can be taken since he is deceased. What evidence are you waiting for?' he asked eagerly, switching off his managerial voice and suddenly reminding them that he, too, had once been a beat officer.

'Some hint that Alec Minton might have been near the site — we're showing a computer-generated facial reconstruction to all the allotment holders and to the guy on the reservoir gate.'

'And Mr Patel, our village shopkeeper — don't forget him,' Mark said.

'And DNA tests are already in train,' Fran concluded.

The chief narrowed his eyes. 'Fran, you don't look your brightest and best, you know. You're not still troubled by what I said yesterday about compulsory retirement, are you?'

She replied to his comment rather than his question. 'To be honest, sir, I'm very tired. Balancing all the admin with running a couple of active investigations has taken it out of me rather.'

'I know which you'd rather be doing. Look, may I offer a solution? Despite all our best efforts, our clear-up figures are very poor. Not compared with other forces', of course: we're right at the top of this blasted new government league table with space to spare. But we all know that there are still cases where it would be nice to get a result, years later.'

They both nodded. Where was this going?

He smiled as he continued, 'What I would like to do is follow the example of a number of other forces and improve our clear-up rate by investigating "dead" crimes with our new technical advances. We'd need someone to head up a small team — very low budget, of course.'

She knew Mark was grinning broadly. Only then did it dawn on her what the chief was offering.

'It's a dead end, Fran. Not the sort of job any young Turk thrusting for promotion would want. But would you think about taking it on? No, it's not even a firm offer. It was something I did intend to put to Simon. How soon he'll be in a position to comment I don't know.'

'Or how impartial his comments,' Mark said quietly.

'However, I think it's only fair to say that that would be my strong recommendation. Ah!' The phone rang. 'I told them not to put any calls through unless they are related to Simon. Excuse me.'

'This calls for a celebratory cup of tea,' Mark said, putting his arm round her shoulder as they left. 'And at least a smile.'

'So it does. I'm sorry.' She produced a weak affair. 'And I never asked how you got on with the valuers.'

'They came, they saw, they jotted. All I have to do now is talk to Sammie about her moving out or at least our moving back in. Tomorrow morning,' he said, hoping he sounded resolute rather than apprehensive.

Her response was interrupted by the sight of Sue Hall running down the corridor towards her, waving a piece of paper. Mark melted away.

'Guv, guv — we've had a phone call you should know about!'

'Yes?'

'A woman who does some volunteer work for a charity shop. Not every day, you know how it is. Anyway, she's seen our TV coverage and — I know, she's not exactly leapt forward — she says she unpacked a black sack full of lovely women's clothes. Some very sexy evening wear.'

'And when was this?'

'A few weeks back. She says she remembers because the sack itself was filthy, as if it had been in a shed or something, but the clothes were still immaculate. But they were the sort of thing she didn't think that Hythe was ready for, you might say, or any other Help the Aged shops in the area. So she sent them off for pulping.'

'Shit! You really had my hopes raised there. Never mind.'

'Well, she did say one other thing. A man brought the sack in. A fine-looking man, she said. And he looked very sober.'

'Sober?'

'That was what she said. Pete Webb got someone to show her that photo-fit. And she's prepared to ID him.'

To her amazement, Fran found herself throwing her arms round her colleague. 'Yes!' they chorused together.

* * *

A double triumph — both this case and, far more important in career terms, a job that might have been designed for her dropping into her lap without any effort on her part. So why was she feeling so empty? She should have been doing handsprings of delight. As it was, there was so little spring in her step she decided to treat herself not to the new outfit Cosmo would no doubt have recommended, but at least to some fresh air.

There was no doubt that she could, indeed possibly should, have delegated showing the e-fit of Minton to Mr Patel to the most junior of Pete Webb's team, but she was going to do it herself. She parked in her own drive and walked down. Yes, this felt good. Villagers were working in their gardens, cleaning their windows, and even applying paint. Why not? The sun was warm, the breeze smelt clean and fresh and all around her was a sense of rebirth. The new job would give her time to enjoy all this at the Rectory and still bring in the income they needed to pull the place into shape.

Mr Patel greeted her by a good approximation of her name, which given the irregularity of her custom she truly did not deserve, and looked with casual interest at the e-fit. He was about to shake his head, she thought, but suddenly his face changed and he called out to his wife. 'Meena! Meena, come and look at the picture of this gentleman.'

Meena also greeted Fran by name, correctly, in her case, as she peered at the piece of paper her husband had laid on the counter. She murmured a name Fran didn't catch. 'His face is a little thinner, but it could be. Excuse me a moment.' She turned to serve a customer.

'We've not seen him recently, Mrs Harmer, that's the trouble. Not for a month, six weeks.'

'I'm afraid you won't be seeing him again, Mr Patel. He's passed away. It's just a matter of identification,' she fibbed.

'Well, his name was Munton or Manton or something. My ears aren't what they were, you know.'

Fran nodded sympathetically. The Patels might be a village fixture, knowing everything about everyone, but that didn't stop them growing old. Stooped and white-haired, he must be pushing seventy-five, glasses on a cord round his neck and a hearing aid in each ear. 'I'm sure they're good enough. And how did you know him?'

'He used to come into the shop quite often. He'd always buy something. Some fresh vegetables. Very keen on his health, he was.'

'But why here?' she pondered aloud.

'Late-night opening,' he said, with ill-concealed triumph. 'And no need to go to a big supermarket.'

But didn't Hythe have a perfectly good Waitrose open all hours? Not to mention a corner shop or two?

'I didn't mean that,' she apologised. 'I meant, why Lenham, when he had a flat in Hythe?'

He smiled graciously. 'I might turn your question. Why have a flat in Hythe when you have a cottage here?'

'Mr Patel, you are a prince among men!' She kissed him on either cheek. 'Thank you, thank you. I don't suppose you know which was his cottage . . .'

* * *

Standing outside to phone, Fran became aware of Mrs Patel approaching her. 'There's more you should know, Chief Superintendent. Poor Ashok is embarrassed to tell you, but I will. He had a fancy woman, that man. I used to see them. She goes to his cottage all plainly dressed on top, but underneath, when the wind blows, you can see that she's not a lady at all. That's why Ashok's upset.'

'And have you seen her recently, this woman?' She was braced for a sad negative.

'Oh, yes. Ms Evans. Ms Caroline Evans. She works in London. She was in the shop two days ago before she went on holiday — she's been looking very sad recently. And now we know why, don't we? She lives just over there, Ms Harman. In that house with the green door.'

* * *

Arms akimbo, Fran watched another scene-of-crime team search another empty house. Not the one with the green door — that could wait till they'd run its owner to earth — but Alec Minton's.

The one-up, one-down cottage — to describe it as bijou would be to exaggerate its size — was on the far side of the village from Lenham, its garden backing onto the reservoir land. There was no sign of the kitchen ever having been used, but then, that was Alec Minton for you. The king-size bed, occupying the whole of the bedroom, with barely enough room to inch round, had been stripped, as she would have predicted. There were no towels in the minuscule bathroom, opening off the kitchen. But if Minton had ever spent time with Janine here, then her DNA must surely be lying somewhere, no matter how efficient his cleaning. And what about other women? Were there others besides Lenham's Ms Caroline Evans in Kentish towns or villages wondering why they hadn't had a call recently, a summons to that big bed? For according to Mr Patel, Minton had been a regular, if infrequent, customer, until what must have been the week of his death. Fran hadn't had the heart to tell him that it was probably the parish magazine bought in the Patels' own shop that had brought about their client's death, bearing as it did the news of the polluted water.

Minton must have known exactly what was polluting the water and feared that somehow his part in it would be traced back to him. He'd set about eradicating all traces of himself—hence, no doubt, his choice of the Mondiale as his suicide venue. She hated it when killers topped themselves and took all their secrets with them.

What about those undies from Minton's gym? No, they couldn't be Janine's, and almost certainly wouldn't be Ms Evans', or she'd have got rid of them herself. There must be another girl, alive or dead, somewhere. Someone whose husband or partner wouldn't approve of his woman wearing sexy clothes for the delectation of a pensioner from Hythe. Fran had better get the MisPer file checked. At least if Minton had ever killed again, the body wasn't stowed in the reservoir, she laughed dourly to herself. No, Janine's death must be a one off. Mustn't it?

There was a call from above her head. 'Guv! Someone's moved something out of the attic here. You can see where it's been from the dust. From the shape it looks like a bag or a sack.'

* * *

She was about to start making phone calls when her mobile rang, making her jump.

Iona Harris!

'I thought you'd want to know I got a really, really rush job done on the DNA samples. We'll be billing you for an arm and a leg, of course.'

'No matter,' she lied. 'What were the results?'

'Alec Minton had sex with Janine Roper before she died. So you can discount whichever of your theories you had here.'

'The barmy one? Thanks, Iona. I'd better get all our other unexplained female sudden deaths checked for Minton's DNA too.' She explained.

Harris was gratifyingly impressed. 'But thank goodness for modern science,' she added. 'Otherwise someone wouldn't half have a lot of work coming up.'

As she strolled back through the village to pick up her car, she decided she and Mark should celebrate, after all.

There might be a load of booze at home — what about all that they'd left at Mark's house? she wondered idly — but she'd do it with a bottle of Mr Patel's best. And a surprisingly good one it turned out to be.

CHAPTER TWENTY-FOUR

Mark stared. At the key, the keyhole, the front door and his house. Why should his key not go in, let alone work? Scrambling less easily than he liked over the side gate, he tried the key from his bunch in the back door. No, he couldn't get that in either. The garage? Not that he'd ever used it for his car, of course. But even that was barred to him.

How could a man not get into his own house?

Because, the answer came painfully slowly but with brutal clarity. Sammie had changed the locks. Sammie and Lloyd had changed the locks. Sammie and Lloyd had changed the locks because their house in Tunbridge Wells was on the market — no chain! — and they had moved into here. Had that been their plan all along or had they simply improvised when presented with a golden opportunity to exploit a naive and indulgent father?

He trudged back to where Fran was waiting in the car, parked cloak-and-dagger fashion round the corner, and slumped into the passenger seat. 'My daughter. My own daughter.' He could feel, not just hear, his voice breaking.

'She's squatting, is she?' Fran took his hand and gave it a comforting but bracing squeeze. 'We'd better get on to a solicitor, then. Now, while the beer is in us.' Without waiting for him to argue — not that he would have done — she turned the car towards Maidstone, all one solid car park on a Saturday.

Funny, he thought he'd been the one who'd driven over here. How did she come to be behind the wheel? 'You guessed?'

'I just had a nasty feeling.'

'My daughter. My own daughter,' he repeated, stupid with disbelief. 'Why don't we just go and knock the door down and throw them out?'

She negotiated a delivery van. 'Because of your security camera. They'd sell the footage to the press, who'd have a field day.' He noticed that neither of them referred to Sammie and Lloyd by name. 'A couple of middle-aged innocent police officers would be no match for them, not if they can conceive and hatch a plan as subtle as this. A top-notch solicitor it is, Mark, and not some man whose sole excitement is conveyancing and wills. We need the most compulsively devious bastard you've ever raged against. Because sure as eggs, they'll have one too.'

* * *

'I feel so soiled,' Mark groaned. 'What a vile woman.'

'Vile indeed. A positive Rottweiler. But I suspect Ms Brent is exactly the sort of solicitor we need. You don't buy suits like that if you don't earn a great deal of money. Come on — it's in her expensively manicured hands now, and we must just let her get on with it. So I'll tell you what we're going to do. We're going to enjoy this gorgeous weather for a few minutes.'

He pulled his face into a smile. 'The Rectory?'

'Where else?'

They weren't surprised to find Paula on site; several other women, presumably other members of the team, were hard at work dealing with flaking paint. As one got a surface clear, another came and rubbed it down. Then a third applied primer.

‘All this double time and we’re going to have to pay an arm and a leg to get our own house back!’ Mark groaned.

‘But Ms Brent’s convinced we will get it back, and soon. She’d scare me into submission, I tell you that. All the same, we need a Plan B, and who else other than Paula can tell us if we can have a Plan B? We have to trust her, Mark.’

‘I trusted my own daughter — invited her in, left her food, left her wine . . . She’s even got that mixer I bought for you, and all your efforts in the deep freeze.’

‘It’s only money.’

‘And I never got round to organising a simple tenancy agreement. I’ve been a fool.’

‘But there’s no legal or common-sense doubt about who owns the property, and to whom it’ll be returned. Come on, let’s see what Paula says.’ She took his hand again.

He looked at it, turning on her ring finger the not quite engagement ring he’d bought as much to soothe the troubled breasts of the hierarchy as to show affection and commitment — they both knew that they had them by the barrel-load. It sparkled encouragingly.

* * *

Paula’s face said as much as Paula’s mouth. ‘Move in here in six weeks’ time? You’re joking!’

‘Alas, no. We know we couldn’t occupy more than a couple of rooms, Paula. And I’d have thought with your contacts you could get a kitchen and bathroom installed before then.’

Her smile was grimly smug. ‘Oh, I’m sure I can pull in a couple of favours. It won’t be much fun for you, though, living in the middle of a building site.’

Mark said, his mouth still stiff, ‘Just think of us as extra security.’

She looked at him with interest. ‘There has to be a back-story. Why don’t you tell me all about it while I brew up?’ She herded them into the scullery. ‘Actually, I wanted to talk to you about Caffy, and not in front of all those interested ears either,' she added, filling the kettle.

'She's been talking to the police shrink?'

'Yes. Shrinks, indeed. They seem to think she has to turn up, and if all goes well to eat with him, quite normally. But somewhere along the line, she's got to make it clear that she's meeting him as an old acquaintance only, and that it's a one off. At the moment they're still belly-aching about whether she should say she's found someone else as being better for Gates' ego.'

'Hasn't she?' Fran asked. 'A pretty girl like that?'

'A pretty unusual girl like that. Most guys of her age are scared by her learning. Those that aren't are put off by her past. That's what happened to her last bloke. When push came to shove he couldn't deal with the fact that she'd been a prostitute.'

'She tells them? What a risk! Some men would find it a real turn-on, a dangerous turn-on.'

'You've met Caffy. Everything up front.'

Mark rubbed his chin. 'Maybe that's what presses Gates' buttons. You never know.'

'So it won't be easy for her to find a decent man,' Paula concluded.

'This ex-pop star—' Mark began tentatively.

'Loves her like a daughter.' The response was emphatic. 'In fact, she insisted that he and his wife were in on the discussions. He wanted to drop her off at the hotel himself, and wait to collect her, but your people insisted on a taxi, driven by cop, of course.'

'Who will no doubt linger in case he's needed. And she'll be wired up?'

'She really wasn't keen, and who can blame her? But the hotel has CCTV, and one of your people will join the security team. There's just one interesting thing you should know, though. Gates is staying at the hotel where they're eating. He's got one of the best rooms.'

Fran's stomach clenched. What would her colleagues do? Thank goodness it wasn't her decision.

Before they could say more, cheery whistling — it sounded like a piece of Mozart or Haydn — announced the arrival of Caffy herself, apparently ready to put in a couple of hours' work.

But instead she sat herself down on the kitchen table. Paula shot her an enquiring look, but said nothing.

'I never told you,' Fran said, to fill what might have become an awkward silence. 'I've got a new job.'

Caffy went pale, as if Fran had punched her. 'You're not leaving this house before you've even moved in!'

'Absolutely not. In fact, as Paula will explain, we're moving in in early July.'

'Brilliant!' Her face was suffused with delight. 'It won't be very pleasant at times, but you'll actually see it improve day by day, organically, as it were. And, talking of organics, I have a friend who would love to help restore your garden. A total sweetie, the nicest bum in the world. Though he didn't like it when I took him up on the scaffolding to see the underlying layout.' She glanced at Fran's shoes.

'Am I properly shod? Oh, Mark, will you come up too? There's not a breath of wind.'

* * *

'You're very lucky, Caffy,' Mark declared, halfway up the second ladder, 'not being afraid of heights.'

'Not afraid? I'm scared rigid. I can't think of anything worse than falling and realising there was nothing you could do about it, that gravity would operate no matter what. It's one thing I shall do to the windows you mustn't tell the planning department about — I shall put on safety devices so you can't fall out accidentally. Ugh. Imagine jumping off the Clifton Suspension Bridge or Beachy Head.'

'Not so nice for the poor sods clearing up afterwards,' Mark said grimly, concentrating on putting one foot in front of another.

'Quite. So what's the new job, Fran?' Caffy asked, pausing on the next platform.

'Investigating murders we've not been able to solve. Now we've got DNA and all sorts of other forensic science techniques—'

'I'm *so* glad you give forensic science its proper name. I hate people calling it "forensics", which means nothing — and forensic only means "of the courtroom", doesn't it?'

'Quite. Anyway, I get to review these old cases and see if we can nick the ones what dunnit.'

'So the miserable swine who think they've literally got away with murder will wake up one morning to find you arresting them! Fran, how wonderful.'

Mark made sure he leant back towards the house but told himself it had been worth the effort to get here. The garden was laid out like a relief map, with ghostly flowerbeds below them, what looked like an ornamental fountain and then a kitchen garden. 'What a wonderful place to hold our wedding reception,' he thought.

And then he realised from the silence he'd said it out loud.

'Aren't you married already? You're so together I thought you'd been man and wife for years,' Caffy said, with one of her warm beams.

'No. But we will be together for years,' Fran said. 'At least I hope so. And you can't back out now, Mark, not now we've got a witness.' She was as pale as he'd seen her; then she blushed, rosily, as if she were a coy girl. It was hardly surprising, considering how often and how hard he'd snubbed her in the past. Would he have backed out even now but for Caffy's presence?

'A witness? At the wedding?' Caffy repeated, with an edge of joy to her disbelief. 'No, you don't mean that. You'll want an old friend. Family.'

Fran bit her lip. She hadn't meant that, had she? She must simply have meant that Caffy had been a witness to what passed for a proposal and he couldn't therefore back out.

Before Fran could right herself, he said quickly, 'I guess we'll be married quietly at St Jude's. We know the vicar there. So we may not need witnesses in the registry office sense. I don't know about Fran needing a bridesmaid, but nothing would give me greater pleasure than if you'd be my best woman.' He managed a courtly bow, but wished he hadn't.

The women, high on their ridiculous perch, hugged each other and him.

'All the same,' Caffy said at last, 'Paula would make a much better best woman. She'd organise everything down to the last flower petal.'

'Well, maybe I do need a bridesmaid,' Fran said.

'You're on. But not if you find someone else you'd prefer: we've only known each other five minutes after all and you must have loads of old friends you could call on.'

Fran was shaking her head slowly, whether in disbelief or because she couldn't think of anyone, he couldn't tell.

Meanwhile, Caffy was bubbling on. 'You know Todd can play the piano and the organ? I bet if I asked he'd play for you — either at the church or here. And some of his mates. He's into piano quartets at the moment.'

'Piano quartets?' Fran echoed.

He let them talk, not eager to think about the imminent descent. He certainly wasn't aware of time passing.

Suddenly Caffy's voice changed. 'Sorry to bring you down to earth, as it were. This new job, Fran. How dead does the body have to be? I mean, would it be a forensic archaeology type of body?'

Fran didn't seem to have picked up the young woman's seriousness. 'Any sort of body. But I wouldn't want one on my own patch. Literally,' she added with an amused glance at Caffy, who responded by licking her index finger and making a mark in the air.

'But you just might have one.' Caffy pointed to the far end of the vegetable garden, where the weeds and grass grew with far more energy than anywhere else in the plot. A strip, two or three feet by six or seven. From here it looked coffin-shaped. Human-body shaped.

'You don't think it's just had more compost than the rest of the place?' Mark asked. 'Maybe it *was* the compost heap!'

Caffy shook her head. 'Have you ever seen a compost heap that shape?'

'Well, no.'

'Quite.' The flat syllable came all the more strongly given her usual loquacity.

'Nor have I,' he admitted. 'Hell, it's the sort of thing they taught us about in one of those courses which you always think is going to be absolutely useless and then . . . Forensic Archaeology,' he explained. 'Didn't you ever go on one, Fran?'

'I should have done but something cropped up.' She shut her lips very tightly.

He guessed it must have been some panic over her parents.

'Even if it is a body, it doesn't have to be a human one, of course.' Caffy was being helpful again. 'It could be a horse or dog or something.'

He laughed. 'I've never seen one of those that shape either. I'm sorry, Fran, but I'm afraid Caffy's right. I'd say we need to get thermal-imaging equipment down there,' he said.

'But — surely—' Fran sounded almost panicky.

'I'd hate my mate to turn up anything that would spoil his dreams,' Caffy said, with jokey reassurance. 'Mind you,' she added, all sober reflection again. 'I'm afraid there's someone's dreams I've got to spoil. And I wish I didn't have to do it. But someone's got to. And it's best if it's me.'

'I'm sure you'll let Simon down lightly, Caffy,' Fran said, taking one last look at the offending corner.

'The trouble is,' she replied, starting down the ladders more nimbly than they dared, and betraying none of the fear she admitted to, 'that in his condition even lightly might be too harsh.'

CHAPTER TWENTY-FIVE

The fifth-floor room was so neat it might never have been occupied. But it was certainly meant to have been. There were baskets and vases of red roses everywhere, even in the marble-walled bathroom. Two near the door had been tipped over, as if someone had blindly run past them. Puddles were only just spreading.

An unopened bottle of vintage champagne was still chilling in a bucket beside the bed, though the ice had begun to melt. A couple of expensive chocolates lay coyly on the pillows.

The heavy curtains had been drawn but tugged slightly apart. They shifted and heaved, driven by the wind. The glass door opening onto the balcony was ajar, despite the sudden burst of rain, which would soon soak into the carpet.

Blue flashing lights were already strobing over the car park below. The slanting rain might have made them look more like lights on seaside rides. Instead, it rendered them even more cold and clinical.

The brightwear of the men and women scrabbling diligently in their intermittent illumination — someone would soon send for incident tape and floodlights — turned a harsh green. As for the blood from the shattered body they were attending, that too a far from natural colour, it was already trickling into the drains and sewers to be borne, via the new and expensive sewage plant that Ofwat had forced upon Invitaqua, to the sea.

THE END

ACKNOWLEDGEMENTS

My thanks to Peter Gambrill and David Whitethread for their watery expertise, freely and generously given.

THE JOFFE BOOKS STORY

We began in 2014 when Jasper agreed to publish his mum's much-rejected romance novel and it became a bestseller.

Since then we've grown into the largest independent publisher in the UK. We're extremely proud to publish some of the very best writers in the world, including Joy Ellis, Faith Martin, Caro Ramsay, Helen Forrester, Simon Brett and Robert Goddard. Everyone at Joffe Books loves reading and we never forget that it all begins with the magic of an author telling a story.

We are proud to publish talented first-time authors, as well as established writers whose books we love introducing to a new generation of readers.

We won Trade Publisher of the Year at the Independent Publishing Awards in 2023. We have been shortlisted for Independent Publisher of the Year at the British Book Awards for the last four years, and were shortlisted for the Diversity and Inclusivity Award at the 2022 Independent Publishing Awards. In 2023 we were shortlisted for Publisher of the Year at the RNA Industry Awards.

We built this company with your help, and we love to hear from you, so please email us about absolutely anything bookish at feedback@joffebooks.com

If you want to receive free books every Friday and hear about all our new releases, join our mailing list: www.joffebooks.com/contact

And when you tell your friends about us, just remember: it's pronounced Joffe as in coffee or toffee!

ALSO BY JUDITH CUTLER

FRAN HARMAN MYSTERIES
Book 1: COME TO HARM
Book 2: DO NO HARM
Book 3: IN HARM'S WAY

DETECTIVE KATE POWER MYSTERIES
Book 1: MURDER THE BOYS
Book 2: MURDER BY THE CANAL
Book 3: MURDER BY ARSON
Book 4: MURDER BY FRAUD
Book 5: MURDER IN DEVON
Book 6: MURDER ON THE JOB

Printed in Dunstable, United Kingdom

78574181R00153